LEE BROOK

The Bone Saw Ripper

MIDDLETON
PARK PRESS

First published by Middleton Park Press 2022

Copyright © 2022 by Lee Brook

All rights reserved. No part of this publication may be reproduced, stored or transmitted in any form or by any means, electronic, mechanical, photocopying, recording, scanning, or otherwise without written permission from the publisher. It is illegal to copy this book, post it to a website, or distribute it by any other means without permission.

This novel is entirely a work of fiction. The names, characters and incidents portrayed in it are the work of the author's imagination. Any resemblance to actual persons, living or dead, events or localities is entirely coincidental.

Lee Brook asserts the moral right to be identified as the author of this work.

Lee Brook has no responsibility for the persistence or accuracy of URLs for external or third-party Internet Websites referred to in this publication and does not guarantee that any content on such Websites is, or will remain, accurate or appropriate.

Designations used by companies to distinguish their products are often claimed as trademarks. All brand names and product names used in this book and on its cover are trade names, service marks, trademarks and registered trademarks of their respective owners. The publishers and the book are not associated with any product or vendor mentioned in this book. None of the companies referenced within the book have endorsed the book.

First edition

This book was professionally typeset on Reedsy.
Find out more at reedsy.com

For my wife, Lisa—
Thank you for reading each and every chapter as I write it.
This book wouldn't have been finished without you.

Contents

Prologue	1
Chapter One	6
Chapter Two	11
Chapter Three	21
Chapter Four	30
Chapter Five	40
Chapter Six	48
Chapter Seven	58
Chapter Eight	66
Chapter Nine	77
Chapter Ten	88
Chapter Eleven	96
Chapter Twelve	104
Chapter Thirteen	112
Chapter Fourteen	125
Chapter Fifteen	136
Chapter Sixteen	142
Chapter Seventeen	151
Chapter Eighteen	156
Chapter Nineteen	161
Chapter Twenty	171
Chapter Twenty-one	177
Chapter Twenty-two	184
Chapter Twenty-three	197

Chapter Twenty-four	206
Chapter Twenty-five	213
Chapter Twenty-six	222
Chapter Twenty-seven	232
Chapter Twenty-eight	239
Chapter Twenty-nine	248
Chapter Thirty	255
Chapter Thirty-one	265
Chapter Thirty-two	271
Chapter Thirty-three	285
Chapter Thirty-four	292
Epilogue	295
Afterword	303
Also by Lee Brook	304

Prologue

Thirty years ago

There were times when Anna Hill hated being a wife and a mother. Yes, it had been her choice, but a choice she realised she had made far too young. One minute she was finishing her O-levels; then, she was married to Timothy and up the duff. In those early days together, she remembered them being almost stuck together for warmth in their shitty, tiny flat in Belle Isle.

Moaning, Anna dropped her swollen plastic bags to the pavement and tried to rub some feeling back into her gloveless hands. She'd been after a bicycle for a while, one with a basket on the front, but they couldn't afford one because she was out of work. Anna longed for one. It would help her in more ways than one. She could cycle up to Middleton and get the shopping done and get rid of the extra weight she had gained during pregnancy. Little Thomas was four, yet the weight showed no signs of budging.

In truth, she didn't mind the extra weight. It had gone to, in her opinion, all the right places. She thought her husband would have appreciated the swelling of her breasts, but Timothy all but ignored the two extra cup sizes. All he noticed was her arse, forever banging on about how fat it was every time she tried it on with him. She was off-limits. He didn't want to diminish her value. She knew others appreciated her body, but Tim didn't. What a wanker.

Anna wiped the cold sweat from her brow and breathed on her hands, rubbing them furiously together. Despite being December, her husband hadn't given her enough money to buy some gloves. She looked around, amazed, seeing each streetlight pop on one after another, illuminating the surrounding darkness. They cast an eerie glow along the pavement, and Anna knew she needed to get home. She rummaged inside one of the bags and came out with a Freddo. Anna took a big bite out of the chocolate, nearly half the bar, and chewed happily. She hadn't had one for fifteen years, and it tasted amazing.

After she finished tonight, she would treat herself to a bottle of wine. Anna knew she shouldn't drink on antidepressants, but she needed to numb the pain. Maybe she'd stay up until the early hours; possibly, there'd even be something good on the telly?

A loud shout shattered the silence, and Anna shit herself. As she turned, a couple of helmetless teenagers on motocross bikes appeared through the fog. The idiots mounted the pavement, missing her by centimetres, their laughter echoing against the houses as they raced down Town Street towards Belle Isle. The stupid kids were getting worse. The teenagers living in the flats on both sides listened to loud music all night. She'd tried complaining to the bloody police, but the arseholes weren't interested.

Christ, twenty-one, and she was already thinking like a middle-aged moaner. It wasn't so long ago that she'd been flirting with boys like that, hoping they'd choose to deflower her. But no, she'd ended up with Tim, a boring banker who couldn't keep a steady job. If only her girlfriends from school could see her now: a whinging mother with a sex-less marriage moaning about loud music and dangerous driving.

Fifteen minutes later, Anna had to put the bags down again, heaving from the journey, the inside of her coat covered with sweat. Her son Thomas tired her as it was, but having to walk into Middleton twice a day meant she was wiped out by seven.

Soon she was outside the front door, rummaging through her threadbare coat for the house keys.

Their shabby Christmas tree greeted her as she entered the flat, the warm air buffeting her, making her heave from the temperature difference. Unfortunately, they could only afford to put the heating on between the hours Tim was home from work and when they went to bed.

Five days a week, Anna would leave Thomas with an elderly neighbour below so she could get to the shops before they shut. They had no fridge, so she had to shop twice daily, so Tim had fresh meals. He refused to eat her food otherwise. She hated leaving Thomas, but it was only for an hour and a half before Tim got home from work. Then, they'd have half an hour of family time together before Tim took Thomas to bed. For Anna, it was strange how one little person could bring joy and sadness into the world.

Anna finished the Freddo in one bite—not wanting Tim to know she'd been naughty—and let herself into the kitchen.

"Tim?"

There was no answer, but she could hear the telly in the living room. "Tim, can you please give me a hand with the shopping? The bloody bags weigh a ton." She dumped the one she had on the floor and then turned to get the others.

A man in a white protective coverall and shoe covers was standing there, a long, silver saw in his hand. His hood was up, and he wore a blue disposable face mask and matching blue disposable gloves.

She was about to scream when he grabbed her.

* * *

"Make sure you swallow it all," he said, the fingers of his right hand finding their way through her hair. The thought of ripping the woman's hair out turned him on, but he took a deep breath and calmed himself. "Fucking swallow it. Now!"

The red-headed Anna Hill gagged. He'd warned her she wasn't allowed to waste a single drop. She gulped. The man removed his mask and grinned. "Did you swallow all of it?"

Anna Hill nodded.

He pulled her up to his level from her knees, his grip on her ginger curls tightening. "Show me." She was weak at the knees and struggled to keep herself upright. He pulled her closer, their noses almost level as he looked down at her, and she looked up. "Open wide." She did as the man told her. Suddenly the man dragged her head down by her hair, her throat taut, the veins bulging. He used the fingers of his free hand to grip it. "Fucking liar. Swallow it, whore. Isn't it what you usually get fucking paid for?"

She nodded, and he relaxed both his grip on her hair and the grip on her throat. He saw her gulp. "Good girl."

The woman stood there, knees shaking, completely naked. The man ordered Anna Hill to put the condom on his hardened penis, which she did with shaking hands. He was still wearing the white protective coverall and shoe covers, and his penis peeking through the white material looked strange to Anna. "On your knees and turn around." She got on her knees as ordered and closed her eyes.

Once the man finished, she tried to get up. "I'm not fucking finished with you yet. Stay where you are."

"Please? Let me go!"

He pushed her back to the floor. She began to speak, but he grabbed her by the hair and pulled her head back. Then, with his left hand, he placed a cloth ball in her mouth before sealing her lips shut with gaffer tape.

Anna Hill was shaking, and he could see the fear in her eyes. All it did was turn the man on more. He grabbed her by her red locks and dragged her into the cellar. It was an ample space with large white walls and a crimson carpet on the floor.

He laid her down on the carpet and tied each limb to the four columns.

From his view, she looked like a five-pointed star—a Vitruvian Woman.

Perfect.

He got to work immediately, retrieving a twelve-inch surgical bone saw from the bag on the floor.

From the ground, the man could see eyes which were wide and staring, filled with fear and dread. She tried to speak but failed. She tried to thrash but failed. He laughed as he raised the saw, and suddenly, there was an explosion of crimson mist against the white walls as the blade bit deep into the flesh. As he began to saw, he chuckled. He was making fine art. The walls were his canvas, and her blood was his paint.

Chapter One

resent day

Detective Inspector George Beaumont rocked his chair in his stiflingly hot office, cursing under his breath as he attempted to decipher the scrawl, West Yorkshire Police called handwritten evidential notes. Every winter, the police were inundated with burglary cases, and whilst these issues were usually below his standing, he had no choice but to trawl through them. Usually, the heating was broken and freezing, but through some twist of fate, the heating, whilst still broken, seemed to be stuck on the molten lava setting.

George's shirt clung to his skin, a thin sheen of sweat acting as the glue. It had been a while since he'd been abroad, but you never forgot that feeling of wanting to peel your skin off and wring it out. He'd already abandoned his tie and had undone the top two buttons earlier in the day and considered rolling up his sleeves in hopes of some relief. But, instead, he yanked at his collar, pulling it away from his slimy neck as he worked through a mountain of paperwork.

Christmas Day had only just gone, and December was their busiest time. It always annoyed George that thieves would target families during this time of year, and he clenched his fists in anger.

CHAPTER ONE

Outside his office, Detective Constable Tashan Blackburn, a twenty-three-year-old who had recently graduated from the National Detective Programme, worked quietly. The rookie was working through his mountain of paperwork, happier than George had ever seen. He'd taken over from Detective Sergeant Elaine Brewer, who hadn't been best pleased about being stuck in burglary for two weeks in December. Some poor detective had to do it, and they rotated the paperwork through the winter to make it fair to everyone on the floor.

Except for George. He'd been on burglary cases since the last week of October, and it felt like an eternity. It was his punishment.

Despite an independent investigation exonerating George in the killing of the Miss Murderer he had been severely disciplined and was grateful that he'd kept his job. It had been a close call, with Detective Superintendent Jim Smith standing up to Detective Chief Superintendent Mohammed Sadiq on his behalf. He had killed a man, saving two lives, and whilst he didn't relish the punishment, he knew damn well he deserved it. Only George's long-standing exemplary service had seen him avoid dismissal. He'd still received a proper bollocking from the Chief Super, who ordered DSU Smith to stop him from overseeing any investigations for the foreseeable future. A two-month suspension with full pay had also been forced upon him after the initial month so that he could do sessions with a psychologist. He came back in August after receiving the all-clear from his psych evaluation. It had been four months since then, and he still hadn't been an SIO.

During his psych evaluation, he'd painstakingly avoided telling the young woman who'd interviewed him about his recurring nightmares. He'd easily fooled the woman, but every night, as George finally fell asleep, he would dream about Adam's face disintegrating beneath his blows, feel Adam's blood speckling his skin.

George's exclusion of his recurring nightmares was why he'd been allowed to return to work. Though many people in the force considered his actions reckless and idiotic, the press regarded Beaumont as a hero. He'd caught the Miss Murderer, saving the life of his pregnant ex-fiancée. But he hadn't felt like a hero, still didn't. Luckily, with DS Wood acting as DI, his team had tied Adam Harris to some of his past victims, meaning the families finally had closure on who killed their loved ones. It also meant that David Clark, the man wrongfully charged for one of Adam's murders, was released from prison.

In the end, George was glad everything was over. Whilst he'd enjoyed the thrill of the chase deep into the investigation, it had changed his life entirely. However, he wondered how long he'd continue to wake up screaming from his nightmares. George shuddered at the memory.

However, the bustling floor outside his office made it difficult for George to feel glad he'd kept his job—leaving DI Beaumont stuck in exile, forgiven but forgotten. He desperately wanted to be the boss again, chasing leads and capturing criminals.

Still, one good thing came from being cooped up in his office all day: Isabella Wood. The fact that they weren't working together daily only made him greedier when he saw her outside work. A cheeky wink through his office window or a sneaky kiss in the stairwell wasn't enough for him.

Beaumont sat back in his chair, his stomach growling as he glanced outside. Other than the orange glow of the streetlights, it was pitch black, and he was on until eleven, the first day of

CHAPTER ONE

his four late shifts in a row. Late shifts meant no Isabella and takeaway food. The fact it was Friday night—their usual date night—and he wasn't seeing her pissed him off, too.

Just two hours left.

Just as his shift was about to end, George's mobile rang, and he glanced down at the number. It was the Detective Super. "DI George Beaumont," he said.

DSU Jim Smith's Geordie accent boomed out of the speaker.

"George, are you still at the station?"

"Yes, sir, is everything alright?" he said, pen in hand, ready to take the details to pass on.

"George, a homeless person scavenging in rubbish bins behind takeaways in Middleton, has found some dismembered body parts wrapped in bin bags. The DCS has permitted me to take control of operations out of Elland Road. I think it's time, George. I want you to lead your team again as the SIO."

SIO. George hadn't heard those words in months. Senior Investigating Officer. "Really?" George struggled to keep the surprise out of his voice and hoped he hadn't messed it up.

"Yeah, this is your chance to get back into the good books with the DCS, George. The ambulance is already there. Patrol officers have begun preservation of the scene with the Crime Scene Co-ordinator, Stuart Kent, and his scenes of crime officers. I understand if you aren't ready yet—"

"I'm ready," George cut in. "Thank you, sir."

DSU Smith grunted. "DS Wood is on her way. As usual, she will be your deputy SIO on this."

"What's the address, sir?"

DSU Smith explained the bins were in the alley at the back of the takeaways on Middleton Park Road.

Heart hammering, Beaumont hung up the call and threw on

his suit jacket and coat.

Guess I'll be seeing Isabella tonight after all.

Chapter Two

Ten minutes later, Beaumont parked on Lingwell Avenue. He could see the bright yellow of an ambulance where the road met the alley. The weather in Middleton was the same as Elland Road, freezing, wet weather they had been suffering with since late October. George thought the weather might have turned the same week he had been forced into working burglary cases. The scents of the differing takeaways hung in the air, a sickly, cloying mix of Indian, Italian, and Chinese food. But George gladly breathed it in, as he soon knew what he would smell. Death.

He approached the end of the alley where police tape fluttered, the telephone poles and streetlights overhead like towering, silent sentries. An officer stepped forward to challenge him. But, other than people watching him from their bedroom windows, all was silent. It didn't feel right.

He flashed his warrant card. "DI George Beaumont, SIO. Is DS Wood here yet?"

The constable nodded and signed him in on the log. "Yeah, she's over there." He pointed to a young woman with long brown hair tied in a ponytail. George had seen little of her that week because she had worked ten-hour shifts during his three rest days.

"Thanks. Keep your scene log going, and don't let anybody through the cordon, please." Unfortunately, DSU Smith had stopped all overtime due to budget concerns, so the Homicide and Major Enquiry Team didn't have the staffing to take over what the constable was doing.

George looked down the alley and saw a police photographer he didn't recognise taking pictures of the scene. He heard the continuous click as he took in the surrounding area. Somebody must have seen something. There were flats above the takeaways and shops, too. Maybe somebody had seen something. He made a mental note.

At the foot of the alley stood DS Wood, a PC, Crime Scene Coordinator Stuart Kent, and a skinny, unhappy woman who was shivering despite being wrapped with a foil blanket. Kent and DS Wood moved further into the crime scene. The PC looked up as Beaumont drew closer, and she introduced herself before sharing with George a list of relevant facts concisely that he appreciated.

"This is Miss Deirdre Haliday. At approximately quarter to nine tonight, she, unfortunately, came across dismembered body parts wrapped neatly in newspaper whilst scavenging in the rubbish bins behind the takeaways. She got one of the takeaways to call the police immediately."

"I just want you to know I didn't do anything," Deirdre said, her muddied face showing concern. "I jus' found t' pieces. You should be thanking me."

A SOCO had made his way over, a tall young man with blond hair. George looked at him, but the young man said nothing.

"Detective?" Deirdre said.

George showed a reassuring smile and ignored the SOCO. "Of course, Deirdre." He scratched his beard, thinking about their next steps. "PC—"

"PC Sally Fletcher," she cut in with a smile. She had already introduced herself earlier, but George's memory wasn't what it was.

"PC Fletcher here will go through the next steps with you to discount you from our investigation. Stay with her for the moment, please."

Deirdre nodded in understanding, and she smiled. She had essential details that George needed to know. The woman wasn't under arrest, but George knew it wouldn't be the first time a killer had stayed close to the crime scene. He'd even known a criminal who called in the crime they'd just committed in an attempt to both hide in plain sight and to acquit themselves. He got the bastard in the end.

"Miss Haliday," he said sternly, his hands in his pockets to fend off the December chill. "Because of what you've found tonight, I'll need to take a full statement from you. So please include as much detail as possible about what happened."

Miss Haliday nodded, and his eyes darted up the alleyway where the body parts lay out of sight. When she spoke, there was a tremble in her voice, and George could see a sadness in her eyes. "I was hungry. The takeaways are busy this time of year. You should see what the pizza place throws away. Full pizzas in boxes. They're hot and fresh."

"So what made you open the bin bags, Miss Haliday?" George asked.

"The takeaways usually throw meat away in black bags. Like chicken tikka from the curry place. Bloody delicious." During the conversation, the woman's voice had become monotone, yet it wobbled once more at the talk of meat and the bin bags. Finally, she turned to DI Beaumont, her face twisted with dread.

"Look, love, it was the smell. I knew something was wrong. At first, I thought the curry place 'ad thrown away a naan kebab. I had one before, and it was long and heavy. I opened the bag, and I was nearly sick from the smell. The newspaper had slid, I saw the flesh, so I dropped it, went into the curry place and told them to call the police." Miss Haliday swallowed and put her head down. "I've never seen a dead body before. I was holding a pale arm."

"The takeaway has closed for the night," PC Fletcher said. "My partner, PC Jamie Higgins, is taking statements."

George nodded and smiled at Deirdre Haliday to continue. He would get DS Wood to take new statements tomorrow and cross-reference them. It could be one of the workers was the killer.

Tears glistened at the corner of Miss Haliday's eyes, and she looked at Beaumont as if she was going to be cuffed and arrested for the murders. "I... I di'n't do anything wrong, did I?"

She looked desperately between PC Fletcher and DI Beaumont. PC Fletcher smiled an understanding smile and nearly placed a hand on Miss Haliday's shoulder, but she hesitated and drew her hand back for whatever reason. "It's alright, Deirdre. Did you touch the body part?"

Miss Haliday shook her head erratically. "No. As soon as I opened the bag and saw what it was, I dropped it."

That meant Haliday's prints shouldn't be on the arm.

"PC Fletcher. When you're done here, will you take Miss Haliday to the station to take DNA swabs and prints for elimination purposes, please? Then you can take her home."

"Sir," she said to George, a grimace on her face. However, when she turned to Deirdre, her scowl had disappeared and was replaced with a smile. "You can't blame yourself, Deirdre. I'm sure this has been traumatic for you—do you have anyone I can call?"

"No. Well, Ali up at Carr Beck will be worrying about me." Carr Beck is a scheme based in Middleton providing 24-hour specialist support and accommodation for alcohol-dependent women. George knew it intended to provide a safe and closely monitored environment where women could get help managing and reducing their alcohol consumption. He also knew women could live in the supported accommodation for as long as required.

"Have you been drinking tonight, Miss Haliday?"

"No. C'u'n't afford to."

"I'll speak to Ali for you, Deirdre, if that's alright?" PC Fletcher said. "With what you've been through, you'll need support. I'll make sure you're taken care of."

"Thank you kindly," Deirdre said, showing a gappy smile.

"Go with PC Fletcher now, Deirdre," Beaumont ordered. "If I need to speak to you again, I'll contact Carr Beck."

"Good luck, love," she said and began chatting away to PC Fletcher.

Around the corner, SOCOs waited with the body parts. As he put on the mask, gloves, protective coverall and shoe covers the guard had provided, he noticed somebody, probably Stuart Kent had set up a common approach path, a designated path everybody used, so they didn't accidentally tread on any evidence. As it usually did, his morbid fascination drew him closer, despite him not wanting to look. Yet, as he took those careful steps, his covered shoes tapping a staccato on the metal stepping plates, closer toward the tall marshmallows in their white scenes of crime coveralls, he found he couldn't look away. First, a pale, dainty foot with emerald nail polish came into view. It was severed at the knee. A second leg was on the ground next to it, a longer, thicker leg with sapphire nail polish anointing each wide ebony toe.

Two arms, one white and one black, were placed side by side as George headed towards the blue and white forensic tent.

As George got closer to the tent, its flaps open, the emergency lights brightened to offer him a view of a golden-brown torso with thighs still attached. There was no head, and it was amputated at the knees. The breasts were enormous; nipples pierced. A tattoo with the quote, 'I may be young, but I'm ready,' was located across the collarbone, heading towards the shoulder. Both arms had been severed, too.

"Sick bastard." An American accent.

"I'm sorry?"

"Whoever did this," the young SOCO from earlier said. "Sick bastard."

"Yeah..." George said as the young man walked away.

From what George could see, all parts were clean; there was no blood. Whoever did this must have cleaned them after killing them. The sick bastard was right. He could tell that at least three women had been killed by their skin colour.

A sharp tap on his back made him jump. He swivelled on the plate and met with DS Isabella Wood. "Looks like we have three bodies. IC1, and IC3 limbs, and an IC2 torso."

The police used IC codes to describe the apparent ethnicity of a suspect or victim. IC1 was White European. IC2 was Dark European such as a person of Mediterranean or Hispanic ethnicity. IC3 was Afro-Caribbean. Though they couldn't be sure without an identification.

"Hey, beautiful," he whispered, a massive grin on his face.

CHAPTER TWO

"I've missed you." He thought better of caressing her hand. It would have been awkward with the blue disposable gloves he was wearing, anyway.

"Hey, babe." She winked at him.

"Any ID?"

She shook her head. "We believe these body parts come from at least three different females because of each skin tone. We can't ID the torso yet. The tattoo might help, and we've taken DNA to send to the lab. Hopefully, she's on the database. We've done the same for the legs and arms. On the white hand, I got a match of seventy per cent on the thumb and eighty per cent on the index finger using a lantern. But whoever this is, isn't known to us." A lantern device was a handheld fingerprint reader they used to ID people, but like DNA, it only worked if their prints were on the database. "Got a hundred per cent scan on the lantern for the other hand, however. She's called Rita Lawrence. I've just phoned it through to the station and got DS Fry working on the background check. Nobody has reported her missing yet."

"Great work DS Wood," he said as a light breeze wafted the unwanted scent of death towards him. It was a thick, pungent scent that met his tongue and nostrils unpleasantly, a sour flavour he couldn't get rid of. He heaved, the smell reminding him of Erika Allen, Emma Atkinson and Eileen Abbott.

"Are you okay, George?"

"Yeah. It's been a while. The smell of death never leaves you, but I guess your memories fade." Death was never easy to deal with. The public believed that police officers or detectives would be used to it, but they were still human. Every time George saw a dead body, it was a brutal reminder of how cruel the human race was to itself.

Who had done this to these women? And why? The bins were a deposition site, and so he hoped the forensics would give him the answers as to where the women were killed. Were the women mugging victims, or was it a sexual assault gone wrong? Were the murders premeditated? How long had the body parts been in the bins? Beaumont nibbled the inside of his cheek and phoned Yolanda Williams, their CCTV expert. George explained the situation and asked her to recover CCTV from around the area to see if they could pinpoint a suspect. Then he needed pathology and forensics to unlock more pieces of the puzzle.

Beaumont ushered DS Wood away from the smell, and they continued their conversation by the police tape. "Any evidence of sexual assault?" George asked, his mouth thinning into a grim line.

An American voice from behind answered him. "There's evidence of sexual activity, but I wouldn't say assault."

George turned. "Who are you?"

"Hayden Wyatt, sir. Nice to meet you."

Wyatt attempted to shake hands, but George smiled and shook his head. "Better not, eh?"

"Ah, Detective Inspector, Beaumont." It was the familiar Geordie accent of Stuart Kent. "I see you've met my new assistant. He's a bit hyper for me."

George grinned. "Yeah, I bet. Any evidence of sexual assault?"

"Activity, yes. Assault, no. I can't check for semen here, but I've found evidence of lubrication, suggesting the culprit wore a condom, anyway."

"It's nice to see you, Stuart. What else can you tell me about the body parts?"

"Not much, Inspector. I can't even advise whether the amputations were pre- or post-mortem. Whoever killed these women is extremely forensically aware."

"No prints?"

"No," Hayden Wyatt said. "Looks as if they were wearing gloves."

"What about the fingernails?" George asked, looking directly at Kent so his assistant understood who he was talking to. "Any DNA from our culprit?"

"Sorry, there's nothing under the fingernails."

"Nothing on the bin bags, sir," Hayden Wyatt said. "We can study the bags under a microscope to compare with any you eventually find. It's quite ingenious. The labs can identify any similarities in the cell structure and effectively match them up to bags from the same roll. Like a puzzle, I suppose. But that requires you having a sample from a culprit."

Wyatt was getting ahead of himself, but George said nothing. "Time of death?"

Kent shrugged. "Sorry. Dr Ross will know more, but it'll be difficult to be sure considering the circumstances."

It began to drizzle overhead, and Kent excused himself and walked off to order his team to erect tents over the body parts. It would be no good for any of them if the rain washed away any forensic evidence the killer left behind.

DI Beaumont hung back with a silent DS Wood, watching Kent go. He could do little until he'd briefed his team and received the forensic results. But, first, they needed to find out who the other two women were.

Before he left, George asked Kent to get his SOCOs to search the rest of the bins in the alley. Then, he'd speak to DSU Smith back at the station to get the refuse collections for Middleton stopped.

As he left the alley, he was sure the young blond SOCO was watching him. There was something intense about him, something George didn't like.

Chapter Three

George drove back to the station, following behind DS Wood. DSU Smith had called his entire team in. They were crowded into Incident Room Four, the largest of their five glass-panelled incident rooms. Like the Miss Murderer case. Yolanda was set up in Five.

This was his room to manage and his room to update as they received information. George went to stand beside DS Wood at the front of the room. She whispered in his ear to let him know she had pinned a photograph of Rita Lawrence on the whiteboard. Underneath was a map, the deposition site circled in red ink.

George breathed in the atmosphere and savoured it. The sound of excited chatter filled the air, an unmistakable buzz spreading through the room. The details of the body parts were being discussed. This made him tick—not sitting in an office doing paperwork. No. It was the thrill of the hunt that was life itself. He was glad to be back, and the look on his face showed it.

"Thank you all for coming in so late," DI George Beaumont said, butterflies in his stomach. "I'm SIO, and DS Wood is my deputy. Detective Superintendent Smith has asked me to remind you there's no overtime, so I will return any hours spent here tonight to you." Everybody's eyes were on him, making his stomach bubble further, and George remembered he felt the same when he first stood up front at the beginning of the Miss Murderer Case.

George pointed at the photograph of Rita behind him, composed his thoughts and took a deep breath. "DSU Smith called DS Wood and me to a deposition site this evening. We found five body parts wrapped neatly in newspaper inside black bags deposited in commercial bins behind a row of shops and takeaways in Middleton."

There was a collective sigh from his team of detectives, especially notable from DS Elaine Brewer. "Stuart Kent couldn't determine whether the bodies were decapitated pre- or post-mortem." He smiled at Elaine, avoiding eye contact with the other detectives but noticing their collective expressions of anger and disgust. "I have little to share with you at this time. The pathologist will clarify everything after the post-mortems tomorrow."

His team was quiet as he explained the evidence of sexual activity and how Kent advised it was most likely consensual. George also explained how the culprit wore a condom and left no trace of themselves. "Whoever killed these women is forensically aware, but most people are these days." He shared Kent's explanation about the lack of forensic evidence on the bags and ordered his team to be on the lookout for any black bags during their duties. He thought samples would be necessary. "I spoke with DS Williams earlier and asked her to recover CCTV from around the area to see if we can pinpoint a suspect." He turned to her. She was sitting in the front row sporting a new straight pixie haircut. George thought it suited her.

"DC Blackburn, you're on CCTV with Yolanda. Learn from her. Trust me when I say it'll be precious in your future years."

Tashan nodded and smiled at Yolanda.

"I don't know what CCTV there is around the back of the shops or takeaways, but see what you can find. Don't just look at tonight, either. With Christmas, the bins haven't been emptied today. So my guess is whoever did this expected them to be. The Super has contacted the council, and they will stop bin collections for Middleton."

Despite being one of the most critical tasks, George knew working with CCTV footage was highly tedious. Most officers hated it, but it had been invaluable during his previous cases.

"DS Joshua Fry is completing a background check on Rita Lawrence. Calder Park is extracting DNA from the swabs as we speak, so they can give us a profile we can run through our databases. Detective Superintendent Smith has asked for the results to be expedited, but with the time of year, it may still take a couple of days."

There were more nods from his team.

"DS Wood is taking DC Scott to interview people working at the shops and takeaways tomorrow evening before they clock off." Wood nodded. "I want DC James to organise three Police Constables to join us on door-to-door duties in the morning." He looked around the room for Oliver and found him. DC Oliver James nodded his understanding.

George pointed at DS Jason Scott. "Your job is to look through the PNC and look for known criminals with an MO or similar MO to the one seen today. Then, check the whole UK, bring them in, and question them if you have to."

"Sir!" he said.

"I also need you to check for any recent mispers, Jay. Get a list of females first, then once you've done that, check for any other gender, and add them to a separate list." George smiled at his team. "I know I don't need to say this, but I am, anyway. Make sure everything is documented on HOLMES. But that's it, thanks, everyone," George said as the team began filing out of the room, talking among themselves. "And remember the message about overtime," he added. He knew his team would do what they could tonight, then all be back during their shifts, raring to go.

* * *

"You wanted to see me, sir?" George asked DSU Smith after entering his office.

"I just wanted to check up on you; make sure you're prepared for this. I know you completed all the counselling sessions, and the therapist advised you were ready. But she also said you weren't sleeping. Are you sleeping better?"

"That depends on how many whiskies I've had," George joked. He wasn't kidding, and the DSU looked at him as if he wasn't so sure it was a joke, either. Nothing got past that man.

"Anything on Rita Lawrence yet?" DSU Smith asked.

"Not yet. Josh is working on it, sir."

"Let me know when you find anything. Keep your phone on. DS Fry is the type to take his work home with him," Jim commanded in his deep, raspy voice. "We could do with somebody to confirm the ID."

George nodded. He agreed they needed somebody to identify Rita formally. "Yeah, that worries me, sir." Smith raised a brow, inviting George to expand. "I'm concerned about the recent budget cuts. If my team can't be in at all hours, we might not get this solved as fast as I'd like. The last thing I want is to slow the investigation down and allow the sick bastard to kill again."

"Watch your language, Beaumont." Smith raised his brow. "Look, I understand your concerns, but there's nothing I can do. This is an order from above, not from me. My hands are tied. Catch him before he escalates."

"Sir."

George got up to excuse himself when Smith stopped him. "I need to talk to you about this case."

Assuming Jim Smith would talk to him about the Miss Murderer or give him a pep talk, George said, "I feel good, sir. You can trust me with this murder inquiry—"

"I wouldn't have put you as SIO if I did not trust you, George. I can see you're ready, and I know you will have learnt from the mistake you made with Adam Harris." George nodded but winced at the name. "I wanted to discuss the MO."

"What about it? All we know is our culprit dismembers his victims and disposes of them. Stuart couldn't even pinpoint the time of death, sir. That's it. He couldn't tell me much at the scene, asking me to wait for Dr Ross' findings from the post-mortem."

"Okay, I need you to listen closely. Thirty years ago, I worked on a similar case. I was a young DS and worked under DCI Peter Alexander."

"Mia's dad?"

"Aye, son, I think he was a DI at the time. Mia told you he died in the line of duty?"

"Yes, sir." He was going to share with Smith that it was one of the reasons why they'd split up but held back. His relationship with Mia was strained because he was a detective like her dad.

Despite being a victim of the Miss Murderer, she felt guilty because not only was she having an affair with the killer, she had survived when others hadn't. In addition, she was struggling with her PTSD, and it didn't help that her due date was New Year's Day, and she was ready to burst. It also didn't help that when he first discovered the pregnancy, he shared his suspicion with her that the baby was Adam's and not his.

George always had the feeling Smith was in his mid to late fifties, the only hint being wisps of grey in his hair, and if the similar case was thirty years ago, his instinct was all but confirmed. "So what happened thirty years ago, sir?"

"Eerily the same situation as now, George. Very similar. A beggar found multiple dismembered body parts of two women initially. We think he killed four women altogether. They weren't placed in commercial bins like yours were George, but were similarly wrapped neatly in newspaper before being placed inside black bin bags and deposited in communal bins outside flats in Middleton, Belle Isle and Hunslet. We found DNA in the mouth of a victim. Semen. Our culprit was killing prostitutes, though he killed a young mother named Anna Hill, who wasn't a sex worker. There wasn't much DNA profiling back in 1994, and the DNA database didn't exist until 1995. We took DNA from men in the area to discount them from the operation, but Leeds was huge even back in ninety-four and ninety-five. It was a fool's errand. We cleared every suspect we had and then had to stop investigating. It was supposed to be a career case for DI Alexander and myself, but we failed everybody."

"So you didn't catch the culprit, sir?"

"No. The killings stopped, and we assumed the culprit had

moved abroad. Then, nearly a decade later, we thought it may have been Anthony Hardy, the Camden Ripper. We cross-referenced his DNA in 2003 when he was sentenced to life but got no match. The culprit's DNA is on our database, so it gets cross-referenced whenever anyone new is added. We even started comparing our profile against familial DNA profiles around the same time we compared it to Hardy's. Nothing. Whoever killed those women got away with it. But this seems similar. Maybe our culprit is bored. Or maybe he's back. Get the bastard for me, will you?"

"Okay, sir," George said as he stifled a yawn. *Tomorrow's going to be a long day,* he thought. "I'll do everything I can."

The Super spent the next twenty minutes detailing everything he remembered about the case, including information about his main suspect, Anthony Shields.

* * *

Detective Inspector George Beaumont's booming voice carried across the room. "I need you all in Incident Room Four in five minutes for another briefing."

"I've just spoken to the Super, and he believes it's similar to a case he worked on thirty years ago. They had no clear suspect but questioned a guy named Anthony Shields. Shields and every other suspect were all cleared, which was difficult considering they didn't have the DNA database," George said, looking around at his colleagues' wide eyes. What he'd said had raised a few eyebrows. "He was a DS back then and shared his memories of the case with me. The press named him Jack the Butcher, Jack because of his obvious choice of victim, and butcher because he dismembered his victims with what they assumed was a saw."

A few people nodded at the name. Elaine and Yolanda were probably aware of Jack the Butcher because of their age, but from the nods, most of his team knew of him, too. "It was a long time ago, but DSU Smith initially found two female bodies that had been dismembered, the parts wrapped neatly in newspaper before being placed in bin bags. Another female body was found a few days later, then the final one a week later. Three out of the four were sex workers. The last one, Anna Hill, was a stay-at-home mum, and DSU Smith is unsure to this day why she was targeted, but believes the killer became alarmed after killing Anna and fled the country."

There was a gentle murmur of surprise.

"The other victims were Nicole Green, Joanne Cox and Stacey Lumb. All confirmed prostitutes. All were white and had red hair. It seems Jack the Butcher had a type. This, again, is very different from our culprit. All were picked up, taken to an unknown place, and were never seen alive again. From what DSU Smith said, they engaged in sexual activity with the culprit, who then killed them and chopped them up. What worries me is the Super said they were picked up from Water Lane, the red-light district, yet there were no witnesses who mention any make or reg of any cars."

"Where were the body parts found, sir?" DC Blackburn asked. Blackburn was a keen athlete who competed at a high level in his university days, a young lad with good manners and great potential. George liked him a lot.

"Good question, Tashan. Now, unlike our culprit, Jack the Butcher disposed of his victims in communal bins outside flats in Middleton, Belle Isle and Hunslet. So it's possible Rita Lawrence and the other two women were sex workers like the original victims, but we haven't finished the background checks yet. So the two cases might not be related. Or we could have a copycat. Once I know more, I'll inform you all."

"What about suspects, sir? Can the Super give us more info on Shields?" Tashan inquired.

"I haven't got that far with the reports yet, Tashan. Your homework for tonight is to familiarise yourself with the original inquiry. All the case files have been scanned and uploaded to HOLMES, and we now have access to them. That goes for all of you. Feel free to print them out if it is more convenient, but I don't want them lying around your homes. This information is confidential. If I hear anything about this in the papers, I'll know it's come from this room." George trusted his team, but the warning still stood. "Finish up, get yourselves home, and tomorrow we'll investigate the local area."

There were nods all around. The ball was in motion. "And remember to log these extra hours so we can give you them back."

Chapter Four

Around 11 am that Saturday, George joined DS Wood, DC Oliver James, and three police constables as they went door-to-door in the area of Middleton surrounding the takeaways.

George, DC James and a female constable scoured Lingwell Avenue and the streets that led east. DS Wood, with male and female constables, combed up and down the area of North Lingwell Road, including the surrounding streets outside the primary school, in their search for information.

House-to-house inquiries drove George insane, and whilst it was below his rank, with the budget cuts, he knew he needed to dig deep and get on with it. The initial hours of a murder inquiry, the so-called 'golden hours' were critical, and George understood the urgency of everything.

George had already searched the houses south of Lingwell Avenue, venturing down Lingwell Crescent, nearly stepping on a piece of hardened dog shit. He got nothing, nothing at all. Nobody had seen anything. He knew it would be a long shot, but he tried anyway.

George gritted his teeth and spent the next hour speaking with residents on Middleton Park Road between Lingwell Avenue and Hopewell View. Still, he got nothing, and desperation was causing his stress to build.

The last area of his to check was Back Mount Pleasant, a long, straight street that stretched away from him, ending at Hopewell View. A row of terraced houses lined his left, with newer semi-detached houses to his right. The terraced houses were back-to-back, each with a walled or fenced front garden about as big as a postage stamp. Some were well kept, but others were littered with wooden fence posts, brick debris, or rubbish bags.

George clenched his fists and approached the next house on his list, taking out his pocket notebook. Nearly every place he visited resulted in silence; most people were out. It was Saturday afternoon, after all. The ones who did answer were no help. They had no suspect to ask about, nothing more than, 'Have you seen anybody suspicious hanging around the alley at the back of the takeaways?'.

After waiting for a minute or two, George turned away from yet another unanswered door, heading towards the bottom of the street ending at Hopewell View. He knew at the end of the road there was a chippy, and his stomach grumbled.

An older man eventually answered a few houses down, glancing up at him through translucent eyes. George doubted that even the non-visually impaired wouldn't have seen anything this far from the crime scene, but he hoped the man may have heard something. George introduced himself and explained they were looking for information on any suspicious characters who lived near the takeaways and the shops.

"Are you as blind as me, lad?" the man snapped back at him. "I can barely see the door, our kid. And my 'earing ain't so good, neither!"

"Yes, well, thank—"

But the older man wasn't finished. "There's that bitch beggar who always steals from bins when it's cold. She's suspicious, isn't she? I caught her rummaging around in my bin the week before Christmas. So I called you lot as I wasn't putting up with it any more. And now you want my help?"

It was true that no one would have taken the older man seriously, but George needed his help. "Please, sir. What's the beggar's name?"

"Deirdre. Bitch. Always in mi bins."

"Deirdre Haliday?"

"Aye. You need to speak to 'er. Tell 'er to fuck off 'way from mi bins," he said, still ranting on.

George nodded his head and asked, "Anybody else, sir? There's been a murder, and we're looking for anybody suspicious." George wasn't sure it was a good idea to tell the older man about the murder, but he needed anything.

The older man turned back into his house, shaking his head. George stepped back and glanced down the road, hoping he'd get some decent information, though he doubted it. "Thank you. Before I go, I need to ask you, have you heard anything unusual in the area? Word of mouth? Anything like that?"

The old man turned his head back towards George and asked, "You say you're on a murder inquiry?" George nodded his head. "There's a murderer who lives 'round here. His name's Tony Shaw. Di'n't used to be, though. Used to be called summat else. Lives in the Park Lea flats at the bottom of Moor Flatts Road."

George knew the flats. "A murderer? What do you mean?"

"Guy changed his name, but not his looks. I remember him from the paper, murdering bugger."

"Can you elaborate on why he's a murderer, sir?"

"Well, about thirty years ago, Detective, he was accused of

killing prossies. But, honestly, it's him. You'll see. The paper said he'd cut them into bits and hid them in bins around South Leeds."

***

George took down the older man's name, address, and contact number. He was called Gerald Baldwin but couldn't give much more information on the rumours about Tony Shaw.

He called Josh Fry, who was back at the station finishing Rita Lawrence's background check. "Josh, I need you to check the PNC for a Tony Shaw. He lives in Middleton. He was brought in during the Jack the Butcher case thirty years ago. He'll be in his fifties or sixties. Get me a picture I can use to identify him with, please." He thought back to the older man and what he said. 'There's a murderer who lives 'round here. His name's Tony Shaw. Didn't used to be, though.' It can't be a coincidence. "You know, the names Tony and Anthony, Shaw and Shields, can't be a coincidence, right?"

"Maybe he changed his name? I'll look into it for you, sir."

"Thanks, Josh. Is the Super in yet? I've been trying to ring him, but he isn't answering."

"Yeah, but he's been in a meeting all morning. I'll ask him about Tony Shaw when he's finished and call you back."

"Cheers, mate."

DI Beaumont approached the burgundy door and pressed a random button, hoping it wasn't Tony Shaw who answered.

A young woman's voice answered, and George said, "I have a parcel for Tony Shaw, love. Can you let me in?"

A buzz indicated the lock had disengaged, but George still didn't know which flat Shaw lived in. He cracked the door open, jamming his foot inside to stop it from closing. "Thanks, love. Which number's his flat? It's rubbed out on the sticker."

"Bottom floor to your left as you get in."

"Cheers, love."

The door flew open before he reached the handle, slamming into his left ankle.

"Ah, shit!" Beaumont said, bending down to inspect for damage. A massive man in his late fifties or early sixties, his coat strained to nearly bursting, had burst through the door in a hurry.

"Sorry about that, mate. Didn't see you." The man's voice was a low rumble.

"No worries. I'm Detective Inspector George Beaumont," he said, flashing his warrant card. "Do you know Tony Shaw?"

"No, sorry, fella, I don't live 'ere."

George watched as the bulky man shuffled away, his big bald head glinting from the low winter sun. A beep distracted George from the man's glowing head, and he pulled out his mobile phone to find a WhatsApp from Josh. In it was a picture of the man who had knocked him over. Tony Shaw.

"Tony Shaw? Stop, Police—" The man turned to face him, but before George could say another word, time seemed to be still, and hopeless panic spread across Tony Shaw's face. And he bolted.

George stood up and raced after him, eventually grabbing onto the man's jacket and tugging him back before reaching Town Street. But Shaw was well over six feet and must have weighed something like twenty stone. Despite having at least twenty years on him, George struggled to tug him back, and when Tony wriggled, it threw George off balance. That, along with his injured ankle, meant Shaw got away.

George exclaimed as he wobbled, falling onto the hard stone flags at the side of the junction. Winded, he scrambled to his feet, a swear word leaving his mouth, and gave chase. George looked left and right but saw no souls; Tony was gone and could be hiding anywhere.

"Bollocks!" George hissed a typical Yorkshire man's curse. He sprinted left towards the church, sure he'd seen Shaw headed in that direction, his ankle smarting from the impact with the door, his knee burning from the collision with the ground—but his pride was hurt the most.

Shaw was gone. He'd fucked it. Again.

Embarrassed, George trudged back to the entrance of the flat to make the shameful calls to DSU Smith and DS Fry. He'd ring Josh first, authorise an alert on the PNC and get him to check the DVLA for any registered vehicles. *The guy might have a mobile phone, too.* He looked around the area, remembering Middleton was a hotspot regarding cell towers and cameras. Josh could set up a mobile trace, and once they knew if he had any vehicles, they could alert ANPR for number plate recognition. George thought about delaying his call to the Super about his failure. They might catch him within the next hour, anyway.

Yet a deep feeling within his stomach made him call the Super, anyway. They hadn't even heard of the name Tony Shaw half an hour ago. They knew nothing about his life, his activities or his haunts. *If Tony were smart,* George thought, *he'd run and keep running or hide until he had gone.* Then, nobody would be stupid enough to come out of hiding and walk straight into George's hands.

He only wished it were so easy. Sometimes.

The Super didn't answer, and he didn't bother to leave a

message. So as George sat on the front step of the flats, he had only one question: Why did Tony Shaw run? But George knew there could only be one reason—Shaw had something to hide. Maybe he was Anthony Shields, and perhaps he'd committed murder.

Beaumont waited outside for another half an hour, just on the off-chance Shaw was stupid enough to come back. While waiting, he called DC Oliver and DS Wood for updates on their searches. Hardly anybody was home, and they didn't have any credible information when they were. People rarely pried into back alleyways behind takeaways.

Oblivious to the shadow behind him, George continued questioning Shaw's motive, means, and opportunity. He was a tall, bulky man who managed to escape him. Yes, he shuffled, but there was no sign of a dodgy gait when Shaw ran. He had the means. But what about motive—

The burgundy door hit him again. George froze, flinched as it hit him again, then turned to see a middle-aged, scrawny woman standing behind him, hands on her hips, her face pulled into a scowl. God knows what she had done to her hair that morning, but it sat atop her tiny head, reminding George of a skunk's tail.

"Oh, sorry, love, I didn't see you there. I'll move," he said, getting up from the step and holding the door open for her. He flashed his warrant card and his best smile. "DI Beaumont. Have you got a minute?"

"Sure, Inspector. What can I help you with?"

A scouse accent. He hadn't expected it. "Do you know Tony Shaw?"

"The smelly bastard who lives there?" she said, pointing to the bottom flat on the left. George nodded. "Weirdo. I don't know him, though, no. I try to keep away from the dirty twat."

"Do you live in the flats, Ms—"

"Miss Carmichael. Eleanor." A beautiful name for a monster of a woman. He shuddered. "Yes, I do. Proper shithole. Do you need anything else? Anything. At. All?" She extended a nicotine-stained finger to caress his chest but thought better. Instead, she raised a brow and smiled, stuck her tongue out and licked her lips. Her intentions were obvious. Instead of flattering him, it repulsed him.

"Can you tell me anything else about Tony Shaw?"

Eleanor Carmichael strode down the step, getting relatively too close for George's liking. The smell of stale smoke suffocated him. "He has a lot of money and likes to pay for sex. I don't doubt it by looking at him. But, on the other hand, I don't think anybody would willingly give up her pussy to him."

"Okay, thank you. If you think of anything else, you can call me." He handed her his card but immediately regretted it as she touched his thumb with a brown-stained finger.

"Can I call you even if I don't think of anything else?" she said. Then, when George didn't answer, she added, "Bye-bye, Inspector."

On a whim, George took a deep breath and stepped into the block. Shaw's door was gently swaying, opening by itself and bumping shut. *He must have left a window open,* George mused, his curiosity piqued. Could he have a brief look? It wasn't as though George was breaking in, especially if the door was already open. He'd be doing Shaw a favour by checking nobody was robbing the place. George thought for a moment, knowing that it would look dodgy without a warrant. George's conscience warred against temptation. He tapped his foot furiously on the grey, carpeted floor and thought, *fuck it!*

But to be sure, he shouted, "Police!" Silence. "Hello! I'm entering this property under the suspicion that somebody is trespassing or a burglary is in progress!"

Again, there was no response. George grinned.

It was freezing inside the dim flat. He slipped on his overshoes and gloved up, just in case. A lack of room meant an old crimson sofa was jammed up against a little plastic table; a chair that had seen better days was wedged under it. Separating the living room from the kitchen was a tiny counter that looked as if it dated from the seventies and matched the finish on the cupboard doors.

There was hardly room to swing a cat, never mind commit murder and cut up his victims. The place didn't smell, either. Death had a distinctive odour that George, try as he might, could never forget.

Yet despite the aged feel and the darkness that loomed, it was clean but messy, if not a tad claustrophobic. George had never enjoyed small spaces, especially dark, cluttered ones.

Letters were strewn everywhere, both opened and unopened. Most were unpaid bills that littered the clumpy velvet sofa. On the tiny table was a stack of paper that looked like a manuscript. *Was Shaw a writer?* Beaumont flicked through it, not intending to read it. The Cleaver Killer—A novel about a serial killer who dismembered prostitutes.

George's conscience warred against temptation once again. Did he allow Shaw's privacy, or did he give in to his professional curiosity? He toiled with the conflict for a minute, but the latter won, and he began to read. Shaw used violent and gory words as if the author got a kick out of sawing off limbs. He knew his stuff, though. Had Shaw managed to get a hold of a detective and discuss the procedure? Could his motive be that he wanted his novel to be authentic? Circumstantial at best.

Scooping up the pages of the manuscript and clipping them back together, he looked around the room for anything else. Finally, he located a small bathroom to his right. George stilled as he turned the knob, the smell of bleach suffocating him.

He pulled the cord, switched on the light, and turned it back off. He urgently called in the incident with Shaw, explaining he entered as the door was open and he thought he could hear noises inside. They needed to arrest Anthony Shaw—immediately.

Chapter Five

George had put out a call for Anthony Shaw's immediate arrest based on what he'd seen in the man's bathroom. The rest of the tiny flat—a small bedroom—had made for quick searching, and there was nothing that stood out.

Then, he left, closing the door behind him. By the time a PC arrived, Anthony Shaw had still not returned. George had taken another look around the area of the flat in case Shaw was hiding, but he was nowhere.

The door-to-door team had finished their questioning around that time, so together, they trawled that area of Middleton, searching as far as the shops at the top of the avenue, Asda and the Middleton District Centre. A steady drizzle had started, dampening George's already foul mood—but still, they saw nor heard nothing of Anthony Shaw.

One of the PCs, a former PCSO called Babou Ola, it turned out, knew Anthony professionally. And from what George found in the flat, he shouldn't have been surprised. From the information filtering through, Shaw had regularly been in trouble with the police during the past ten years.

So George left PC Ola to it, with strict instructions to find and arrest him urgently, whilst they headed to Tony's work to see if he had gone there.

But George hated to admit it. He doubted Shaw was at work and assumed instead that he'd disappeared.

* * *

DI Beaumont slowed his Honda and turned into the centre of a small industrial estate near South Leeds Stadium to find the correct address. The older orange brick buildings contrasted against the newer blue and silver prefab warehouses made of stone and corrugated metal.

The courier company Tony Shaw worked for was situated in one of the newer prefabs. The signage fixed on the spiked metal fencing proudly displayed the words T. Myles Delivery Experts in blue writing and on a white background, which Beaumont could hardly read through the deluge that battered the roof of his car. Many delivery vans clogged the yard, though the road leading up to a large warehouse with huge open roller doors was clear. This was where the vans were parked to be loaded or unloaded.

George parked on the road outside due to the lack of visitor parking. It was annoying because of the constant rain, but what could he do?

Holding a brolly over their heads, the detectives exited the Honda and walked through the open gates. It was freezing, and George wished he had put his coat on. He could smell fuel in the air. George hated these places, preferring to be in the open with nature around him.

By the looks of it, the small building to the right of the warehouse contained the reception and back office. They walked towards it, closing their umbrellas and shaking off the excess water. George held the door for Wood, who smiled at him as she entered. Despite not having long to get ready this morning, she looked incredible.

Inside was an older woman waiting behind a desk. "DI Beaumont and DS Wood. We would like to speak to the owner, Tommy Myles." They both held out their warrant cards.

She frowned a look of prolonged contemplation before raising a brow at the two detectives. Wood, her brown hair tied up in a bun, did not attempt to say anything and simply stared through the rude woman. The elderly lady soon got the message and quickly called Tommy. With a quiet voice, she explained two detectives were here to see him. Wood nodded. The lady hung up.

"Okay, he will see you now. Follow me." She opened a waist-height wooden swinging door and moved to the side to allow them in. "He's in the upstairs office behind me, waiting. Take the stairs to your left."

They entered the door and headed up the steps, the pattering rain on the metal roof amplified, hurting George's ears. It was colder inside than outside, and George regretted not wearing his coat once again.

They didn't knock as they entered the first office, but George noticed a large plaque stating, 'Tommy Myles CEO'.

A man was sitting behind the desk, devoid of a suit, wearing a blue polo bearing the company logo. He didn't get up when they flashed their warrant cards and introduced themselves. He didn't offer them any drinks, getting straight to the point. "Tommy Myles," he said in a baritone Yorkshire accent. "What can I do for you, officers?"

"We're detectives, actually, and we're here about Tony Shaw. We tried calling you repeatedly but had no answer."

CHAPTER FIVE

"Yeah, well, it's hectic this time of year. We deliver about the same number of packages in the weeks after Christmas as before. Did you not leave a message?"

Tommy Myles stood up, his balding head glinting in the harsh light. He was a chunkily built man with the start of a beer belly. He offered a tattooed arm and hand to George and Wood, crushing George's hand, hopefully not crushing Wood's. Up close, Myles' shoulders, arms, and thighs were bursting with muscles, though more akin to a weightlifter than a bodybuilder. He smiled, and overall, George thought the man oozed strength and confidence.

"We're here about one of your employees, Tony Shaw," George said whilst the rain picked up, increasing the battering sound on the roof.

"You get used to it," Myles said, nodding to the roof. He was speaking to Wood, who was looking up. "What's Shaw done now, darling?"

"Excuse me?" Wood asked.

"Shaw, love. He said you were here about him. What's he done?"

"Is he due to work today?" George asked.

Tommy didn't take his eyes away from Wood. He saw in her precisely what George did, and George moved closer so they were shoulder to shoulder. He wasn't usually jealous and clenched his fist, counting down from ten in his head.

"Answer the question, Tommy. Is Shaw due in today?"

"I need you to tell me what this is all about first," Tommy said, still looking at Wood.

Purposely, George answered before Wood could. "We're investigating the murder of three women. We'd like to ask him some questions."

"Oh, shit!" Tommy's mouth dropped, and he looked horrified. "You think he might be involved? How'd they die?" He was still looking at Wood.

"We can't divulge that information as we are in the middle of an inquiry."

He nodded his understanding. "Do you think he killed someone then?" he blurted out.

Wood shared a glance with George. "As my partner, DS Wood said, I'm afraid we can't comment on an ongoing investigation. We can only tell you we are investigating the deaths of three women at this point."

Tommy pursed his lips and nodded furiously, arms folded across his sturdy chest. "Right, let's get down to business, eh?" He shook his head again. "I knew he was dodgy, but murder..." He trailed off.

"When is Shaw next due at work?" Beaumont asked again, his tone oozing annoyance.

"You want to know where Tony Shaw is?" Tommy asked, walking towards one of the floor-to-ceiling windows. "Well, Tony Shaw is down there as we speak, filling up his van for the late deliveries."

"We appreciate your help," Wood said, sharing a look with George. "Unfortunately, this is a warrant for his arrest." With a smile, George continued to let her lead; their differing strengths during an investigation were necessary, and this was her time to shine. "That means he won't be fulfilling those deliveries, as he will be coming with us."

They turned and left the office, walking down the steps before Tommy Myles, out of breath, confronted them. "Stop! Do you have any idea what this will do for my business? He can't be a killer. We vet everybody."

CHAPTER FIVE

"Sorry, Mr Myles," Wood said. "We have the right to retain him for twenty-four hours. I suggest you find some cover."

Tommy's face dropped once again, but he nodded his head. He gulped deeply and said, "Tony Shaw's a nice guy. But, unfortunately, I think you're barking up the wrong tree."

"You called him 'dodgy' and asked what he'd 'done now.' Clearly, you think well of him but are aware of his background. Yet now, he's suddenly 'nice', and we're not doing our jobs right," George countered.

"Did he work last night?" Wood asked.

Tommy glanced at her, then back to George, as though confused that they had changed direction. "Aye."

"What days does he normally work? How many hours?" She crossed her arms over her chest. Somehow, the temperature had plummeted even more.

Tommy winced. "We're swamped around Christmas, as I said. He probably worked every night since the first of December. Probably only had Christmas Day off."

Wood looked at Beaumont, who nodded. "What hours does he work?"

Tommy unfolded his arms and closed the distance. He pulled out his mobile and started tapping. "He's been working three until midnight, hence why he's here now." Wood jotted notes in her pocket notebook.

"How's his behaviour been to you recently? Nothing different about his appearance, or owt?" George said.

Tommy shook his head emphatically. "He's been the same as he usually is. And I've noticed nothing unusual. He gets to work on time, loads his van efficiently, and delivers to customers until 10 pm. Then, from 10 pm until 12 midnight, he picks post up from the Royal Mail. We have a contract with them, you see. He has had no negative feedback. No fines. He's been alright." Tommy looked like he had little else to say. "It's always tough this time of year, especially now because we've had a few drivers off, and the rest of us have to pick up the slack. Hence the hours he's working." The dark shadows under Tommy's eyes gave his tiredness away. "But it's all legal, detectives. We have the hours logged, and it might look like it, but no one's going over their maximum hours. I have made sure appropriate breaks are in place."

George wasn't convinced, especially considering what he had told them about the shifts Shaw was working. But it wasn't why he was here. *At least Shaw will get twenty-four hours' rest,* he thought with a chuckle. "Do you have anything else to tell us?"

Tommy shrugged. "No, sorry. Better take you to him, yeah?"

"Yeah," both detectives said in unison.

DS Wood followed closely behind Tommy Myles, with DI Beaumont following her. She smelled like a mix of vanilla and coffee. She left that perfume at his place, and he'd never admit it to anybody, but he was guilty of spraying her pillow with the scent when she wasn't there. The last six months had been difficult for George, and he wasn't sure he would have coped without her. "Thanks for your help, Mr Myles," Wood said. "We'll be in touch if we need anything else."

He nodded and then led them towards a man filling his van with parcels. "Tony, mate. Some people are here to see you."

Tony Shaw looked up quickly and cleared his throat. "Who, boss?" He saw George Beaumont, dropped a package and sprinted away.

Beaumont took a deep breath and ran after him. Again. *Why*

the fuck did criminals insist on running away?

"Stop, Tony Shaw, you're under arrest. You do not have to say anything, but anything you do say—"

Shaw suddenly stopped, realising he had sprinted into the warehouse instead of out of it. There was nowhere for him to hide, and George slammed into him, the once dulling pain in his ankle increasing with fervour.

"Come with us, Shaw," George said with a smile that reached his eyes but held no warmth.

Shaw nodded, but his gaze was troubled as he left in cuffs, glancing back at his boss, his eyes pleading.

Chapter Six

Detective Superintendent Jim Smith came and knocked on his office door. "We're ready for you, George," he said.

"Sir."

George followed Smith towards his office, but Smith came to a sudden halt. "I just wanted to let you know that you're not in trouble, George and that I'm sorry I've been secretive since you got back."

George gave him a smile and nod and accompanied him to his office.

"DI Beaumont," DCS Sadiq said in his north-eastern twang, made famous by Gazza and Ant and Dec. "It's been a while. How are you?"

George was about to sit in what was usually an empty chair, but a tall, solidly built man with a thick head of blond hair, sharp brown eyes, and a pleasant face occupied it. His muscles bulged, threatening to rip free from his shirt. "I'm well, sir. Hope you are too." He turned to the guy in the chair. It was the stranger's sharp nose that drew George in. It made him look familiar, especially with the blond hair. "DI George Beaumont, nice to meet you." George looked at Smith with questioning eyes.

CHAPTER SIX

"Likewise," the stranger said in a Geordie accent not too dissimilar to Stuart Kent's or Jim Smith's. He didn't get up, nor did he offer to shake, but he did offer a smile, revealing two perfect rows of white teeth.

The stranger turned to Smith and smiled, his boss looking uneasy, and George immediately felt a sense of déjà vu. It was rare for Smith to look this uneasy. George could only think of one time when the boss had looked so dishevelled.

Smith took a drink from his mug and said, "George, meet another of our Geordie detectives, DCI Alexander Peterson."

"Let us get straight to the point," DCS Sadiq said. "Jim advised me on the triple murder case you're investigating. I believe it is too similar to the Jack the Butcher case from thirty years ago, especially as you already have one of the original suspects in custody. But, for all we know, the cases could be connected. As such, I've appointed DCI Peterson as lead on this."

"Wait, does that mean—"

"You'll remain SIO, DI Beaumont," Sadiq said, interrupting George. "Instead of asking Jim for support with warrants and everything else, you'll turn to DCI Peterson instead. He'll be involved in every step, so I need you to brief him on the situation. Are we clear?"

George took a deep breath before he responded. It would be no good to argue with the Chief Super. At least he was still the SIO. "Crystal, sir."

He spent the next twenty minutes explaining they had four limbs and one torso believed to be separate parts from three different women. Forensically, not much was picked up from the crime scene, as they thought it was a deposition site only. However, they were waiting on the Calder Park lab to carry out an environmental profile which would give them an idea of where the women were killed and could be used later as evidence for a conviction.

Next, George advised DCI Peterson about the DNA profiling they were waiting for, as they couldn't currently identify two of the victims. He also reported how they'd used a lantern device on the two hands, and whilst they'd achieved decent scans, only one gave a result. Rita Lawrence. They had procured her driving licence from the DVLA, and DS Joshua Fry had finished with her background check.

"DS Fry finished briefing me on Rita Lawrence just before you called me here. The file has been uploaded to HOLMES. Rita had been arrested as a kid for shoplifting before progressing to mugging an older man. She was involved in a burglary where her partner at the time assaulted the resident. Rita was incarcerated but was let out for good behaviour. She then worked in a supermarket cleaning for six months before quitting and joining an escort agency." He handed over a paper file to DCI Peterson.

George was about to explain further, but then he hesitated. Peterson would probably already be aware of Tony Shaw.

"I've read most of your reports on HOLMES, Inspector. So you have Tony Shaw in custody. So he assaulted you and resisted arrest?"

"Yes, sir."

"Fucker has something to hide, eh?" Peterson said.

George looked at the DCS, who laughed. They must be close, George assumed. Foul language had always got him into trouble. "I believe so, sir."

"I'm not the kind to pull rank, George, so you can get rid of the sir. Alex is just fine."

CHAPTER SIX

"Okay, thanks, Alex. We're waiting on the Royal Courts of Justice to confirm whether Tony changed his name from Anthony Shields to Tony Shaw."

"It'd make sense that the sick bastard changed his name after what happened thirty years ago," Smith said. "You got an ETA?"

"Not yet, sir. DS Fry is working on it. With the budget cuts and the cancelled overtime, we can only go so fast—"

"I get it, Beaumont, but it's out of my hands—"

"It's even out of my hands, DI Beaumont," the Chief Super added.

George felt as if a sledgehammer had hit him in the chest. He hoped pleading to his boss's boss would work. "I'm just worried he's going to kill again whilst we stick to set shifts," George explained.

"If it's too difficult for you to investigate this case under usual circumstances, we can get somebody to take over as SIO?"

DCI Alex Peterson was nodding his head.

Not for the first time, it felt as if DCS Sadiq wanted him off the case, and after what he'd done to the Miss Murderer, he knew that disobeying the DCS could be the end of his career. "That won't be necessary, sir. I only meant—"

"I think what George is trying to say, Chief Superintendent Sadiq, is he wants to capture the culprit who did this ASAP," Smith interrupted. "Whilst I agree George should report to Alex instead of myself, George has both my trust and my respect, and I believe, given a chance, he will solve this murder inquiry."

"Thank you, sir," George responded, unable to disguise his delight at the boss having his back.

"I have no doubt, Jim," DCS Mohammed Sadiq said. "As I said, he will continue as SIO reporting to Alex. But as for the overtime, it's out of my hands, too."

A rare, faint smile formed on Jim Smith's lips. "Do you have anything else to add, Beaumont?" Smith asked.

He shook his head.

"Good. Detective Chief Inspector Peterson, Detective Chief Superintendent Sadiq, and I have other matters to discuss. I'll speak with you later."

Dismissed, George rose from his seat. "Thank you, sir," he said to DCS Sadiq. Then, he repeated the same farewell to DSU Smith.

"I'm going to take some of your team to visit Shaw's flat whilst you interview him. Kent and his team of SOCOs are on their way. I'll come and find you after, Inspector," DCI Peterson remarked as George exited the office.

* * *

It was never a dull moment working on the HMET. George, shocked with the contents of his conversation with the DCS, the DSU and the DCI, went straight in to interview Tony Shaw as he'd already filled DS Wood in on the way to Shaw's workplace. He omitted entering Shaw's apartment without a warrant, knowing he could be in big trouble if anybody found out, and it worried him that DCI Peterson was currently on his way to search the address.

"I didn't do it," an angry Tony said the moment the pair of detectives walked into the interview room. He was already waiting with his lawyer, a tiny woman who sat as far away from him as was humanly possible. Shaw's thick, muscled arms

CHAPTER SIX

folded on the table, his head was down, and he was slumped in the chair as though he couldn't be arsed. His long, black beard was greasy, a pungent odour of sweat lingering in the air. Being in an interview room hadn't ruffled him. Yet the guy was sweating profusely, and the cloying smell was intensifying. DC Blackburn had purposely turned the heating to the lava setting. He may have put up a stoic façade, but his body language told the opposite. George was confident they had their man.

Shaw looked up at Beaumont, who stared at him for nearly half a minute until Shaw turned his rebellious glare back to the table. He took his seat opposite the suspected killer in silence, and Wood sat beside him. George wanted her to lead the interview—show the superiors what she was made of and possibly get her the promotion she was due. Wood pressed the recording button to start and introduced everyone in the room.

"Why run away, Mr Shaw?" Wood asked, her voice soft and calm.

"It's obvious. You think I killed and butchered those women?" Tony said, his mouth pulling into a scowl. He balled his fists up on the table and shook his head. They'd fingerprinted him and taken DNA swabs, and forensics would try to match him to anything they found at the scene.

"What women, Mr Shaw?" Wood asked. She shrugged her shoulders and held up her hands.

"You bloody well know which women. There are no secrets in Miggy. Word got out last night. Facebook is rife, or so my neighbour tells me."

"Fine, Mr Shaw. Did you kill these women?" Wood asked, inviting Shaw and his lawyer to look at documents two to four, images of the body parts found in the bins.

Shaw and his lawyer didn't look at the images. "No! I did not!"

"Then why did you run away, Mr Shaw?" she asked. "Look at document five, which shows an image of Rita Lawrence. Did you kill this woman?"

"No. I've never seen her before. And I didn't run away. But, when the inspector showed me his warrant card, I panicked."

"Help me understand, Mr Shaw," Wood said, smiling. "From my point of view, you assaulted a police detective to escape. You know that carries a heavy sentence? If you're innocent, then why did you do it?"

Tony's flushed complexion deepened, and a bead of sweat dripped from his greasy beard. "No! I didn't assault anybody. It was an accident. It didn't happen the way you said. I just, just—"

"Just be honest with me, Mr Shaw!" Wood said, leaning forward, running a hand through her brown hair. "I want the truth because the stuff you're giving me now isn't getting us anywhere. The fact is that you caused Detective Inspector Beaumont's injuries by escaping him. That's correct, isn't it?"

Tony nodded and shifted in his seat before shaking his head. "Yes and no, Sergeant. I opened my door at the same time he did. I apologised," he said, looking at George to confirm the story. Beaumont stared at him impassively and said nothing until he darted his eyes between the two detectives. They both stayed silent. He had been advised of his right to remain silent, yet for once, their suspect was speaking without being prompted. *Let's hope it continues,* George thought.

"Where were you between 5 and 9 pm on Thursday the twenty-sixth of December?"

"Work, probably."

CHAPTER SIX

"What time did you get to work?"

"3 pm."

They already knew this from the information Shaw's boss Tommy had given them, but it was always best to check. It could have been that he dumped the bodies earlier. They were checking for CCTV footage of the entire week. "Okay, Tony, let's ignore that you assaulted me for now. You lied to me when I asked if you knew Tony Shaw. And you resisted arrest. Twice. Why?"

Tony's scowl deepened. "I've already told you. I panicked because of the women that had been killed—"

"Because you were a suspect thirty years ago in a similar case?" Wood interjected.

Tony said nothing, glaring at Wood.

My, my if looks could kill.

"Well, it's true, isn't it? Although you were Anthony Shields back then, right?" The information they were waiting for had been uploaded to HOLMES 2 whilst George had met with the DCS, the DSU and the new DCI. Along with a team of SOCOs, the DCI, his DC, and a few of George's team were searching Shaw's house, legally, with a warrant this time, whilst they conducted the interview.

Both detectives watched Shaw like a hawk. They saw the flaring of his nostrils and the widening of his eyes, which Shaw quickly hid. His entire body tightened, as did his mouth. "No comment."

"We know you used to be named Anthony Shields, Tony. Information from the Royal Courts of Justice has confirmed this. See document nine in your folder."

Shaw did not look, but his lawyer did. She was fuming as if Shaw hadn't disclosed this to her. "No comment."

"So you deny being involved in a similar case thirty years ago?" Wood asked.

"No comment."

Wood looked at George, a look of annoyance in her eyes. She had expected him to talk, but clearly, he'd changed his mind.

"What do you do for a living, Tony?" George asked, changing pace and the type of questioning. Shaw looked shocked.

"You know what I do. I work for Tommy Myles."

"Ah, well, an honest answer. Good for you." He hoped Shaw was going to confess to writing serial killer novels. "So what do you do when you're not delivering parcels?"

"Nothing. The cost of living is too high. I can't afford to do nothing."

"Nothing at all? You don't frequent escorts?" He shook his head, and George made a note. The man was lying, especially considering what Eleanor Carmichael had told him. "Some things cost a pittance. I like to draw, though I'm not very good. A pencil and an art pad are pretty cheap. What do you like to do, DS Wood?"

She thought for a moment, her initial look of confusion replaced with a cheeky grin. "I like to work out. I can go out for a run for free. What do you do, Tony?"

"I write."

Bingo.

Wood, at her leisure, slowly smiled and asked, "You write? Wow! What do you write? Books and stuff?"

He nodded.

"What genre? I'm partial to a good romance myself," Wood said evenly.

Silence.

"For the tape, Tony Shaw remains silent—"

"I must protest," his lawyer cut in. "This bears no relevance, and if you keep asking irrelevant questions, I have no choice but to advise my client to answer 'no comment' to every question. You haven't disclosed one piece of evidence, detectives."

"As we have already advised, we arrested Mr Shaw for resisting arrest, which he did twice. Once at his flat, and once at his place of work."

"Please disclose the reason for the initial arrest," his lawyer asked.

"The assault of a police officer. He caused physical harm to Detective Inspector George Beaumont."

Shaw spoke. "It was an accident—"

His lawyer cut him off, glaring at Shaw, forcing him to shut up. "You have no proof of this. No eyewitnesses. My client has advised it was an accident. Repeatedly! This is absurd. I would like a break with my client. Now! We will also seek damages for wrongful arrest."

Chapter Seven

George was late for the post-mortem, something which, annoyingly, was becoming a bit of a habit.

Dr Ross, the Home Office pathologist, glanced up at George standing up in the viewing gallery. Ross was a vigorous, no-nonsense guy who was great at his job. George both liked and respected the man greatly. He and his young blonde assistant were wearing scrubs, gloves and masks. Dr Ross nodded a greeting at George before he finished work on the limbs.

"So great you could make it, George," Dr Ross said. "I'll be honest, son. There's not much I can give you. I'm just about finished with the limbs and will be starting on the torso soon."

"Thanks, Dr Ross."

"The victim is an unknown female, aged between twenty and thirty. She has been dismembered. Her arms, legs and head are currently missing."

"She was found naked, wrapped in newspaper and placed in a black bin bag. Internal inspection suggests she had intercourse just before death—no signs of sexual assault. Lack of sperm and semen suggests the use of a condom," Dr Ross said, leaning in at the bottom of the torso. "Internal swabs were taken."

CHAPTER SEVEN

He'd only recently found out Rita Lawrence worked for an escort agency. It must have been a customer or a partner if the sex was consensual. He texted DS Elaine Brewer, who was working late, to ring the local agencies and see if Rita worked for any of them.

"Who killed you, Rita?" he whispered. "Whoever you are, I'll get you, you sick fuck."

George listened as Dr Ross described the wounds in more detail and gave measurements.

"The flesh of the wounds has been shredded, suggesting a saw of some kind." Dr Ross looked up at George. "I can tell you it's not a hacksaw, son. That's it. Sorry."

"Why not a hacksaw?" George asked.

"They have fine, shallow, closely spaced teeth which make a mess of the amputations. These are clean."

He gave Dr Ross a thumbs up. It was hard enough as it was without a possible murder weapon.

"Full rigor mortis. To be able to ascertain the time of death, I'm going to need to open her up," Dr Ross announced.

George didn't want to see that and depressed the audio button so Dr Ross could hear him speak. "Thanks, Dr Ross. I'll leave you to cut her up. If you find anything, let me know. Otherwise, I'll wait for the report."

He looked up and nodded. "Okay, son. Will do."

His phone pinged, and he glanced at his messages. It was an update from the DCI. Their team had been out all afternoon, and he was now busy relaying the results. No one in the Middleton area knew anything about either Anthony Shields or Tony Shaw. The occupants of the bail hostels around South Leeds and North Wakefield had all been traced, interviewed and eliminated from the inquiry. Nothing had been flagged up for further investigation. DCI Peterson was undoubtedly efficient. As soon as a new line of questioning was identified, the DCI followed it up.

DI Beaumont exhaled as he left the viewing gallery. He needed to get outside and away from the stench of death.

* * *

George sat at his desk. He wasn't supposed to be in his office this late in the evening, but no one on the night shift was surprised to see him there. He'd proven to everybody how relentless and persistent he was when solving cases, with some remarking they seemed to get solved because he wouldn't give up. For George, there was always a new way of looking at things or a new line of questioning.

He thought about giving Wood a ring, but it was too late. She was on earlies and would be in bed ready for her shift. He wished he was with her, but the case needed solving. People were counting on him.

He sent her a text instead: Missing you, Gorgeous. Once this case is over, I'll take you somewhere special. X.

It felt weird messaging Wood like that, on WhatsApp, where a warrant would be required to look. They took their secrecy seriously as; if anybody found out, they could lose their jobs.

Was that why he was so wary of late? No, it must have been something else. Things were out of balance for him, and George felt it every morning when he woke up. There was a kind of restraint in him. Before Adam Harris, he was full of energy and confidence. Now, that former boldness was fading away. He'd lost his instincts when solving a case and wasn't sure things would get resolved. He knew it was only a matter of time before he captured the Miss Murderer. Yet now, he wasn't even sure if Shaw was their guy. What happened to his optimism? It used to be there in bucket loads. Not now. Now all there was, was alcohol: alcohol and doubt.

Whatever change had happened, whatever doubts he had, a career change was on his mind. He just didn't seem to have it in him any more. But what else could he do?

DS Josh Fry hadn't gone home yet. He was supposed to be working late, so George had returned to the station after speaking with Dr Ross. Along with several printouts he'd produced over the last hour, Tony Shaw's phone sat on the desk. He picked up the phone, found it was locked and could do nothing because Shaw refused to give them the code. It made Shaw look guilty, but Josh would sort it soon enough.

The printouts on his desk were from where he'd checked the DVLA for Shaw's Vauxhall: it was a silver Astra, registered in his name. His work van was registered to Tommy Myles' company. He also had the ANPR data for the car and the van for the last couple of months. All sightings of the number plates were traced onto two separate maps of Yorkshire. The borders of West Yorkshire were coloured yellow, and the Leeds HQ boundary was blue.

By the look of it, Tony didn't work in Leeds. He studied the maps. His personal car's journeys were less frequent and were indicated by green lines. His work van's journeys were red, and the thicker the line, the more frequent the trip. From looking at the other printouts and cross-referencing the logs of journey times, George could see that Shaw only used his Astra to go to the shop or work. The computer system had flagged up nothing for him to investigate further.

Most of the trips in his work vehicle had taken him south

down the M1 to Wakefield, around the towns and villages of Horbury, Ossett and Lupset. But every night, the ANPR data confirmed Shaw headed back to Hunslet to collect the mail.

The system had also printed out other trip logs, including longer stops, for frequency and timings. George was disappointed, but most were pretty regular. As his boss had mentioned, Tony Shaw appeared to have a fixed schedule. There was nothing suspicious about any of it. Not even the fact that Shaw's car appeared to stop outside the Lingwell takeaways between half-eleven and midnight seemed out of place most nights. He'd been doing it for months, and George bet if he got an entire year's worth of data, it would show a similar trend. So unless Shaw had planned this, they couldn't use the data in court. It wouldn't show anything other than Shaw's innocence.

He checked his watch. Josh was taking his time getting to him. Did he ring him again? No. George wasn't supposed to be in the office, anyway. Josh probably had other jobs he needed to do first. He was doing George a favour, after all.

With a sigh, he looked through the information he already had. Tony Shaw's police record was limited to a few cautions. One was for paying for sex with a prostitute subject to force and coercion. That meant a pimp had forced the woman to have sex with a paying Shaw. Whether Shaw knew the woman had been forced was not precisely the point.

The other two were for shoplifting and being drunk and disorderly in public. But that had been five years ago, and since then, he'd been clean. That PC had mentioned knowing him professionally, but he couldn't see why from his record. He'd ordered his DWP file to see what benefits he had claimed over the years, but that wouldn't be available until the morning. He rifled through the rest of the printouts, one of them being the police record for Anthony Shields. Again, he'd been cautioned for paying a prostitute who had been subjected to force and coercion, the only information on there being the information he knew about the Jack the Butcher case thirty years ago. The guy was pretty much clean. So why did George have a strange feeling? And why, if he was innocent, did he escape?

Think George: you saw the blood in the bath. Everything you know about killers who dismember their victims leads you directly back to Shaw.

DS Josh Fry strode into the squad room and knocked on George's office door. He was a slim man, usually unshaven, who wore black Ray-Ban rectangle glasses with such thick lenses that his eyeballs looked as if they were protruding from his face. Yet despite the permanent yawn and a bird's nest atop his head, Joshua was the best-qualified person in Leeds Police HQ regarding tech. He'd studied Forensic IT at Leeds University and was George's go-to guy.

He was wearing his usual navy Burton suit and brown shoes. "OK, sir," he said, "I'm here. What did you need, again?"

George held up Shaw's phone.

"Tony Shaw refused to give us the passcode, so I need you to unlock it for me. Please."

He nodded. "Yep. Easy. Anything else?"

"Once unlocked, we can track the movements of this phone going back since its first use, right?"

"Yeah, of course. You want me to do that for you?"

"Please, Josh."

"Okay, sir. It'll take me about half an hour or so to get inside the phone. Then I need to retrieve the data, print it out and bring it back," he said. Then, as he left to go downstairs to the forensics lab, he shouted from the door, "Easiest job I've had all day. You know there's software for all this stuff, right?"

George knew. They had software for everything. He used the programs for vehicle tracking, CCTV face and gait recognition. DS Yolanda Williams was in touch with a gait analyst for two reasons. One, to see whether the guy they'd found on CCTV walked that way on purpose, and two, to see if it matched the way Shaw walked.

There was the obvious phone tracking software, fingerprint recognition, and card and bank transactions. It reminded George he needed to get Josh to get the forensics done on Shaw's accounts. He emailed the Super asking for a warrant, copying in Josh.

He put his feet up on the desk and closed his eyes, fed up with looking at data that wasn't getting him anywhere.

A knock at his door shit him up, and he saw Josh. He checked his watch. The DS had taken a startlingly short time to finish the jobs he'd given him.

"Didn't need the software to unlock the phone in the end, sir," Josh said by way of explanation. He'd seen the shock on George's face.

When George said nothing, Josh explained. "His date of birth. After all the advice on the TV or the internet, you'd think that people would come up with a random password rather than an easy one. His loss, I guess."

"And the tracking."

"It's a lot of data. Especially as you want it from the life of the phone, it's quite old, you see. A data support officer is on it. It'll be ready by and on your desk by the morning. Sir."

"Thanks, Josh. Appreciate it. I need the forensics on Shaw's accounts, as he has a couple of bank cards and credit cards in his wallet. I've emailed the Super asking for a warrant. I've copied you in too, Josh. You let me know as soon as you get the information tomorrow, yeah?"

"Okay, sir," he said as he prepared to leave. "What kind of things are you looking for?"

He thought back to the blood in Shaw's bath. Nothing had been typed up on the system about the official search yet, but George suspected Shaw was killing and dismembering his victims in a different place. "The usual stuff. Unusual transactions. See if he's paying rent for other properties, storage containers, and the like."

Josh nodded. George looked up to express his thanks, but all there was, was a space where Josh had been. He shut his office door, watching as the navy Burton suit glided soundlessly away.

He opened an email from the DCI and read through the information. It seemed they'd found many exciting things in Shaw's flat. The DCI wanted to lead an interview with George as his deputy tomorrow morning, first thing. But unfortunately, there were no details about what they found, and nothing had been updated on HOLMES 2.

But one thing was sure: Tony Shaw would get the shock of his life during the DCI's long and detailed interview tomorrow.

Chapter Eight

George switched the television to the sports channel, and the highlights of the footy were on. But, despite concentrating on the goals, his thoughts kept returning to Tony Shaw. Once the data came back from the lab, he knew he'd be able to charge him for Rita's murder, along with the other victims', but something didn't feel quite right.

Why had Shaw disposed of the bodies in a busy place? And why a day earlier? Did he not know that the bins would be collected a day later? George had received a leaflet from the council informing him and assumed Shaw would have been sent one, too.

His phone rang. He reached for it from the coffee table. It was Dr Ross. "Hi, Dr Ross. It's nice to hear from you."

"Sorry to call so late, son," Dr Ross said, his tone as friendly as usual. "I've written the post-mortem report on Rita Lawrence, and I thought you'd like it."

"Thank you. Send it through to my email, please."

George heard the clacking keys. "Okay, son, it is on its way," he said. "I know you were keen to know all the details. Shall I give you the highlights?"

"Yeah, please."

"I'll be honest, I struggled, son," Dr Ross said. "I can't give you the cause of death for any of them. I can't tell you what the culprit used to dismember them, either. There're two reasons for that. First, human bones are too big to observe during an autopsy using a regular stereo microscope. It's because of the limitations of viewing distance."

"You mean the distance between the plate and the lens?"

"Correct, son. I couldn't get a decent magnification because of that. It's the same for your two Jane Does' limbs. Two, because of that limitation—the viewing distance—it's challenging to measure the marks made by the implement. In this case, a saw. I'm certain."

"You told me earlier it wasn't a hacksaw. Do you have any idea now what kind of saw was used?"

"At this time, no." George thought the pathologist sounded disappointed. "I need a special piece of equipment to help me determine what kind of saw the murderer used on Rita Lawrence, and your two Jane Does. If I could see the saw marks on and in the bones better, I could identify any unique incisions or markings which could provide details about the type of saw used."

"Shit! How long will it take for you to get the device?"

"It's a specialised piece of equipment, a portable palm-sized device that can take digital images from magnifications of five times up to fifty times. I've been asking for one for years, but murderers rarely dismember their victims with saws these days. And with the budget cuts—"

"Don't talk to me about budget cuts, Dr Ross. I was supposed to go home after seeing you earlier but went back to the station and started grafting. I need the evidence to get this guy."

"I'm sorry, son. But unfortunately, I cannot determine whether the victims were dead or alive during this dismembering. The limbs were dispatched from the torso rather quickly, and as such, I cannot say whether she died from being sawed alive or whether it was exsanguination."

"I need something, Dr Ross. Especially if this goes to trial."

"Your only hope is to find the murder weapon and hope we can extract the victims' DNA from it. Hopefully, the culprit's DNA is on the weapon too. I could also do some test cuts with the saw and identify those unique incisions or markings I mentioned earlier. But, without the portable microscope, I can't do that, either."

"It's like they don't want us catching killers in this bloody country!"

The line went quiet, and George rebuked himself.

"Sorry, Dr Ross, that was extremely unprofessional," George said once he'd calmed down.

"You're passionate, son. There's no need to be sorry for that."

"I'll speak with the Super tomorrow, see if he can pull any strings and get you what you need. Is there anything else I need to know, Dr Ross?"

"Well, son, it's why I was calling. We've made some progress, especially regarding your IC2 Jane Doe. Initially, it was difficult to determine the time of death because when a body is discovered over seventy-two hours after death, the usual details we normally examine, such as body temperature, skin colour, and muscle rigidity, have all plateaued. Because of that plateau, we have to use other techniques like examining the decomposition of internal organs or looking for evidence of blowflies."

George knew all about blowflies and how they laid eggs within minutes of someone dying. Because of that, they

CHAPTER EIGHT

could use the growth timeline of blowfly maggots to find out exactly when a person died. "Have you spoken with a forensic entomologist?" A forensic entomologist was someone who studied bugs found on dead bodies and was invaluable in cases such as this one.

"Should have the report by tomorrow for you to look at, son. But, unfortunately, I couldn't get a rectal reading on the arms and legs, so the Glaister Equation was no good."

"Thank you, Dr Ross," George said. Knowing the time of death was crucial evidence that could support or deny the stated actions of the suspect. "Is there anything else you can tell me?"

"For Rita Lawrence, we don't have a torso, so I cannot examine her organs. It's the same for your IC1 Jane Doe. However, I examined the organs from the IC2 torso you found. It's not much, but because of the decomposition of her internal organs, your IC2 Jane Doe died mid-to-late afternoon on Christmas Day."

* * *

The following day, DI Beaumont and DCI Peterson sat knee to knee in the interview room whilst DS Wood watched from a live video link. Before bringing Tony Shaw and his lawyer back in, DCI Alex Peterson wanted to discuss with George what they'd found in Shaw's flat. Hopefully, they'd seen and smelt the same things in Shaw's bathroom George had seen. His smug smile grew with every word the DCI spoke, detailing what the SOCOs had found.

DCI Peterson, George noticed, was armed with a stack of paperwork containing evidence, research, and questions he was going to ask. He wondered whether this was what DCIs did or whether Alex was just a meticulous guy.

"Excellent, Alex," he said when DCI Peterson had finished. George sat back in his chair, arms folded across his chest. "I just wished I could have been there. What a piece of evidence to find!"

A knock at the door interrupted George's celebration. Tony Shaw entered with his pixie of a lawyer, trying his best to exude confidence. Shaw had spent the night in the holding cells at Elland Road Police Station, but how much sleep he had managed was debatable. George thought they both looked like shit.

They sat down, and George handed out the document folders whilst DCI Peterson started the Digital Interview Recorder.

"Interview of Tony Shaw in the presence of his solicitor by Detective Chief Inspector Peterson and Detective Inspector Beaumont, at 9 am on the twenty-ninth of December." He asked each participant to identify themselves for the DIR.

"You remain under caution, Mr Shaw," DCI Peterson said. Shaw glared at him, but if it had any effect, he didn't show it. "Mr Shaw, what's your current permanent residence?"

"I live in a flat in Middleton," Shaw explained.

"And this would be the Park Lea flats?"

"Yes," Shaw replied, confirming the number of the flat.

"Please see document eleven in your folders. Document eleven relates to a legal search of your Park Lea flat yesterday on the twenty-eighth of December."

George could feel the tension rising in the sweltering room. They hadn't turned the heating down, and George had begun to sweat, too. The DCI seemed unaffected.

"Do you recognise the item in document eleven, Mr Shaw?"

"Bin bags?" he said, more of a question than an answer. "I thought I'd run out. Guess an expert search team will find anything, though. Save me a few bob at any rate, thanks." A smirk stretched from ear to ear on Shaw's face.

Cocky bastard. George knew the smirk would soon be long gone. "So to confirm," George said, "those bin bags we found during our lawful search of your premises are yours?"

Shaw looked at his lawyer, who shrugged her shoulders. "Yes. If you found them in my flat, they're mine."

George grinned and said, "Please see document twelve in your folders. Document twelve is a report from one of our forensics specialists. The report shows the bin bags used to dispose of dismembered female body parts found on Friday the twenty-seventh of December were from the same roll found at Tony Shaw's Park Lea flat on Saturday the twenty-eighth of December."

"Lies!" Shaw screamed. "They're not my bin bags."

"Calm down, and less of the shouting, Mr Shaw," DCI Peterson said, raising his brow.

"I'll fucking calm down and stop shouting when I'm not being accused of being a murderer."

"There's no argument, is there, Mr Shaw? We have detailed forensic analysis proving the bags came from the roll you confirmed was yours. The paper wrapping also shows you purchased them from Sainsbury's. DI Beaumont—"

"You can't prove anything! Anybody could have easily planted them," Shaw quickly supplied, interrupting the DCI. A scowl appeared on Alex's face for a split second before being replaced with a smile.

"My client is telling the truth. He strenuously denies ownership of the item in document twelve," his solicitor said.

George mirrored Alex's grin and continued, ignoring Shaw's solicitor. Shaw was sweating again. Beads of sweat dripped down from his shiny, bald head. "Please look at document thirteen in your folders. Document thirteen is an image of a receipt found in Tony Shaw's flat. Said receipt lists bin bags and cleaning products purchased from Sainsbury's on Middleton Park Avenue on Boxing Day this year. Do you recognise the receipt?"

"No," Shaw said.

"Well, a SOCO found it in your flat," DCI Peterson said. "DI Beaumont?"

"Document fourteen shows the exact cleaning supplies as listed in document thirteen. All have prints that match the samples you provided yesterday. We're in the process of cross-referencing your DNA."

"Of course you found my prints on my cleaning supplies," Shaw said. "There's no proof I purchased them on Boxing Day in Sainsbury's."

Ignoring him, George continued to disclose their evidence. "Document fifteen shows an image of a bin with a newspaper inside. Document sixteen shows an image of said newspaper that had been disposed of. It is the Boxing Day edition of The Sun. If you look back to document thirteen, you will see The Sun newspaper is listed."

"And?" Shaw was getting angry, and George thought Shaw looked terrible. Dark rings were under his eyes and giant sweat patches under his arms.

"Documents seventeen to twenty show a set of images captured on CCTV. Using the time and date from the receipt, we have isolated CCTV images of the person who bought the products. Is that you, Tony?"

CHAPTER EIGHT

Tony Shaw looked gravely down at his copy of the document. He scrutinised the images, which were images of a broad, tall man with his hood up, wearing gloves, purchasing the bags and cleaning goods with cash. "No!" exclaimed Tony, finally uncoiling his hands and raising them emphatically. "I didn't buy those products! I didn't kill anyone!"

"Where were you at this time, then?" DCI Peterson asked, pointing to the time and date stamp on the receipt. "We know you weren't at work because we've already spoken to Tommy Myles."

"I'm being framed. Please, you have to believe me."

"Framed by who?" DCI Peterson asked.

In his silence, George continued. "Document twenty-one is a statement given to DC Blackburn by Sainsbury's worker Chantelle Watts on the twenty-eighth of December. Yesterday. In her statement, Miss Watts claims she remembers serving a 'tall, bulky man who walked with a waddle. Under his hoodie, I saw he had a shiny bald head. Other than his brows, the only other hair on his face was a long, black beard tinged with grey hairs. He spoke little and didn't say thank you. The man paid in cash, which was strange. He was wearing gloves, which wasn't strange because it was freezing.' How do you explain that, Tony?"

"That could have been anybody," Shaw's solicitor said. "And I must repeat that my client insists he's innocent."

"Document twenty-two in your folders," DCI Peterson said. "We set up an identity parade where an officer unfamiliar with the suspect showed Miss Watts pre-recorded video footage of nine unrelated men of a similar appearance and age. She made a positive ID for number six."

"See document twenty-three," George cut in. "Document

twenty-three is said image of male number six. It's an image of Tony Shaw taken yesterday when he was booked in. Can you confirm this is a picture of you, Tony?" George leaned back, a cocky but triumphant sparkle in his eyes.

"You're going too fast for me, detectives. Please slow down and let me think. I'm not as sharp as I once was."

As if, George thought. The man was under pressure and would soon break. They couldn't afford to let him get his composure back.

"Is that you, Tony?" George asked again.

"Yes, that's me. I often go to Sainsbury's, so she could just have remembered me." Tony's voice held an edge of panic.

"Document twenty-four," George said, "is an image of your bathroom. That is an image of your bathroom, right, Tony?"

"It looks like my bathroom, yes, but then all the bathrooms in the flats look the same," said Tony. George could hear a raw edge in the middle-aged man's voice.

"Documents twenty-five to twenty-nine show more images taken yesterday during the lawful search of your home," DCI Peterson cut in. He was straight to the point, with a harsh tone to his voice. "Can you confirm these are images of your bathroom?"

"Yes. Fine. It's my bathroom. I can tell by the tiles."

"Good. I like it when we're on the same page," DCI Peterson said. "Forensics performed a luminol reaction to locate potential blood evidence that would be unnoticeable through visual inspection. Document thirty shows an image of your bathroom, Mr Shaw. A large luminescent pattern is visible in the image. Your attempt to clean up blood is obvious. Explain yourself."

Tony swallowed and shook his head, the sharp jerks erratic.

"For the DIR, Tony Shaw is unresponsive. As you can see by the image, a lot of blood has been cleaned up, Tony," George said. Can you explain this?"

"No comment."

"Is this the blood of one of your victims?" Alex Peterson stabbed his forefinger at the offending image. He allowed the question to hang, but Tony gave him nothing.

"Okay, Tony," George said. "See document thirty-one. Document thirty-one is an image of the newspaper used to wrap up the victim's body parts before being placed in the black bin bags. Do you recognise the newspaper in this image, Tony?"

"No. Of course I bloody don't!"

"You can't see the date?"

Shaw's eyes flickered to the large S. Underneath was the date. Thursday, December 26.

"I'm being framed," he cried.

"Tony Shaw, the threshold test has been passed and therefore, it is my lawful right to arrest you on suspicion of the murder of Rita Lawrence. I will also seek guidance from the Crown Prosecutor on how to charge you for the two other lives you have taken. Is that understood?" George asked.

"No! I'm not having it! No!" Shaw screamed, banging the table with his hand.

"We will hold you in custody while we gather further evidence against you," DI Beaumont said. "If you are not charged within twenty-four hours of your original arrest, you may be released. However, if that happens, I will seek the authority for a twelve- or seventy-two-hour extension. Do you understand, Tony Shaw?" George's voice took on a harsh edge that had Tony staring at him in disbelief. As the SIO, it was up to him to present his case to the Crown Prosecutor.

"No! Please, detectives, what is happening here? I'm being framed! I'm telling you, I'm being framed!" If Shaw had anything to do with the murders of those poor women, there was no way he could worm his way out of being charged.

"Interview ended," DCI Peterson said. They left the room, replaced by two PCs.

Chapter Nine

There was a knock on George's office door. "Sir," Yolanda Williams said, popping her head around the door. Her cheeks were flushed as if she had just sprinted to see him. "I think I have something from the CCTV near the bins for you." Yolanda was their CCTV expert. Other forces were starting to outsource their CCTV work, but Leeds district HMET didn't need to. With operations like this, with no witnesses, Yolanda was invaluable. He'd worked closely with her on the Miss Murderer case, and they wouldn't have caught the sick bastard without her. "Shall I notify DCI Peterson, too?"

"I'll do it," George said, getting up from his chair and grabbing his mobile. "Go get everything set up. The DCI likes efficiency."

"Sir," the DS said and followed him out of his office. George paused outside Incident Room Five and called the DCI, asking him to come down.

George didn't bother to wait for Alex and entered the room where two large monitors were set up next to one another. Paused CCTV video footage of a man in a dark coat was shown on each. *Jesus, that was quick.* George's heart hammered deep within his chest; the adrenaline continuously surged during these moments.

"What am I looking at?" DCI Peterson asked when he arrived.

"Paused CCTV footage of our culprit, sir," she said.

"What, already?" The DCI gave her a look of surprise and then smiled.

"If you also look here, sir, I've printed out a map of the area surrounding the alley. I've circled all the CCTV cameras we have harvested footage from. Each has CCTV at the back, and I've circled those in different colours so we can cross-reference the footage with the camera. They're also of decent quality and in full colour."

"Smart. Well done, DS Williams."

She blushed and blew a stray strand of hair from her face. "Because of these details, it makes little sense, sir," Yolanda said.

"What doesn't and why not?" the DCI asked, turning towards her, his brow raised.

"Well, the cameras are large. Obvious. They have lights on them, too, so they would be seen at night. Our culprit would have seen them, so why would he dispose of the body parts in any of these bins, sir?"

"Good question. Maybe Shaw assumed he wouldn't get caught. If it weren't for Miss Haliday, the remains wouldn't have been found. George, do me a favour and check the bin collection days."

"Sir, if I may?" Yolanda asked. "Inspector Beaumont mentioned the bins when he briefed us on Friday night and advised that because of Christmas, the bin collection days were askew."

"I remember, Yolanda. I guessed whoever dumped the body

parts expected the bins to have already been emptied that Friday. As soon as we returned to the station that night, I got the Super to contact the council and stop all refuse collections for Middleton."

"Correct, sir. Well, I checked up on them, and you were correct. Because of Christmas, the council collected them a day early at the beginning of the week, whilst they pushed the end-of-the-week collections back a day. The council should have collected them Friday, but they didn't—"

"They were due Saturday," Alex Peterson interrupted. "This is how you isolated the CCTV footage so quickly?"

"Correct, sir."

"Amazing job, you two. So this footage is from Thursday the twenty-sixth?"

Yolanda nodded. "Boxing Day. The Indian takeaway closes at half-twelve on Thursdays but isn't very busy. So perfect time for dumping, I'd say."

The DCI nodded. "Thanks, DS Williams. Let's have a look at this footage then, shall we?"

The footage showed a tall, bulky man wearing a black hoodie and black jeans walking through the open gate of the Indian takeaway, pulling a large suitcase behind him. He was wearing black gloves and black boots. It certainly seemed to George the culprit wanted to blend into the night. The guy kept his head down, but after opening the suitcase and hefting the bags into the bins, George was sure he could see what looked like a dark-coloured beard once he turned to leave. The images were extremely similar to the ones from Sainsbury's.

"He's got a distinctive walk," Yolanda said.

George nodded. "I don't remember a suitcase. Was it taken away for evidence?" George asked.

The DCI shook his head. "No, I don't think so. After arresting Shaw, I went through everything last night to see if there was any other evidence you could put to the Crown Prosecutor. But, unfortunately, there was no suitcase in the inventory."

"Bollocks!" George said, slamming his hand down on the table.

"Don't be so hasty, DI Beaumont. Run the video on DS Williams, please," the DCI said. They saw their culprit bathed in light as the security light switched on. The culprit was smart enough to keep his head down, though, so the detectives could not identify him.

George scrutinised the screen. "It's impossible to ID the guy. He might as well just be a shadow. Everything he's wearing is black. He knew what he was doing. We need to put this fresh evidence by Shaw, right?"

The DCI nodded. "Where does our culprit go next, DS Williams?"

"I don't know yet, sir. He closes the gate behind him, blocking any footage of the alley. There's no CCTV footage of the alley at all. DC Blackburn is currently scouring the area for more CCTV. I've asked him to check for footage from both the east and west of the alley, Lingwell Avenue and North Lingwell Road, respectively. I'll be able to home in on him once I know which direction he went immediately after dumping the body parts."

"You'll also be able to see whether he has the suitcase," George said.

"Exactly, sir. Whilst I'm waiting for DC Blackburn, I'll keep looking. Perhaps I can get something of the culprit without his hood up."

But George was doubtful. He knew their culprit was being

careful to conceal his identity. His clothes and boots were all black, with no identifiable logos.

"The rest of the bins have been checked, is that right, George?" the DCI asked.

"Yeah. Nothing of note. We checked all the bins around the takeaway the night we found the body parts. Detective Superintendent Smith stopped all collections."

"How far did you check?"

"Just the alley and the shops and takeaways Friday night. Then Saturday morning, we checked all bins in a hundred-metre radius."

"Who allowed this? Detective Superintendent Smith?" Alex looked pissed.

"Yes, Alex. We're low on staffing because of budget cuts. We got some PCs involved, but they have their jobs too."

"Did you order any searches of the bins outside Shaw's flat? From what I remember, they have communal bins. What about other flats in the area? Jack the Butcher disposed of his victims in communal bins."

"The Super did, Alex. He ordered them when he asked the council to stop all collections. These things take time but would have been done already if overtime had been granted. You were there when I asked the Chief Super."

"Well, which areas did you prioritise?" the DCI asked.

Yolanda sat there, looking uncomfortable. "Go on, Yolanda, get a coffee. You've been working hard. Thanks," George said.

She nodded and silently left the room, shutting the two detectives in.

"We used a radius, to begin with, and steadily increased it. Most killers stay close to home, as I'm sure you well know."

"Exactly. Shaw lives what, three-hundred metres away from

the alley?"

"Yeah, but we told the PCs to avoid the flats."

The DCI bristled. "Why on earth would you do that, DI Beaumont?"

"I assumed the SOCOs would check the bins when they searched his flat. Did you not ask them to do that?"

"Are you questioning my decisions, Inspector?" the DCI bellowed.

Arguing with his new boss would not get him anywhere. George ground his teeth before saying, "No, sir, I assumed they would get checked. I thought there was no point wasting money doing multiple searches."

"That's sloppy, Inspector. With your reputation, I expect better from you. You better buck up because I won't hesitate to speak to the Chief."

"Sir, I made a mistake," George said. "I understand that now. I should have checked with you, and I won't let it happen again."

"I'd recommend you cut down on the drinking too, DI Beaumont."

"Sir?" A look of confusion spread across George's face.

"I could smell it on you when we were interviewing Shaw this morning, and to be honest, I can still smell it on you now. I'm surprised nobody has mentioned it to you."

George closed his eyes, defeated. "It's mouthwash, sir."

The angry DCI stood up, shook his head and left, slamming the door shut and leaving George to ponder the CCTV footage alone.

It still didn't sit right with George, especially as Yolanda had similar doubts. The cameras weren't exactly hidden. Why would the culprit dispose of the body parts in that specific bin where three cameras could pinpoint him? It made no sense. It was as if he wanted to be caught.

* * *

George didn't let what the DCI said bother him. It was true that he'd been drinking last night, but it was also true that he hadn't told anybody about his drinking. The nightmares of him killing Adam Harris, the Miss Murderer, would only stop when he drank. George felt lost, but he had a job to do.

It was getting close to the twenty-four-hour deadline, so George rang the Crown Prosecutor and received confirmation that he could extend Shaw's custody to ninety-six hours.

They took Shaw out of holding and told him this after starting the interview. They also informed him he was still under caution. DS Wood and DCI Peterson were watching from a live video link.

"Beg your pardon?" George asked. Tony Shaw jumped at the unexpected sound of his angry voice and fixed him with a watery look. The man was crying.

DC Holly Hambleton stared at Shaw, too, dumbfounded. A suspected serial killer breaking down was unheard of.

"I'm being framed," Tony repeated in a whisper. "Please. Let me go. I'm innocent."

Hambleton cleared her throat and shared a look with George. The DCI had wanted her to lead the interview, so George gave a sharp nod of his head. "Then tell us. Who is framing you, Mr Shaw?" she asked.

"Probably the same detectives who tried to frame me thirty years ago. DI Alexander and DS Smith. But I was let free then, and you'll let me free soon, too. Shit sticks. I'm innocent."

"Explain," Hambleton said faintly.

George could tell her reaction was the same as his—what the fuck? That was not what he had expected. A dead detective and DSU Jim Smith framing him? Bullshit!

"Well, thirty years ago, they tried to say my DNA was on one of the bodies. It was all the evidence they had, other than eyewitness testimony. People can be mistaken about what they've seen, but DNA can't. DNA is the best evidence you can get." Shaw smiled a rather large, toothy grin, his teeth stained yellow. "I provided blood for them to use. I did that because I was innocent. They let me go because my DNA didn't match."

George knew this, of course, having read the files. Smith and Alexander had found semen in the stomach of a victim named Stacey Lumb, but her stomach acid had made it so they couldn't use it for DNA purposes. Luckily, they'd found the heads of their victims. One woman's mouth hadn't been bleached, removing all traces of semen, so they'd stored it. The young DC Holly would have been aware of it, too.

"That's an absurd accusation, Tony," George advised. "As detectives, we have no bias. We'd move on if we didn't have any evidence to charge you. We don't care about gender, race or creed. All that matters is that three women are dead, and the trail leads back to you."

"We have already disclosed to your solicitor that the DNA sample you gave back in 1994 wasn't viable. So it's why we took a fresh sample from you," Holly said.

"Once your DNA profile returns, we can match it, Tony. DC Hambleton." He wanted to move on because Shaw's DNA profile was already taking longer than usual to return.

"Documents thirty-two to forty show a set of images captured from various CCTV cameras from Boxing day, the twenty-

CHAPTER NINE

sixth of December at eleven fifty-three. Is that you, Mr Shaw?" Holly swept a strand of black hair behind an ear, exposing her many earrings.

"No. I was at work."

"At eleven fifty-three? Can anyone confirm this?" Holly asked.

"No. My job is very solitary. I'm on my own once I leave Tommy's place. The only people I see are customers."

"And between 10 pm and midnight," Holly said, "you gather post from the Royal Mail?"

"Yes. That's correct."

"Where do you gather the post from, Mr Shaw?" she asked.

"Hunslet Delivery Office, just off Belle Isle Road."

"Explain to me your routine, Mr Shaw," Holly said.

"Well, I travel to Hunslet as soon as I've finished delivering my parcels, load up the van with mail and then go back to Tommy's."

"And you finish there at exactly midnight, every shift?"

"Well, not exactly, love, no. Sometimes I get off earlier," he said and winced. He quickly added, "But most times, I finish later. Probably ten or fifteen minutes at most. Not enough to complain about. I get in my car and go home. So, I'm not the man in those images because I would have been at work."

"Can anybody vouch for you, Mr Shaw? Do you leave the van with somebody to unload the mail? Or do you lock it away?"

The middle-aged man chewed on his lip. "Probably. We were shut on Christmas Day, so we were inundated with shit from Royal Mail."

DC Hambleton looked to George, who nodded. Usually, George held the highest rank during interviews, so one of his team would check. But this time, the DCI outranked him and had put Holly in charge. So, George slipped out to quickly ring DS Brewer—he'd get her to check Shaw's alibi with Tommy Myles.

"What forensics do you have linking my client to the crime scene?" Shaw's pixie solicitor asked Holly as George silently entered the interview room and took his chair.

"The bin bags used to dispose of the victims match the roll belonging to your client. Your client's prints are on the cleaning products purchased at Sainsbury's, alongside said bags. In addition, we have the Boxing Day edition of The Sun newspaper, which was bought from Sainsbury's. This was listed on the receipt. Forensic scientists are currently linking the pages that wrapped up the body parts with those found in Mr Shaw's flat."

"Were my client's prints found on any of the remains or bin bags?" the pixie asked.

"No," Holly said. "But we know the culprit wore gloves, so your client's prints won't be on them." Holly turned and looked at Shaw. "What we have is damning, Mr Shaw. Confess."

"At the time of my client's arrest, his clothing was seized for forensic examination. Were any traces of the victims' DNA detected?"

"Other than traces of his own, no. We seized all his clothing, and our labs are examining them," Holly quickly supplied. "But anyone with half a brain would know to dispose of their clothing. Your client has all his mental faculties and can think clearly and logically. See document fifty, for example. Document fifty is an image of Mr Shaw's novel transcript found during the lawful search of his flat. It's clear as you read this that Mr Shaw is intelligent. It's also clear he is well-versed in

CHAPTER NINE

police procedure and extremely forensically aware."

"Where is this clothing my client disposed of?"

Holly turned to Tony Shaw and said, "Yes, where is it, Mr Shaw?"

"I have not disposed of any clothing. I have killed nobody, and I am innocent. Believe me; I know how damning forensics can be. I have no motive, either," he said scathingly.

"Oh, come on, you killed thirty years ago and were desperate to kill again. It's clear from the way you have written your novel. So don't bullshit us, Mr Shaw."

"I did not kill thirty years ago, and I did not kill those three poor women. So my novel is irrelevant."

"As explained yesterday, forensics carried out a luminol reaction to locate any invisible blood evidence," Holly said. "Document thirty-one shows an image of your bathroom where a large luminescent pattern is visible in the image. It's an attempt to clean up the blood. Now's your chance to explain yourself. We're waiting on a DNA profile, but once that comes back as one of your three victims, it's game over."

Tony shook his head and clamped his lips shut. His fingers fiddled with the edge of the table.

"For the DIR, Mr Shaw isn't responding," George said.

"I guess we'll leave that there for now. We'll find out whatever it is you're hiding," Holly said. "Interview terminated."

Chapter Ten

George hadn't been asked to do the press conference. His interim boss, DCI Alex Peterson, sure did things differently to DSU Jim Smith. Smith didn't do any fieldwork at all, no interviews other than ones at the station, no searches of properties or crime scenes, no nothing. DS Elaine Brewer had told him the DCI hadn't done much other than point out the roll of black bin bags from the doorway, having spoken to his DC, Holly Hambleton, from across the cordon. He was the managerial type. The face, the organ grinder. It was why George watched Alex giving the press conference on television rather than being allowed to do it himself.

"Good afternoon. I'm Detective Chief Inspector Alex Peterson. The bodies of three women were discovered in Middleton on Friday. I will not be confirming their names until next of kin have been notified. We have a suspect in custody, and we will notify the press once charged. Thank you."

The DCI turned to leave, but the usual questioning began.

"Were they victims of sexual assault?" A female reporter shouted from the front row. George knew from experience it was going to be the first question asked.

DCI Peterson furrowed his brow and gave a barely noticeable shake. "No. Thank you and goodbye."

CHAPTER TEN

The reporters wouldn't let the DCI leave and fired off question after question, wanting to know the suspect's identity and how they'd murdered their victims.

"As this is an ongoing investigation, I cannot comment on the matter," the DCI said to each question.

It wasn't until a reporter known to George asked, "How do you feel about having another serial killer on the loose?" that the DCI took the press conference seriously.

That reporter was a woman named Paige McGuiness. She had dyed her hair golden brown and wore a black skirt and white blouse—the consummate professional, as always. The dark makeup made her look older, yet George knew she was barely out of University.

"As I said, we already have a suspect in custody, and no serial killer is on the loose. Thank you."

"Why haven't you mentioned that you found the women in pieces, Detective Chief Inspector Alex Peterson? A source tells me the three victims were dismembered, wrapped in newspaper and disposed of in bin bags. Is that correct?"

For the first time, the DCI looked agitated. Paige's knowledge had shattered his confident demeanour. Then, George saw Juliette Thompson, the press officer, step toward him and whisper something in the DCI's ear.

"As this is an ongoing investigation, I cannot comment on rumours, Miss McGuiness. However, anyone with information is asked to contact me, or DI Beaumont, at the Leeds District Homicide and Major Enquiry Team quoting reference 1537435149 or online via live chat. We are currently pursuing all lines of inquiry. That's all we have to say for now. Thank you."

***

It was time for George to go home. He'd worked too many hours and wouldn't get paid for them. It was shit business, but it was what was expected of him. George was expected to work ridiculous hours during a case for his usual salary, all because he had the gall to ask for paid overtime and was threatened to be removed. The police system was becoming a bit of a joke, and George considered his future.

A knock at the door interrupted his thoughts. A short, balding man in a shirt and trousers was looking at him. It was Stuart Kent, and he looked distressed.

"Stuart? Come in. Are you okay?"

"No, George, I don't think I am."

George shook his head, unsure how to deal with Kent. "What's the problem, and how can I help?"

"OK, the case against Tony Shaw," Kent said. "Have you charged him yet? You haven't, right?"

"Right. With it being a triple homicide, we were given an extension to hold Shaw for ninety-six hours. But I can charge him. I can call the CPS now, and they said they would authorise it."

Kent nodded. "The crucial findings at the crime scene were the bin bags and the receipt that linked the purchase to Shaw?"

"Yeah? The receipt is less so because we can't prove Shaw was in the shop then."

"Aha. Yep. I've read the reports." George thought he sounded nervous. Kent slid two forensic photographs across George's desk, showing the bin bags and the receipt. He also slid the report that contained the details of the forensic scientist's findings. "Two forensic scientists matched the bin bags from Shaw's flat to the ones used to dispose of the body parts."

"Yeah... I don't understand where you're going with this, Stuart? It's substantial evidence."

"Solid evidence. No. Not for a person such as myself. It's significant. And sound. And a jury would probably go for it if not for what I'm about to discuss with you."

George frowned. "Explain, Stuart. Please?"

Kent coughed and went to speak before he stopped for a brief moment. "Shaw supposedly bought the bin bags found in Shaw's flat from Sainsbury's on Boxing Day and the newspaper, right? And then, Shaw used that newspaper to wrap up the body parts before being placed inside the bags. Is that right?"

"Right, though, why supposedly? The checkout girl recognised Shaw."

"Come on, Inspector Beaumont. You know that's not a solid piece of evidence. It's sound, yes. But come on, George."

George held up his hands. "We're still investigating all angles, Stuart. But, look, what's this all about? Really?"

"Now be honest with me, Inspector. How forensically minded are you?"

I—I'm okay. I manage. It's why I have you and Dr Ross, right?"

Kent smiled and nodded his head. "I'm not being funny, but some detectives believe they are God's gift. They think the forensics are clear cut. But that's just not the case, George. Like with Tony Shaw and the evidence from his flat, for example. You can find the forensic evidence, document it, and decide how you want to use it in court. But honestly, I believe that forensics has to be interpreted carefully. Extremely carefully.

A, because they can be easily interpreted the wrong way by the defence and cause doubt with the jury, and B, they can be interpreted wrong by the Crown and put the wrong man away. You see what I'm saying?"

"Not really, Stuart."

"Okay, so I noticed DCI Alex Peterson did little with the evidence from the flat other than ask for it to be checked for prints and DNA. That wasn't enough, George, so I asked the Submissions Team at Calder Park to carry out an environmental profile on the bin bags, the newspaper, and the receipt. For comparison purposes, I also got them to profile Shaw's manuscript, a random sampling of his clothes, amongst other items we had taken in for evidence," Kent said and slid another stack of photos across the table. "Now environmental profiling will detect—"

"Tiny amounts of carpet fibres that as residents walk around their properties are thrown into the air and settle on objects which show you how long the objects have been in the locations."

Kent smiled and did a sarcastic clap. George used to like the guy, but there was something off about his behaviour. "Exactly, George." He slid across another report. "That report shows that no carpet fibre deposits were found on the bin bags, receipt, or newspaper, which matched the deposits found on the manuscript, Shaw's clothes, and the like. You already know those three solid pieces of evidence bore none of the suspect's DNA. Now I don't know about you, but I'm worried. The three items, those sturdy pieces of evidence, had deposits on them, some specifically from the material used to make the uniforms the Sainsbury's staff wear. But, sadly for us, they also found carpet fibre deposits from an unknown place. So, to be the bearer of bad news, I'm worried, you know, that someone planted them there."

"Planted by who, Stuart? Every person who entered that flat was part of a team. You're never on your own." George thought for a moment about who had been there during the search. Kent and his team. DCI Peterson and some of George's team. That was it if you didn't include the officer manning the log. "You were there, with your team. Did you see anybody acting suspiciously?"

"Here's a list of who entered," Kent said, sliding over yet another piece of paper. "The log shows my team and me. DS Brewer, and DCs Blackburn, Morton and Hambleton."

"Morton?" George knew the DCI's protégé, Holly Hambleton, had been seconded to his team whilst the DCI took over. "And not DCI Peterson?"

"Yes, Morton." Morton didn't do much fieldwork, so his inclusion was odd to George. "Now, I'm sure you know the Police and Criminal Evidence Act 1984 like the back of your hand, George." George smiled and nodded, not knowing where Kent was going with it. "There was an amendment made in 2015, and from the first of April that year, some police forces have been permitted to take DNA samples from 'serving police officers and special constables, who are likely to come into contact with, and therefore have potential to contaminate the physical evidential chain', and these 'officers are asked to provide a DNA sample to generate a DNA profile for inclusion on the Contamination Elimination Database.'"

"Yeah, I'm aware. But our force doesn't require it. So I gave mine voluntarily."

"Of course, as many detectives would. I asked your DCI why he wasn't leading the search, and he told me he wasn't on the

CED."

"So what you're saying, Stuart, is that you think one of your team, or one of mine, planted the bin bags, newspapers and receipt whilst they searched Shaw's flat? And you think one of those individuals is the killer?"

Stuart Kent shook his head and shrugged his shoulders. "I've no idea, George. That's your job, not mine."

"How well do you know Hayden Wyatt?"

"Why?" Kent questioned. "Has there been a problem?"

"No, but he... I don't know how to say this, but he gives me the ick."

Stuart laughed. "Wyatt's intense and doesn't have any boundaries, either. But he's good. He was the SOCO collecting and bagging evidence. He's efficient and knows what he's doing."

"He strikes me as suspicious."

"Okay, George, I'll keep an eye on him. When Calder Park carried out the environmental profile on Shaw's manuscript, they found something interesting. A microscopic blond hair. Fortunately, there was a follicle, and a forensic scientist at Calder Park is profiling the DNA from the hair as we speak."

George inhaled sharply and sat upright. "Blond hair?" Kent glanced at him, a concerned expression on his face. "Are you okay, George? Anything wrong?"

The DI's face had turned pale, and Kent could see a visible shake in George's hand. It wasn't like the DI.

"Yeah, fine. Nothing's wrong," George said, shaking his head. "I just can't believe there's a chance we have the wrong suspect. I need to speak to the DCI and find out what to do next."

"DCI Peterson?" Kent said, interrupting George's thoughts.

CHAPTER TEN

George nodded back, concerned his voice wouldn't work. "I wouldn't. Maybe you should speak to Detective Superintendent Smith instead."

"Why?" His voice was croaky. He needed a drink. George picked up his mug to find the contents were empty.

"There's something I don't trust about DCI Peterson," Kent said.

"I do. I trust the man fully. DS Elaine Brewer told me she never saw the DCI enter the flat. So it can't be him if that's what you're thinking. I know he's blond, but he never entered. Wyatt's blond, too. Maybe it's his hair?"

Kent shook his head and shrugged. "Crime scenes are busy places, as you well know. But, I don't know about you; George, a DCI who isn't on the CED, is suspicious, no? He's blond. Instructs his own DC to attend the search despite her having no prior knowledge of the case. And from what you say, he's the one who points out the bin bags? I could be wrong, and I hope I'm wrong. But, I've been trying to contact the officer who guarded the cordon, a PC Sally Fletcher, with little success. Somebody had been in that flat, somebody with blond hair. There's something strange going on, George. And I don't like it."

Chapter Eleven

"He said what?" DCI Alex Peterson said, sitting in DSU Smith's chair. It was Sunday, and so, of course, the DSU wasn't in the office. "Let me tell you about Stuart Kent. He's a self-obsessed forensics freak. Honestly, George."

George hadn't said a word about Kent's suspicions but had told him about Kent's theory that Shaw was being framed.

"Framed?" The DCI laughed. "Framed by who?"

"He said that was my job to figure out."

"Yeah, of course, he did. You want a brew?" George nodded. He called down to DC Hambleton, who was typing up reports. "Two brews please, Holly—"

"No sugar for me, please," George added.

"The usual for me, and white tea, no sugar for DI Beaumont. Thanks, love. Right, let's go through what Kent said, then, yeah? See if he's right."

George spent the next twenty minutes explaining how Kent had asked the Submissions Team at Calder Park to carry out an environmental profile on the bin bags, the newspaper, and the receipt. Then, for comparison purposes, Kent also got the lab to profile Shaw's manuscript, a random sampling of his clothes, and other items that SOCOs had taken in for evidence.

CHAPTER ELEVEN

"Right. And so what did the report show?" Alex asked, finishing his cup of tea.

"The reports show zero carpet fibre deposits from Shaw's flat were found on the bin bags, receipt, or newspaper. However, they were found on the manuscript, Shaw's clothes, and the like."

"Kent also reminded me that the bags, newspaper, or receipt bore none of the suspect's DNA, either. However, they found fibres from the uniforms the Sainsbury's staff wear. And, Kent pointed out, they found carpet fibre deposits from an unknown place."

"Well, there you go. That solves it."

"Sir?"

"Look, George. After watching the CCTV footage with you early, I got angry with you. That was my mistake, so I apologise. I spoke with the Super, and he admitted it was his error. I'll be honest with you. I'm up for Detective Superintendent in Bradford. This case could make or break my chances, so as you can imagine, I'm under a lot of stress. And as for the alcohol, I thought I could smell; you were right; I'm sorry. It must have been mouthwash. And I also wanted to apologise for making you Holly's deputy when interviewing Shaw. She needs the experience, but I could have put her in with DS Wood or another one of your team. I disrespected you, and I'm sorry."

"Thank you, Alex. I didn't take offence."

"Of course you did," he said with a wink and a laugh. "But it's good of you to shrug it off. Anyway, back to Kent. It's obvious what's happened, right? The scenario? The situation?"

"I don't think I follow?"

"Tony Shaw's flat, we know from Kent, isn't the place where

he killed and dismembered his victims. Right?"

"Right," George confirmed with a nod of his head.

"It's not a stretch to say the bin bags, newspaper, and receipt were also stored elsewhere."

"The place he killed his victims?"

The DCI smiled. "Bingo."

George stared at the blond DCI longer than necessary, an awkward silence building between them. "Are you sure we haven't met before, Alex?"

"I don't think so. Why?"

"The way you smiled. It was like déjà vu. I felt like I've seen it before."

"Dunno, mate. Sorry. Anyway, back to Shaw, yeah?" Alex said. "It makes sense that Shaw stored the items elsewhere and brought them to his flat. He might have brought them the day you arrested him. Hence the lack of fibres. Kent said they found carpet fibres that didn't match the ones from his flat?"

"Yeah, so that means he has a second property, somewhere else he frequents, somewhere with a carpet?"

"Exactly. Forensics have impounded Shaw's work and private vehicles. They've searched and found nothing. I'm sure Kent would have told you if anything matched. So that means he meets his victims there. Wherever 'there' is."

"Right. We find the place, take samples and bingo; our evidence is tight."

"Exactly, mate. Exactly. Did Kent give you his opinion of what kind of fibres they were? Whether they had any pollen on them or anything else? We might be able to narrow the area down a bit, that's all?"

"No. Kent didn't give me his opinion, though I didn't ask."

"Of course, he didn't. He creates a problem and doesn't help

CHAPTER ELEVEN

with the solution. So typical. Right, I'll speak to him tomorrow. I'm not officially in, but I'll be in tomorrow morning to finish some bits. That alright with you?"

"Yeah, it's probably better coming from you. Coming to you means I took Kent's concerns seriously." The DCI nodded. "Thanks, Alex. I've gotta say I was worried about bringing this to you."

"You shouldn't have worried, mate. It's my job. I'm not here to take over, you know. You're still SIO. I'm only here to give you advice and help, yeah?"

"Yeah."

* * *

After driving home, George settled on his comfortable Ikea sofa, a microwave meal on his lap, and switched on ITV News at 10 pm. They showed the replay of DCI Peterson emerging from Leeds HQ to deliver the news. He watched it until the footage cut to Alex being questioned by Paige McGuiness. The press had already dubbed the killer the Bone Saw Ripper. George didn't think it was original nor particularly catchy. Luckily, they hadn't linked it to the murders from thirty years ago. It was inevitable they would, though.

His phone rang. He reached for it from the coffee table to find it was Dr Ross calling.

"Hi, Dr Ross. How are you?"

"Sorry to call so late again, son," Dr Ross said, his friendly tone welcoming. "The forensic entomologist has sent me their report on Rita Lawrence and your IC1 Jane Doe, and I thought you'd like to discuss it?"

"Sure, thanks, Dr Ross." George got a pad and a pen, putting the pathologist on speaker. "Go ahead."

"Okay, so to get straight to the point, the forensic entomologist estimates your IC3, Rita Lawrence, died Christmas Eve. They suggest this because the blowfly eggs, which had been laid in the open wounds where the parts were dismembered from the torso, had grown into maggots. Said maggots had produced an enzyme that broke down the proteins of the flesh. I'm afraid they can't be specific about what time on Christmas Eve. However, if you eventually find a torso, I can check the organs for decomposition."

"Thanks, Dr Ross. What about the IC1 Jane Doe?"

"Your IC1 died on Boxing Day. Eggs were visible but hadn't reached the larval stage. That's it. Again, get me a torso, and I'll check what I can. If you find it sooner rather than later, I should be able to check for body temperature with the Glaister Equation. I can use that as well as skin colour, muscle rigidity and even the decomposition of her internal organs to give you a more accurate time of death."

"Thanks, Dr Ross. That's extremely helpful."

"My pleasure, son. I'll email them over. Take care."

George said bye to Dr Ross just as the news item ended. Their final image was a photo of George taken by the press while hunting the Miss Murderer, the image only on screen for a couple of seconds. They'd used it because George was the SIO. At that moment, he saw how he was back then: He had the face of a younger man, of someone else, eyes bright and hungry, and a confident, experienced aura. Is that what he used to be? Whatever George was, he wasn't like that any more. Adam Harris had knocked that right out of him. What was he now? An older, unsure man with weary eyes and a tiring aura?

It made him sick.

CHAPTER ELEVEN

George put his plate to the side, realising for the first time it was lasagne and poured himself a whisky, unaware that the news had moved on. He sat there and took a long slug, the liquid burning pleasantly as it slid down his throat, a warmth he only associated with alcohol spreading through his body, soothing his mind immediately. What Kent had shared with him still worried him, despite assurances from the DCI. Why was that? They must have been missing something, but what? George turned off the news with a sigh and started double-checking all the evidence they had on Shaw.

He began by writing a timeline, reminding himself of what he'd found and when. They found the body parts on Friday. Saturday, they arrested Shaw but only questioned him lightly about the three women. On Saturday night, George had gone through the ANPR data for Shaw's private vehicle and his work van. That data showed nothing other than Shaw using Astra to go to the shop or to go to work, and the computer system had flagged up nothing for him to investigate further.

It was the same for Shaw's work van, as most of the trips had taken him south down the M1 to Wakefield before the ANPR data confirmed Shaw headed back to Hunslet to collect the mail per Myles' contract.

They'd received the location data from Shaw's mobile phone, too. It showed nothing. It was switched off most of the time, which was suspicious in George's eyes. Without concrete evidence, though, his suspicions meant nothing.

He was still waiting on the forensics on Shaw's accounts. George knew they would be invaluable, especially now that Kent had shared his concerns. The DCI had made an excellent point, and so he hoped the accounts would shed some light on whether Shaw was renting perhaps another property or a storage container.

The autopsies for all three women had been busts, with Dr Ross not even being able to determine whether the victims were dead or alive during the dismembering. Without the specialised microscope, they couldn't even guess what kind of saw was used. But one thing Dr Ross could confirm, at least, was that IC2 Jane Doe died Boxing Day.

The forensic scientists had matched the ones in the bins to the roll in Shaw's flat. They had the newspaper, too, and the receipt that proved they were bought from Sainsbury's. Not only that, though, they had a statement from the young woman who served Shaw and a positive ID for Shaw during the pre-recorded video identity parade she took part in.

Shaw still hadn't explained the large luminescent pattern in his bathroom, either, but a report uploaded by Kent showed it was blood from a male with an AB-negative blood group. So Shaw was AB-negative, which may explain things. Yet if it explained things, why did he reply with 'no comment?' *What was Shaw hiding?*

Next, George thought about the CCTV footage at Sainsbury's and behind the Indian takeaway. They looked like the same person. So if it wasn't Shaw and he was being framed, they were doing an excellent job of looking and acting like Shaw.

They had enough to charge him. Easily. Yet what Kent had come to him with still bugged him.

An hour later, he was still there, a half-empty bottle of whisky by his side. His living room floor was covered with a mess of paper that may have once been in some sort of order. It was past midnight, yet he continued to search the room for page one, knowing that between the thickly etched lines and brightly coloured circles, he'd find something he'd forgotten.

CHAPTER ELEVEN

There was a link he'd not made yet. He was sure of it. Looking down, he couldn't help but chuckle as he found it. It was a mind-map of a madman.

For the first time in a while, he fancied a cigarette. Instead, he took another slug of whisky and continued reading.

The drinking, the reading, the etching and the circling continued like that throughout the rest of the night.

Chapter Twelve

"You're late," DCI Alex Peterson said with a wink, throwing his guttural voice across the office. "I'm on leave today, so I need you to take charge, Beaumont."

He was only two minutes late and not what George needed to improve his mood. "Sorry, sir," he said, not wanting to point out he'd already worked a ton of unpaid overtime and clenched his jaw to stop him from saying something he might later regret. However, the DCI had apologised to him yesterday, so George had decided it was better they worked together rather than against each other.

"Have you spoken to Stuart yet?" George said, but the DCI was gone. It was probably best if he messaged him later with an update. So, with a sigh, George headed to the canteen to grab a brew. After that, he needed to find DC Terrence Morton. Terry was a recent transfer to his team, a man in his fifties who, it seemed, didn't have the ambition to climb the ranks. Despite that lack of ambition, Terry was a decent detective, but all he did was moan about his wife.

George found him already sitting at his desk, a steaming Greggs takeaway cup beside him—and a toffee muffin.

"Morning, Inspector," Terry said with a grin as George entered the shared offices. Unlike himself and the other high-ranking detectives, the constables and sergeants didn't have their own private offices.

"Thought you were cutting down after Christmas, mate?" George nodded to the muffin with a grin, raising an eyebrow for good measure.

"You what?" Terry said, instantly on the defensive, which was typical of him. "Piss off." He grinned and gave George the finger. "I normally have two, so this is cutting down."

George snorted with laughter and shook his head. "Ah, okay, mate, fair enough. For a moment, I thought you were trying the see-food diet. You know, the one where you see food and eat it."

Terry snorted coffee from his nose. "Bloody wife's starving me at home, mate!" Terry said between chortles. "You know what she cooked me for tea last night? I say cooked—she gave me a fucking salad, George. I'm not a bastard rabbit! Winter's 'ere, and it's fucking freezing. A man doesn't need salad; he needs pie and peas! Chips and gravy! Beef stew and buttery mash. Fuck salad!"

George laughed again. "Hear, hear. But you'll be no good chasing criminals eating that shit all day. And, err, you are a grown man, you know. So, bloody, stand up for yourself!"

Morton looked at George in amazement. "I can see why you're single, pal. If there's one mantra in life, it's this: A happy wife means a happy life! And don't I fucking know it?"

George winced. Isabella Wood wasn't like that, not that he would volunteer that information. Having a relationship with a detective in his team wasn't strictly kosher.

"Enjoy your muffin, mate," George said and grinned. Terry looked sorry for himself, but George knew Terry worshipped the ground his wife walked on. Young DC Jason Scott had taken the piss out of the dinner Terry's missus had packed him one afternoon a few days after Terry had transferred. The young lad immediately regretted it. Terry wouldn't hear a bad word against her. They'd been together for over three decades and had three kids older than DC Scott. George had gotten in the middle of them that day, and Terry was quite strong for a chunky fellow.

"So you didn't want anything from me, boss? You came over 'ere to mock my malnourishment, eh?" Terry raised a brow.

"Right you are, Terry. I saw the Greggs cup and the muffin and couldn't help myself."

"Ah yes. Pick on the fat bloke. Don't you have anything else you could spend your time on? Why you 'ere, anyway? Thought you were on lates?"

"Yeah, I am. But I'm SIO…" George shrugged and took a sip of his brew. "The new DCI wanted me in. He sai—"

At that moment, DS Wood called his name from across the office. She was already standing up, grabbing her bag and pocket notebook. He saw her slip some gloves and overshoes into her bag, too. "Sorry to interrupt, George, but the SOCOs sent to Shaw's flat have found something. So the DCI has ordered us to get there at once."

George turned back to Terry. "See? Good job I was here, eh?"

"Later, mate, ring me if you need owt."

"Thanks. Call Calder Park for me and get an update on the DNA profiling of the body parts, yeah? Ring me as soon as you get anything."

"Sure, boss, no probs."

George sighed. He liked to call Calder Park labs himself and usually led his team by example rather than delegate. But the cuts HMET had suffered recently meant he no longer had the

CHAPTER TWELVE

luxury of managing cases his way. And if he didn't play ball, he knew the DCS could quickly take the case away. The Detective Chief Superintendent had said as much.

"Let DCI Peterson know, too. If he's not around, call him. He's supposed to be on leave today, but I'm sure he'll want to be in the loop."

Terry flicked his eyes around the office. "Between us, he's a ball-breaker, that man."

George wasn't sure he liked the new DCI, either. Yes, he was efficient, but the way he'd ordered George to handle the Shaw interviews was too robotic. George liked to talk and tease out information. He didn't enjoy referring to documents every minute, not giving the suspect a moment to clarify anything. Despite his feelings, though, it had worked, and they had enough to charge Shaw, he was sure of it. "Cheers, mate."

George quickly chugged his brew, the lava running down his throat and heating his stomach, and dumped the mug on his desk—he'd wash it later. He shrugged his coat on and checked his pockets for his phone, car keys and wallet before doing precisely what DS Wood did and loading up on gloves and overshoes.

He crossed the room to where Wood waited and said, "Morning, DS Wood." She smiled a genuine, warm smile that showed she cared for him. He mirrored it, hoping she could see how much she meant to him. Hopefully, he'd work with his partner more during this murder inquiry as he had on the Miss Murderer case.

"Morning, George. Are you ready?"

"Not really." He got close and whispered, "I'm just glad I get to spend some time with you."

Wood smirked and walked out. George watched her as she

did.

"Good-looking woman," Terry said as George walked past to follow DS Wood. "I won't lie and say I'm not jealous you get to work so closely with her,"

"What? Oh, DS Wood. I can't say I noticed," George lied.

Terry raised a knowing brow. Not that George saw because he'd rushed towards the door to hold it open for DS Wood. She put a hand on his chest and thanked him with a bright smile.

George couldn't help but smile back. He felt like a giddy teenager. Despite being together since April, for him, the honeymoon period hadn't ended yet.

Terry watched the entire exchange with a knowing smile.

"What have the SOCOs found, anyway?" he asked as they left the station. Then, without any pool cars to choose from, they headed over to his Honda.

"Another torso and four limbs," she replied.

* * *

They arrived ten minutes later, and George parked up on Town Street. It was the same PC who guarded the cordon on Friday night. They flashed their warrant cards. "DI George Beaumont, SIO. This is DS Wood."

"I remember you, sir," the constable said with a nod and signed them in on the log.

"Thanks. Keep your log going and guard the cordon, please."

They suited up and followed the common approach path to find the usual blue forensic tent. Inside was a pale torso laid on a table. The thighs were still attached, and ginger pubic hair was visible. George couldn't see any tattoos or identifying marks such as moles or scars. As before, both arms

CHAPTER TWELVE

had been severed. Two other tables held the other body parts, two golden-brown arms and two golden-brown legs. *Were those body parts from the torso they'd found on Friday?* George questioned.

SOCO Hayden Wyatt told them the body parts were wrapped in the same Boxing Day edition of The Sun newspaper as the others. However, George still didn't trust him. To George, that meant there was a high probability it was the same culprit. Shaw. Because of that, the killer probably dumped them on the same day, which was good evidence because Shaw was still the most likely perpetrator.

Forensic scientists had harvested DNA and fingerprints from the newspaper but had no hits on the DNA database. As the killer had bought the newspaper from Sainsbury's on Boxing Day, it was likely the newspaper had been cross-contaminated. George would always pick his newspapers and magazines from the back but would usually handle the first copy to see if it sparked an interest. He did the same with milk, as the longest dates were generally at the back. Though recently, George thought the shelf stockers had gotten lazy, with some dates often being better at the front. They knew their culprit had worn gloves on his trip to Sainsbury's, so his prints and DNA would likely not be present.

If the same guy dumped the parts on the same day, it was a race against the clock for Stuart Kent's SOC team to capture all the evidence they needed from the scene.

Kent let out a long sigh as he approached George, taking off his blue mask and blue disposable gloves. It was clear he'd been looking at the body parts. "It's the same as before, Inspector Beaumont. I can't advise whether the amputations were pre- or post-mortem. But, as before, whoever killed these women was extremely forensically aware. We'll extract DNA from the body parts. Make sure you only have three victims rather than six. Dr Ross will investigate, but he probably won't be able to tell you much."

"Culprit could be a SOCO," George said, looking at Hayden Wyatt. "Could even be a Crime Scene Co-ordinator." Kent smiled. "I'm thinking about people who are extremely forensically aware. Blonde people, who are extremely forensically aware."

"Guess the same could be said about you, DI Beaumont. A blond person who is extremely forensically aware," Hayden Wyatt said, clearing having been eavesdropping.

George ignored him and walked away. There must be something they could get from the scene as he didn't believe in coincidences. They were due to be collected on the same day as the Indian Takeaway's bins.

But it didn't sit right with him. Why would somebody dump body parts outside their own home? George's thoughts were interrupted by the constant click of a camera, and he saw the same police photographer he didn't recognise before taking pictures of the scene.

"What are you thinking, Inspector?" Kent asked.

"Any distinguishing marks on the torso?" George said.

"Nothing on the front. A butterfly tattoo on the small of her back."

"Can you send me the image?" Kent nodded. "What's the decomposition like?"

"Further on by a day or so, suggesting the culprit dumped them around the same time as the others. We won't know until Dr Ross investigates. The cuts to the bones look very similar to the other body parts, but without the proper equipment, it's hard to be certain."

"Cuts made by a saw?"

"I'd say so, yeah. But as Dr Ross told you, without a handheld microscope, it's difficult to be certain."

Chapter Thirteen

"Sarah Lawson. Twenty-six. Lived in Hunslet." George stared at the WhatsApp image DC Morton had sent of her driving licence. A redhead. The DNA results had come back just as they'd finished looking at the remains found in the bins behind Tony Shaw's flat. He called Terry immediately.

"She's on the DNA database then," George said.

"Not even a 'hello,' boss?"

"For once in your life, Terry, take something seriously. Was she—"

"Yes, sir. She was on the database, but not because she had committed a crime. She was a sex worker involved in a pilot scheme where sex workers voluntarily gave DNA samples because they were deemed as potential high-risk victims but the DNA collection ceased as the money ran dry. Rita Lawrence's remains have also been identified by DNA collected from the same scheme. The torso came back as negative, sir."

"Shit. At least we have two IDs, though. Speak to Josh, DS Fry, and ask him to do a background check on Sarah. It might be that the two women worked for the same agency?"

"Twenty-six… Too young to die, and particularly like this," Terry said. "My youngest is twenty-six. I can't imagine her being murdered. Think of her poor parents. It's awful, just awful."

"Did you hear what I said about the background check, Terry?"

"Yes, sir. I'm writing it down as we speak."

"Good. Let the DCI know, yeah?"

"Sure, boss."

George hung up the phone. It had been a long and cold morning, the chilling cold stiffening his bones. He wasn't getting any younger and knew he'd suffer when trying to sleep that night. The steel-grey clouds above were threatening to burst, and they were all frozen. George shivered. The weather was getting colder day by day. Wood had popped up to the café on Middleton Park Road for a coffee run. After an intensive search by his team, George was satisfied the takeaways and shops weren't involved in the murders of the three women found in their bins.

A sharp pain erupted from his back where Adam Harris had stabbed him. He'd managed to reduce his painkiller intake but was relying on alcohol more and more, especially with the nightmares.

Stuart Kent and his team combed through every inch of the undergrowth and surrounding area for anything the culprit had left behind.

They would need to search for witnesses in the area and work from there. For example, maybe a resident of the flat had seen Shaw dumping the bin bags that night.

"Did you find any CCTV cameras?" Wood asked once she was back.

George took a sip of his coffee, the strong, bitter flavour tingling on his tongue. It was a welcome tingling, as was the warmth that spread down his throat and into his stomach.

He sighed and folded his fingers across his cup to keep them warm. "Nothing. Behind the flats is the park. 200, 194A and 200A have CCTV on the front but not on the back or the side. Same for 202. I rang Tashan. He's searching Brandling Court. If one of the houses had CCTV on the right side and was high enough to see over the fence, they may have caught something."

"In other words, probably not, then?" she said—a rhetorical question.

"Anyway, we have an ID: Sarah Lawson, twenty-six from Hunslet. I've got DS Fry on the preliminary checks. The sooner we find out about her next of kin, the sooner we can visit them." Rita Lawrence had no family, but they had contacted a close friend who said she would identify any remains.

"I'll ring the office, George, and get DC Scott to pull up any social media accounts. We need to find connections and build a picture of her life."

Stuart Kent's team were beginning to pack up as George rounded the back of the flats, packing up the tent that had preserved the scene and the body parts.

"Okay, so DC Scott's on that," Wood said, approaching the scene. "Did Kent give you anything else after I left?"

George shook his head. "Not really. No defensive wounds. No sexual assault. All fingernails are clean."

"No sign of a suitcase or murder weapon?"

George shook his head again, a look of defeat in his eyes.

Wood glanced at the black body bags behind them, the sad remains of what had been at least three women.

"Kent's going to fast-track all their finds, but even that could take a day or two."

CHAPTER THIRTEEN

Wood dragged her eyes away from the body bags and planted them on George.

"But we got nothing?"

"Nothing, yet. The sooner we get Sarah's next of kin information, the better." His phone pinged. "Wood. I've got an address for Sarah Lawson's parents."

* * *

On the way to see Sarah Lawson's parents, DI Beaumont sped the Honda down Belle Isle Road towards Hunslet, on the outskirts of Leeds city centre. George hated this part of the job the most. After all, there was no easy way to tell somebody their loved one had been murdered.

Beside him, Wood reviewed the notes George had taken whilst talking to Stuart Kent. She looked at the sky; the low sun hid behind a featureless white blanket of low clouds. Winter was well and truly here. It was cold enough to snow.

Belle Isle Road changed to Balm Road as they flew underneath the M621 motorway bridge, headed towards The Oval estate where Sarah's parents lived. It hadn't been long since George had been down here, he remembered, watching a rugby match with one of his mates.

He glanced at the clock in the car as they reached the traffic lights at the junction of Balm Road and Church Street. "Fancy a quick dinner stop?"

"Absolutely," said Wood, smiling at the suggestion. "I'm proper starving."

George grinned. "KFC or Morrisons' hot counter? What'll it be? I think I want a sausage butty from Morrisons."

"Are we doing that thing again where we eat fast food daily

whilst working on a case?" Wood said, her voice oozing sarcasm.

He held his hands in surrender and said, "If you prefer to go somewhere else, then just let me know. "

"Nah. Sounds good to me, George. I'll have the same."

"Anything to drink?"

Wood smiled. "Yeah, I'll come in with you."

George turned right into the expansive supermarket car park and switched off the Honda's engine.

* * *

Soon, the Honda smelled of brown sauce, peppery Cumberland sausage, and strong coffee as they tucked into the hefty butties with enthusiasm. George savoured the warm, tender sausages, the pepper and brown sauce tingling and warming his tongue.

Wood made sure the takeaway cups were secured in the holders between hers and George's seat, and as soon as both were belted up, George drove through the car park to the other exit and turned right towards The Oval.

"I think I overate," she said with a laugh, holding half the butty in its wrapper. "You finished yours, yet don't look half as pogged as I do."

"I don't mess around with food, you know." He grinned at her but kept his eyes on the road.

"Please tell me you at least chewed the food before inhaling it?"

"What does chewing mean?"

Wood shook her head. "You'll end up like Morton."

"All I need is a bit more exercise. You up for some?"

Wood's laugh turned to a choke as she took another delicate

CHAPTER THIRTEEN

bite of her butty. He'd never seen her with sauce on her chin or grease on her shirt; somehow, she always made eating look vaguely elegant. "Be careful with that brown sauce. I'd hate for it to get on that white blouse you're wearing."

"Looks good, doesn't it? Though it'll be a shame when I decide not to let you see what's underneath." Wood sent a fake glower his way.

"You're right. It looks good," George said with a nod. He turned right once again and sped down Grange Road. The Lawsons lived right at the end of the road in a semi-detached terracotta-coloured house. As he slowed to park beside the kerb, he winked and said, "It'd look better on my bedroom floor."

An extensive set of bushes and a bed of flowers ringed the unfenced house. The front lawn was flawlessly cropped, and the paved path to the front door was immaculately weeded. Unfortunately, the same couldn't be said for the conjoined house to the left. That house looked a complete mess. As DI Beaumont and DS Wood approached the front door, sheltered from the hail that had begun to fall, he saw movement from the bay window to his right.

He took a deep breath. George hadn't even knocked on the door before a squat, chunky woman in her late fifties flung it open. Sarah Lawson's mum. It must have been because George stopped and stared for a short moment. It was as if a broader and older Sarah was staring at him.

"Mrs Lawson?" She nodded. The detectives held out their warrant cards. "Detective Inspector Beaumont, and Detective Sergeant Wood. We're sorry for visiting unannounced. Can we come in, please?" As he spoke, the red-headed woman looked at them with worried eyes.

"That was quick. Has something happened?" she asked before realising the detective had asked to be invited in. "Sorry, where are my manners? Please, come in."

George smiled at her, and she led them inside, pausing at a door that proudly stated, 'Gregory's Office.' "Greg," she said. "Can you come out? The police are here."

Greg came out from his office, the wooden door slamming against the wall, as Mrs Lawson led them into a humble living room with leather sofas that she invited them to sit in. The faint smell of bleach hung in the air.

Greg scratched his head as he followed them in. "You guys were quick. We only reported her missing half an hour ago. And to send two detectives? I would have thought you had better things to do with your time. I'm grateful, though. Sarah means the world to us."

"Absolutely," George said. The fake smile he had managed faded immediately.

"Would either of you like a drink?" Mrs Lawson asked.

"No. Thank you. Could you both please sit?"

Mr and Mrs Lawson shared a curious glance. It soon turned to worry when George explained he wasn't here to take the missing person's details. "I'm sorry to bring you such sad news, but your daughter Sarah has been murdered."

There was a stunned silence that lasted for nearly a minute.

A tear dropped from Mr Lawson's eye. "Repeat it?" His face turned pale.

George nodded and repeated his sentence. Then he waited for his sentence to sink in—he didn't want to repeat it.

Mrs Lawson couldn't have looked any shorter as she shrunk into the leather sofa. Greg's hand found hers, and George saw the dam was about to burst.

CHAPTER THIRTEEN

"How? When? What happened? Are you even sure it's her?" Greg asked, his voice hoarse. He was fighting back the tears. His wife sat there in stunned silence and looked to have aged a couple of decades, wilting even more as the seconds ticked by. "We haven't heard from her since Christmas Day, which was strange. But—but she can't be. She can't be dead."

As Wood spoke, Mrs Lawson burst into tears.

"We're investigating the murders of three young women—"

"Can we see her?" Mrs Lawson interrupted.

Wood looked at George, who briefly shook his head. "I'm sorry, but—"

"But what?" Greg asked.

George put his hand on Wood's and smiled. It was unusual for her to struggle during these types of situations. However, he removed it quickly when he realised it probably didn't look professional. "Out of respect for the both of you, I'll be frank," George mumbled. "Whoever murdered your daughter dismembered her."

He waited for his words to sink in.

"Dismembered. How? Why?" Greg asked.

"We are still in the early stages of the investigation, but the pathologist cannot determine whether Sarah was dismembered pre- or post-mortem. Either way, we believe our suspect dismembered his victims so he could dispose of them more easily."

A moan of anguish escaped Mrs Lawrence's mouth. She stared desperately at George, begging for answers but not wanting to know the truth. Grief manifested in many ways, and who was he to judge? All he could do was tell them the truth and get them justice.

George stood up and took in the view of the room. Family

photos showing the trio's smiling faces were sprinkled around the room. No other children were present in any of the pictures, and he suspected Sarah was their only and most treasured child.

Thud, crash. Thud, crash. Thud, crash.

He started shaking and felt physically sick. What was happening to him? He'd never let the emotions of a family get to him before. Finally, he stood up, and Wood looked at him. "Are you okay?" she mouthed.

He nodded and took a deep breath.

"I think I need a drink," Mrs Lawson eventually said as she pushed herself up. She fell forward, and her husband caught her. "Carry on with your explanation, please, detective."

Greg looked at the detectives with pleading eyes.

"We found a leg and an arm that we now know belongs to Sarah on Friday night, wrapped in newspaper and thrown in a black bin bag. The perpetrator tried to dispose of them in a commercial bin behind a takeaway."

"A leg and an arm?" Tears flowed like rivers down Greg's cheeks.

"Yes. This morning, we found a torso. Would you mind looking at this picture and letting us know whether it belongs to Sarah?" He gingerly took out his phone and pulled up the image Stuart Kent had sent him.

"That looks like her tattoo to me. Why was she killed?"

"We don't know. Yet. But I can promise you we're doing everything we can to understand what happened, why it happened, and be assured we're close to bringing the person responsible to justice."

"You have a suspect already?"

"Yes. But I must stress that if you know of anyone with a

motive, please let us know. At this early stage, any information can be beneficial. For example, did Sarah have any enemies, anyone with a grudge? Do you know if she'd recently fallen out with anybody?"

Greg stared at the floor and shook his head, tears splattering on the laminate floor. "I doubt it very much. Sarah's a good girl and always has been. She loves life—she loves people." Greg shuddered, and more tears fell from his wide eyes. "I can't think of one person who would want to hurt her," he said and smiled sadly.

"Did she have a partner or ex-partners who would want to harm her?"

Mrs Lawson entered the living room and dropped her steaming mug of tea on the laminate floor. She didn't flinch as the river of tea ran under the leather sofa, but with a voice full of hatred and anger, she said, "Not a single person on this planet would want to harm my Sarah!"

"What did she do for a living?"

Mrs Lawson stepped closer to her husband and put a hand on his shoulder. "We're well aware of what she did," she said. "It wasn't our business, and so we didn't judge. She told us it was safe." She stared at George with a look of desperation in her eyes. She needed someone to blame. "You don't think... you don't think one of her clients killed her?"

"It's a line of inquiry we are following, yes. Do you have any information on Sarah's clients or who she had been with the past week or two?"

"No," Mrs Lawson spoke again, glaring at George still. "We don't ask. It's none of our business. She's well-looked-after at the agency."

"And which agency is this?" DS Wood asked.

"Red Light Green Light," Mr Lawson supplied. "Something to do with a popular Netflix show."

George saw his DS scribbling notes in her pocket notebook. "Do you know what name she used?" Wood asked Mr Lawson.

"She didn't say, and we didn't press her. As my wife told you, we didn't judge, and it wasn't any of our business."

"Do you know if she had any problems at work?"

"I thought we were being clear when we said it wasn't any of our business," Greg retorted.

George got the impression that despite knowing about her job and what it most likely entailed, they didn't exactly approve of it. That was their right.

"We don't know anything else, detectives," Mrs Lawson said and once again burst into tears.

"We're sorry to have put you through all of this, Mr and Mrs Lawson," George said. "Do you have any contact details for her work?"

"No." He had a stern look on his face. "Is there anything else?"

George shook his head and stood. "I'm sorry to have brought you such awful news. We'll do everything we can to give you answers and bring the perpetrator to justice."

Mr and Mrs Lawson stood up and clung together.

"I'll arrange the visit of an FLO," Wood said to George, pointing at her mobile. She respectfully said goodbye and stepped outside. This had affected her more than George had initially realised. It had affected him, too. He could barely look at the images on the mantle without shivering. He wondered why.

"We'll send a family liaison officer to see you, Mr and Mrs Lawson. It'll be a woman named Cathy Hoskins, and she will be

CHAPTER THIRTEEN

your main point of contact with us. Think about what we asked you earlier, and if you can expand on your answers or even think of anything else that might help with our inquiries, then you can pass that to us via Cathy. That also works in reverse, so Cathy will keep you informed of any developments. Cathy won't be visiting you to intrude but to offer you any support you need. Don't hesitate to ask her, Mr and Mrs Lawson." He looked between them to check they understood, and they nodded, their eyes dull and glazed over.

"If you need anything else before Cathy gets here, here are my details." George handed them a card from his inside pocket. He began to give his thanks when he was distracted by Mrs Lawson's movements. The mourning woman hadn't been paying any attention to George. Instead, she had moved towards the mantle and had gently picked up a photo of Sarah as a toddler. In the image, Sarah was grinning a gappy smile.

Thud, crash. Thud, crash. Thud, crash.

As Mrs Lawson clutched it to her chest and sobbed quietly, George started shaking and felt sick.

Greg saw George watching his wife, stepped forward and took the card from George's outstretched hand. "I'm—I'm very sorry for your loss," George finally managed.

George thought for a moment as he was about to show himself out. "Did Sarah have a mobile phone?"

"Of course she did."

"Can I have her number?"

"Yeah, okay," Mr Lawson said. He pulled out a mobile phone from the pocket of his denim jeans. He scrolled for a moment. "Here."

He took Sarah's mobile number from Mr Lawson and stored it on his phone.

Outside, George found Wood. "I got her mobile number. So we can get a warrant and pinpoint her last moments with the phone," he said. "That, and we get her call records."

She smiled woefully. "Great idea," she said, heading for the Honda and getting in.

George called DS Joshua Fry and supplied him with Sarah Lawson's mobile number and asked him to get a warrant for her records, requesting if Josh could track it.

"As you asked, the FLO team has assigned Cathy," she said.

Chapter Fourteen

Red Light Green Light was run out of a small office on Bath Road just before the junction of Water Lane, in Holbeck, a stone's throw away from Leeds City Centre. It was next to an old printing factory, and the street was deserted during that time of day. A grey-steel roller door covered the front of the office. George did not know the place existed, and he got the impression that many other people would have thought the same. "Practically invisible is this place," said George. If not for the video doorbell, George would have continued past, lost. Apart from that doorbell, there were no identifying features, no plaque beneath the doorbell, and no sign on the roller door.

Yet it was Wood who pointed out the reference that George didn't understand. The roller door was decorated with graffiti, a female doll with black hair wearing a yellow blouse and orange dress. Above were a red circle and a green circle.

"It's from a Netflix show. I'm surprised you haven't seen it," Wood remarked.

He shrugged and pushed the button. A moment later, a husky female voice said, "Yes? Can I help you?"

He held up his warrant card to the doorbell. "We're detectives from the Homicide and Major Enquiry Team. I need to ask you a few questions." But, of course, the Super was working on a warrant, so technically, the woman with the husky voice didn't have to let them in if she didn't want to.

"CID?" the voice inquired.

"Technically no, but plain-clothes, yes." She had been expecting them to be vice, rather than CID.

"What's this in connection with?"

"I need information about one of your agency workers."

"We don't give out that kind of information," the voice replied. "We have a confidentiality agreement in place."

"I appreciate that, but this is about one of your agency workers who was murdered last week."

George looked at Wood, who nodded. "It's a homicide inquiry," she said. "We're not with the Vice Squad."

A temporary pause. "Fine. Come in."

The roller door gave way to a door painted the same steel-grey as the roller. George pushed it inwards and held it open for DS Wood. There was a musty smell as they climbed the steps, his feet sticking to the manky, threadbare carpeting. The walls were covered with ripped, outdated wallpaper. He wasn't expecting the place to be so worn. Yet, as soon as they reached the landing, the décor was different. It was like night and day. The walls were painted a brilliant white; the floor was made of ebony polished tiles. It looked like a professional place. Classy, even. Directly in front of the stairs was a glass door with black lettering that read Red Light Green Light Escort Agency. George wasn't expecting it. Another doorbell blocked access to the inner sanctum.

George pushed the button of the doorbell and was immediately granted access. The glass door swung open, and the pair of detectives walked across gleaming black tiles

CHAPTER FOURTEEN

toward the front desk. Behind the counter sat a blonde young woman wearing a white long-sleeve button-up shirt and black trousers. George showed her his warrant card, as did Wood.

"I'm DI Beaumont. This is DS Wood. Can we speak to the manager, please?"

Her eyes widened. "Yes. Sure. Of course." It was a different voice to the one who let them in.

A door at the back opened and a middle-aged brunette, wearing the same shirt and trousers as the young blonde, came out. George could smell the sour tang of nicotine mixed with a fruity spritz spray he was sure he recognised. "Come through, detectives," she said in her throaty voice.

The blonde opened a swinging partition, and they were allowed through the front office into the back office. It was a small, tidy room with a large rectangular desk and two visitors' chairs. They looked uncomfortable, whilst the brunette's chair was padded and looked welcoming. In the corner sat a printer next to a giant shredding machine. The sound of it shredding paper made George suspicious, and he raised his brow at the brunette, who gestured for them to sit down.

"Thank you for agreeing to speak to us," he said, offering his hand and name. She didn't take it but nodded. The Super hadn't called with confirmation of the warrant, so she could easily have refused them entry. They could be asked to leave at any point, and so he quickly planned in his head.

As George decided what questions to ask, the brunette lowered herself into the comfy chair and examined them. "You're sure you're not from Vice?"

"We're from the HMET, the Homicide and Major Enquiry Team. We're investigating a trio of murders."

She gave a terse nod.

"This is DS Wood. And you are?" asked George.

She smiled. "They call me Brielle."

He wanted to ask her who calls her Brielle but thought better of antagonising her. It was obviously not her real name. "Thank you again, Brielle."

Before he asked about Sarah Lawson, she cut in. "Listen, detectives; I'm sure you understand I can't divulge information about my girls." She puckered her lips and stuck her tongue through them. "Their identities are kept a secret for a reason."

Up close, she was younger than he had first thought. She had intelligent, green eyes, and he found her rather attractive, something Wood must have noticed because she coughed.

"I just need information about Sarah Lawson. Her parents have already told us she works here." George took out his mobile and found the photos Stuart Kent had sent him. He slid his phone across the table. "Is this Sarah Lawson?"

She stared at the torso for a long time. "The tattoo looks familiar." He leaned over and swiped the photo of Sarah's driving licence. "Yes, I know Sarah Lawson." She hesitated.

"We know from her parents that she works here. You're not giving away any confidential information. We just wanted confirmation."

Brielle nodded. "She hasn't been in contact with me for a while. She owes—owed me some commission from her last client. I guess this is the reason."

George saw little emotion on the woman's face.

"Are you able to give us the information on who her last client was?" Wood asked.

She was already shaking her head. "We take our clients' confidentiality seriously, Detective. And anyway, they never use their real names."

"When was her last client? Which date?"

Again, she shook her head. "Sorry."

George moved on quickly. "Do you know a woman named Rita Lawrence?"

"Without a warrant, I can't say much."

"All you have to do is tell me whether you recognise this woman. We're not here about anything other than to get information from you to solve their murders. So here," he said, swiping back to an image of Rita's licence. "Do you recognise this woman?"

"Why do you want to know?"

She was playing games now, and George was short of time as it was. "Three young women have been killed, dismembered and then disposed of. We know the identities of two out of three. One of them works here. The other two might have worked here, too. We believe one of your clients has murdered the women. Who was Sarah's final booking? Please, Brielle."

She pursed her lips. "Fine. Rita Lawrence was also one of my girls."

Brielle said nothing else. George met her gaze head-on. She didn't reply—she knew she didn't have to.

"Do you do bookings over the telephone or have clients coming into the office?"

"Both. However, few of our clients know where we are based. Only the regulars come here. But all they do is meet the girls before going elsewhere. We're not a brothel, detective."

He held up his hands. "I'm not from vice. I couldn't give a shit right now. All I want is to catch the bastard before he kills again. You might lose more of your girls if I don't catch him."

She fell silent. The penny dropped. The shredder had stopped a few minutes ago, and the only sound was the soft hum of her laptop. Then, finally, she said, "I will check our booking system for you."

"Thank you." George met Wood's gaze, who gave a slight nod. He saw her exhale. Something about this case was bugging her, and she wouldn't share with him why.

At least Brielle was cooperating. He retrieved his phone and messaged Detective Superintendent Smith for an update on the warrant whilst Brielle began tapping away at the keyboard. A few minutes passed before she raised her head again.

"I can confirm that London and Scarlet were booked out recently, but I can't say with who and on which days."

"Why?" enquired DS Wood.

Brielle shook her head.

"Was it Christmas Eve, Christmas Day or Boxing Day?" George asked.

Brielle's eyes flickered to the screen, and her face went pale. She would have made an awful poker player.

"I'm right, aren't I? It's one of those days. Maybe they were booked on separate days?" It would explain the autopsy results. "This is important, Brielle."

She gave a slight nod. "But I'm not giving you the name of the man. I can't. Our clients trust us."

George met her gaze. "Man? They saw the same man?"

Brielle closed her eyes and shut her laptop with a definitive snap. "I'm sorry, but I've already given you too much. You'll have to come back with a warrant if you want anything else." George blew air from his mouth and shook his head. There wouldn't be any point in pressing her for more information; she knew her rights. He met her gaze again, but the steely glint that stared back told him she wouldn't budge.

"Thanks, Brielle. Before we go, have a look at this image."

CHAPTER FOURTEEN

He found the image of the unidentified torso with the Beyoncé quote tattoo. "Do you recognise this tattoo?"

Brielle shrugged as George's phone pinged. The warrant. "Okay. Thank you. Do you know the name, DCI Gates?" She nodded. "He told me confiscating equipment and searching the premises would be bad for you, and I agree. Now that ping you just heard means I now have a warrant that allows me to send in uniformed officers. But I don't want to do that, Brielle. All I need is for you to answer some questions. We leave. Nobody knows."

Brielle nodded her head, a scowl on her face.

"Thank you for your cooperation."

She scoffed. "Oh, save me the bullshit, Inspector. What choice do I have? You could ruin my business, you know."

He shook his head. "All you had to do was give us the information we needed. We catch the sick bastard, and nobody knows it's you who gave us the information. I'm offering you the same deal now. Okay?" She nodded. "Good. I need you to confirm the name of the woman with the Beyoncé tattoo on her—"

George's phone rang. He held up a hand and answered. "DI Beaumont."

"Yes. Yes. Right, okay. That's interesting. I bet Dr Ross had a field day. Germany? Crazy. Yeah, if that's what her mum said, send a team of SOCOs to the house. Don't let Hayden Wyatt anywhere near the place. Why? Because I said so. They can take some of her belongings and harvest the DNA for a profile. Yeah, send them over." His phone pinged three times, and he checked the images he'd been sent. "They're good, thanks, Terry. Go over to her house. Yes, Mrs Hall's house. I want you to take an official statement. Well, take DC Scott with you then."

He slid the phone across the table after hanging up on the idiot DC. "Do you recognise this woman?"

She picked his phone up and studied it. George noticed she had long, perfectly manicured nails. He wondered whether she had ever been an escort herself. "Yes, that's Roxy. She's the woman with the Beyoncé tattoo. Alina Hall."

"Thank you. Her mother reported her missing this morning." He turned to Wood. "Dr Ross noticed scars on her breasts during the autopsy, suggesting she'd been under the knife. When he cut her open, he noticed the implants had serial numbers. Dr Ross traced them back to the company who did them, and they took some convincing as they're in Germany and we're no longer in the EU, but they finally gave us the information we asked for. He sent it to the Super, who gave it to Terry minutes after he'd finished speaking with Alina's mum. She confirmed all the details over the phone about Alina's breast enlargement surgery, as she had been the one who paid for it."

"So we have three bodies all identified?"

"As soon as they can get a profile to match the Jane Doe, yes." He turned to Brielle. "So I need information on Rita Lawrence, Sarah Lawson and Alina Hall. Specifically, who their clients were. You mentioned earlier it was the same man. Does he have the same contact information?"

"Rita and Sarah—"

"London, Scarlet and Roxy," said Wood, her tone one of impatience. George was impressed, though. He'd forgotten their agency names already.

Brielle gave a forced smile and tapped away at her keyboard. "All three were booked out recently. Rita Lawrence, London, on Christmas Eve. Alina Hall, Roxy, on Christmas Day. Sarah Lawson, Scarlet, on Boxing Day."

"Same guy?" asked George, just to be sure.

She nodded her eyes on the screen. "Yeah. Different name but the same number."

"What kind of number is it?"

"A mobile number," said Brielle. "We take them down as our girls contact their clients themselves."

Wood nodded. "Is he a regular?"

She shrugged but tapped her keys furiously. Then the printer in the corner came to life with a jarring, whirring noise. She gestured for Wood to collect the print-out. "I've isolated all bookings associated with this number," she said.

Wood nodded again but bit the inside of the cheek. "I'll rephrase the question. Do you recognise the guy from his mobile number?"

Brielle looked genuinely surprised. "No, why would I? I've been out of the game for a long time."

"Who owned this place before you?" Wood asked.

"My mum. She opened it about thirty-five years ago."

"And your records only go back five years?" Wood gestured to the print-out.

"We did everything by hand back then. It all got shredded. Saw little point in transferring the data over."

Too expensive, more like, Wood thought.

"What's with all the questions, Sergeant? You've got what you wanted, now do one!"

"Do you mind if I ask how old you are, Brielle?" Wood asked, a smile on her face.

"Yes, I bloody well do!" she snapped back.

"Well, I'll put it another way. Do you remember anything

about a murderer they called Jack the Butcher? It would have been about thirty years ago. He—"

"killed prostitutes and then dismembered them. Yes, I know of the case. Was never solved, right?"

"Right."

Then she clicked, understanding Wood's questions. She slid an image of a younger Tony Shaw across the table. "You know this guy?"

"Sorry. It was before my time. I was only a youngster back then."

George sighed. "Okay, Brielle. Could you give me the contact details for all three women and their client history?" It might be worth calling their clients and getting alibis from them to exclude them from the investigation. They would probably know where the police got their contact details from. Whilst it wasn't ideal for Brielle, he was done with strolling around, and he needed to decide whether to charge Shaw. Per his call with the CPS, they had until Wednesday to charge him, but George thought it would be over soon.

She closed her eyes and sighed loudly. "If you insist, Detective," she said. "But you should know, this might put me out of business, you know? Our clients will know who gave their info to the police."

"Whether you like it or not, your agency is involved in a murder inquiry," said George. "One of your clients has murdered three of your escorts. I thought you'd want to catch the fucker!"

"I do. Of course I do. Give me a minute." They waited for her to look up the information.

"Last question. Do you currently have girls you can't account for?" George asked.

CHAPTER FOURTEEN

Brielle's gaze darkened. "It's Christmas. Some take holidays; some spend time with their families. I can give you three or four names I haven't heard from for a week. It's not unusual."

"Could you give me that list of names? And check your system for a guy named Hayden Wyatt. Give me all data regarding any partial matches to Hayden Wyatt," he asked.

Wood looked at him with confused and questioning eyes.

"Sure. Why don't I just let you access every single fucking record?"

"I'd also like a list of all December bookings, past, current and future ones. We may as well have the first two weeks of January, too," Wood asked.

Brielle studied her; her teeth ground together. "Shall I email these over, or do you want to wait whilst I print them?"

"We'll wait." Wood leaned back in her chair and crossed her arms. The printer made the whirring noise once more.

She's found something, George thought. He gazed at her, making eye contact, wanting to know.

Chapter Fifteen

"What did you find?" George asked DS Wood as they walked towards his Honda.

"Tony Shaw. He's a regular. The first name's always Tony or Anthony, and the surname's always Shaw or Shields. He mixes them up," she said as she opened the Honda's door. "This is proof he's your guy, George."

"Do you think this is all a bit too easy?"

"No. Look at the timings. Shaw hires escorts before his working hours. His mobile number keeps showing up as noon bookings. Now we need to know where he's killing and dismembering his victims. Then we have a strong case. But what we have so far more than meets the threshold test. So let's get back and charge him."

"Yeah, you're right," George said with a grin. Wood was right. They'd already had enough to charge Shaw, but something had been holding him back. Now, there was nothing. They could spend months leading up to the trial trying to find the kill site.

George sped down Water Lane and Holbeck Lane towards Dunelm when he received a call from DS Joshua Fry. "Sir," he said, his voice booming out of the speaker. "I have the forensics back on Shaw's accounts."

CHAPTER FIFTEEN

"DS Wood is here with me, Josh. And good. Go on."

"Sir, he takes out a lot of cash each week, which isn't odd. Everything else seems legit, bar one thing."

"And that is?"

"He's paying for a storage container each month. I've traced the payment to one on Gelderd Road. Unfortunately, they won't speak to me without a warrant, so I've asked the Super for one. Is that okay?"

"DS Wood is going to send you three mobile numbers. They're the numbers for the three victims. Engage with the providers and see if they'll give you any information without a warrant. If not, get the Super to provide one. I'll clear it."

"Okay, sir. Anything else?"

"No, great job, Josh. Once the warrant for the storage place comes in, take DC James and a SOCO team with you. Oh, and get statements from the staff. I want this documenting fully."

"Yes, sir."

"Cheers, Josh. We're heading back to the station now. I've got some work for you to do whilst your warrants come in." He pressed the button and chanced a glance at Wood. She was beaming, and he was too.

* * *

Once back at the station, George took the print-outs and gave them to DS Elaine Brewer. He ordered Elaine to work with DC Terry Morton and DC Holly Hambleton to check all alibis for the men who had been their victim's recent clients. George asked that any who couldn't provide an alibi be brought into the station for questioning.

The names Hayden and Wyatt never showed up. Was he

wrong about the young blond American?

Then, George checked in on DS Yolanda Williams and DC Tashan Blackburn, who was working on CCTV.

"Nothing to report, sir," Tashan said. "There are still a few blind spots on Town Street and the surrounding roads. People are on holiday, with it being Christmas, too."

"We'll keep you informed, sir," Yolanda said.

George soon found himself back in his office after checking in on his team's progress, logging updates to HOLMES 2. They'd got a lot done. All three bodies had been identified, with them just waiting on the DNA profile match for Alina Hall. They'd manage to link the bodies to the Red Light Green Light agency. And with that match, they'd linked all three women to Shaw. The dates and times matched those of the autopsy results. He consulted the printouts in front of him. Rita Lawrence, London, was booked out and was killed on Christmas Eve. Sarah Lawson, Scarlet, was booked out and died on Boxing Day. Alina Hall, Roxy, was booked out and was killed on Christmas Day. All three had noon appointments with Shaw. That would easily be enough time to have sex, kill, and then dismember his victims before going to work.

He grabbed the other printouts he'd taken copies of and looked at the mobile numbers for the three victims. Josh's trace on Shaw's phone hadn't given them much. He turned it off a lot, especially during the hours of noon and midnight. The van he used had GPS, and once Tommy Myles had provided them with the data, it matched the ANPR data they already had. He called Josh into his office, offering him a seat once he arrived.

"Any luck with the providers yet?" George asked. Sometimes, phone companies would release information to the police without a warrant, but that wasn't always the case. It was undoubtedly more helpful and quicker than procuring a warrant. And from experience, even if they had a warrant, some providers were awkward, waiting for ages before they complied.

George needed them to comply. And fast, because it would give them invaluable insight into any communication between Shaw and his victims that no statement of his could ever come close to in terms of the truth.

"I did, sir. I should have something back by the end of today." Josh Fry sounded as unhopeful as he did. Even so, it was better than nothing. "I noticed something weird with Shaw's data, though, sir. If you remember, I checked his on Saturday night. He hasn't used that phone to contact the agency in months."

"Shit. Really?" He'd been so busy yesterday interviewing Shaw that he forgot to check the data. He knew he needed to delegate more and was happy to have such an experienced DS working for him. "Give Red Light Green Light a call and ask for Brielle," George ordered. "Ask her whether they document the number that called or their client's number on their booking system when they book an appointment."

"Will do, sir," Josh said. "I'll let you know once I've found out. I assume if they take the number their client provides, you want me to get them to email over any info they have about the actual number that's called?"

That's what George wanted. He took a sip of his now cold coffee and smiled. "That's what I want, Josh. Thanks."

When George loaded up his emails, he realised for the first time that tomorrow was News Year's Eve. Shit, the day after was Mia's due date. He wasn't ready to be a dad yet. But then, who was? Being a parent was hard work. He worked long, unsociable hours. Mia knew this, of course, and said they'd sort out him having their child when he could. She'd broached them getting back together about three- or four months in. But he had Isabella; to be honest; he knew he didn't want to be with Mia any more. He couldn't live with her for the sake of their child, even if that sounded selfish.

A knock at the door interrupted him from his thoughts. "Shaw's solicitor wants an update," Wood said, smiling.

"Don't know why. The CPS gave us until 4 pm on Wednesday…"

* * *

On the way to the interview room where Shaw and his solicitor were waiting, DS Josh Fry called him over to his desk. "Hiya, sir." At the tone of his voice, Wood came over. Terry did too. "The network provider has come through. All three were on the same network and didn't require a warrant."

"What a result," George said, rushing over to his desk and clapping him on the shoulder. "Go on, then. What we got?"

"Sir…" Josh's voice sounded grave. "All three phones disconnected from the network just after noon on the day they died."

"Do they have a location when they were switched off?" George searched through the ream of data displayed on three windows on the screen. He soon realised the files were histories which were a pain in the arse to cross-check.

"Yes, sir." He scanned the email from the provider and downloaded three images. Each one showed a large yellow circle. "Holbeck area—we can say they turned them off when meeting their clients. They were booked in for noon, right?"

CHAPTER FIFTEEN

"Right," George said.

Terry came bounding over. "Ey, isn't it supposed to be more accurate than that?" he interjected.

"I'm not Tom Cruise, and this isn't Mission Impossible, Terry," George said with a laugh. "It's cell tower triangulation, not satellite. How long have you been on the force?"

"Oh, I'm kidding, I'm kidding. I know they can tell which cell towers it's pinged, and based on the signal strength, the provider makes an educated guess at the location. But it's just a guess, isn't it?"

George sighed. "Yeah, a guess. Without the phone, the location data is impossible to get. Now, if we had it, we could use the location history to track its exact movements. Terry, work with Josh and learn something. Josh, I need you to comb the records for any clues. Look for numbers we can match to friends, colleagues, and places like her bank, utilities, or even takeaways. I want a list of numbers that pop up a lot and a separate list of numbers that appear on all three call logs. I know it's shit work, but it'll keep you busy until your warrant for the storage company arrives. The more stuff we have on Shaw, the better the case will be."

Chapter Sixteen

Shaw and his solicitor were waiting. They had only two hours to charge him or release him. The detectives sat down without a word, and Wood handed out the document folders whilst George started the Digital Interview Recorder.

"Interview of Tony Shaw in the presence of his solicitor by Detective Inspector Beaumont and Detective Sergeant Wood, at 6 pm on the thirtieth of December." He asked each participant to identify themselves for the DIR.

"You remain under caution, Mr Shaw," George said. "Tony, do you frequent escorts?"

The room was still too hot for his liking, and already Shaw was sweating. He looked at his solicitor, who nodded. "There's nothing illegal with frequenting escorts, is there?" Shaw asked.

"No, but lying and obstruction of a murder investigation are. So answer the question, Mr Shaw," Wood said. She had a ferocious look, a steely glint in her eye. She was pissed off.

"Yes," Shaw replied.

"Both now and thirty years ago?" DS Wood asked.

"Yes," Shaw replied.

"See document sixty-four. There are four images on there.

CHAPTER SIXTEEN

Do you recognise these women?" DS Wood asked.

"Three of them," Shaw said, covering up Anna Hill. "I don't know her."

At least he was beginning to incriminate himself, George thought. But admitting to recognising three sex workers wasn't enough by a long shot. "Have you ever been a customer?"

"Yes. A customer of all three." Shaw replied. "That doesn't mean I killed them."

George nodded. "So you're admitting now to frequenting sex workers and prostitutes?" Shaw nodded. "For the DIR, Shaw is nodding. So tell me, how do you get in touch with said women?" George asked.

"Well, I called the number. I got quoted a price. I visited them and paid them with cash once we were done. They request cash. There's nothing I can do about that. Both now and thirty years ago. And every time in between."

The man, George could see, was on his last legs, volunteering information rather than having to put pressure on him. At least they now had a solid link to Shaw and three of the four original victims.

"Please see documents sixty-five to seventy in your folders. Documents sixty-four to seventy are copies of your bank statements. You take out a large sum of cash weekly, as circled in blue. Why?" George asked.

"Well, to pay for the escorts, as I said."

"You visit escorts weekly, Mr Shaw?" Wood asked.

"Yes?" he said, more of a question than an answer. "I'm not attractive enough to get the companionship of a lovely young woman for free. So I spend my money how I want to spend it." A sad smile stretched from ear to ear.

"How else do you spend your money, Mr Shaw?" Wood asked.

Tony Shaw looked confused, so Wood said, "See documents seventy-one to seventy-seven. These are the same bank statements. What charges are circled in red?"

Shaw looked at his lawyer, who looked at the statements and shrugged her shoulders. "I don't know. A direct debit?"

George grinned and said, "A direct debit for what?"

"I..." Shaw stopped speaking and looked down at the sheets of paper. "Honestly, I'm not sure."

"These are your bank statements, Mr Shaw?" Wood asked.

"Well, yes."

"And you can't tell us what these monthly direct debits are for?"

"No. I'm sorry. I can't." He looked towards his solicitor for help.

"Can we come back to this line of questioning, detectives? My client says he doesn't know what the charge is for, and he's telling you the truth."

"Fine," George said with a grin. He nodded to Wood.

Wood mirrored George's grin and continued. Shaw was sweating even more. Beads of sweat dripped down from a long, scruffy beard. "Do you know of a place called Red Light Green Light?"

"Yes, it's an escort agency. It's the one I use."

"Can you confirm for the tape your mobile number, Mr Shaw?" asked Wood.

He confirmed it for them. "You have my mobile phone locked away as evidence, right?"

Wood nodded her head but otherwise ignored the question. "Thank you for confirming your mobile number. Please look at document eighty in your folders. Document eighty is a print-out from Red Light Green Light's booking system. Said print-out shows all bookings for the number you have just provided. Can you confirm for the tape?"

"Yes. But some of these bookings aren't mine. I haven't booked an escort for a week or so. Especially not Christmas Eve, Christmas Day and Boxing Day. Please, you have to believe me."

George raised his brow and said, "You expect us to believe you when it's there in black and—"

"Where's the evidence of this from my client's phone? All you have is a print-out from a booking system that could have been doctored," Shaw's solicitor quickly supplied, interrupting Beaumont. A scowl appeared on her face.

She had him there. Josh hadn't come through with the information from the agency yet.

He ignored her. "There's no argument, is there, Tony? That's your mobile number, right—"

"No," Shaw interrupted. "Well, it's my mobile number, but I didn't call and make those bookings!"

George said, "This document proves—"

A loud knock on the door interrupted George's question. "For the DIR, Detective Constable Terry Morton has entered the room."

"Sir. DCI Peterson wants a word with you." He handed George his phone.

"For the DIR," Wood said as George left the room. "Detective Constable Terry Morton has replaced DI Beaumont, who has left the room."

"So as the Inspector was about to say, Mr Shaw, this document proves otherwise." She was straight to the point, with a harsh tone to her voice. That look was still in her eye. "Moving on, documents seventy-eight and seventy-nine are images of two women. Do you recognise these women, Mr Shaw?" Wood asked. She wondered why the DCI needed to speak to George on his day off.

Shaw picked up the images from his folder and scrutinised them. "I recognise image seventy-nine," Shaw said. "It's Scarlet. She's my regular escort. I don't recognise seventy-eight, sorry."

"Document five in your folder shows a woman known as London. Seventy-eight shows an image of a woman known as Roxy," Wood added.

"And?" Shaw was getting angry again. The dark rings under his eyes were getting bigger and darker, as were the enormous sweat patches under his arms. There was a sour smell coming across the table.

"Do you know these women, Mr Shaw? Perhaps you were a client of theirs?" she asked.

Tony Shaw, a grim look on his face, looked down at his copy of the documents. He scrutinised the images, which were images given by the DVLA. "No!" exclaimed Tony, finally uncoiling his hands and raising them emphatically. George entered the room again just as Shaw said, "I didn't know these women! I didn't kill anyone!"

"I never said you killed London or Roxy," George added after announcing for the DIR that DC Morton had left and he'd replaced him. "What's the matter, Shaw, feeling guilty? Tell us the truth, and spare their families a long trial. Come on, be a man and own up to what you've done!"

"Stop trying to antagonise my client, Inspector," his pixie of a solicitor said.

CHAPTER SIXTEEN

"For the record," DS Wood said. Scarlet's real name is Sarah Lawson, London's real name is Rita Lawrence, and Roxy's real name is Alina Hall."

"I'm being framed. I'm innocent."

"So you keep saying. Framed by who?" George asked.

In his silence, George continued. "Do you recognise the names, Rita Lawrence and Alina Hall? You've already admitted to knowing Sarah Lawson, though you know her as Scarlet."

"I know Sarah Lawson. She told me her name after our third or fourth time together. As for Rita Lawrence, I know her name because you told me about it in a previous interview. However, I did not know her as London. And as for Roxy or Alina Hall, never heard of them."

"I think that's enough," Shaw's solicitor said. "I must insist we move on. My client has answered your questions about this repeatedly. You haven't answered mine. So disclose the evidence showing my client called the escort agency on his phone."

"We already have. Document eighty in your folders," George said. "If you take another look at document eighty, you will see a list of client names. Do you recognise any of these names, Tony?"

The man was under pressure and would soon break. George didn't like this way of interviewing, but the DCI wanted a conviction, and he couldn't afford to let Shaw get his composure back. "My name is Tony Shaw. I used to be called Anthony Shields. The names there is a mixture of the two."

"What does this have to do with my client, detectives?" Shaw's solicitor cut in. "Anybody could have given the escort agency these names and mobile numbers. This kind of evidence will certainly be inadmissible in court. I'll make sure of it! Move on."

"Is this you, Tony?" George asked again. "Did you make these bookings?"

Tony's voice held an edge of panic. "Some of them. But not those." He pointed towards the most recent three. George didn't believe him. It made no sense why he would regularly be a customer, only to stop for a week. Sex was a drug. There was just no way.

"Okay, Tony, this is your last chance," George said. "And by last chance, I mean last chance. See documents seventy-one to seventy-seven. These are the same bank statements as earlier. What charges are circled in red?"

Shaw looked at his lawyer, who looked at George with a furious state. "My client has already explained he does not know."

"I don't know about you, Tony, but I know every penny that goes out of my accounts. Most people would say the same. So it's not an error, is it? It's not a company taking the money by accident? Otherwise, you'd have noticed, right?"

Shaw shook his head. "For the DIR, Tony Shaw is shaking his head. He doesn't know where his money is going. I do. See document ninety-three. It's an image of a well-known Leeds self-storage company on Gelderd Road. That's what this charge relates to," George said, stabbing his finger at the paper. "Am I right?"

"I must have forgotten to stop the direct debit," Shaw said. "I haven't been there in years. No need. Cleared it out."

"No. I disagree. DCI Peterson needed to speak to me, and I'm glad he did because DS Fry was waiting outside, and DS Fry provided me with some new evidence. I'm going to disclose this to you both now. Here," he said, handing out four more documents to each participant. "Documents ninety-four to ninety-seven say otherwise. Ninety-four shows CCTV footage of you at the storage company this week. Christmas Eve, to be exact. We're waiting for additional footage and a warrant to search the place. Document ninety-five shows a direct debit mandate with your signature on it. Ninety-six is a statement from the manager who says he spoke with you on Christmas Eve. Document ninety-seven is a transcript taken from a detective unknown to the case. They set up an identity parade where they showed the storage manager, Jason Perkins, pre-recorded video footage of nine unrelated men of a similar appearance and age. He made a positive ID for number four."

When Shaw said nothing, George continued. "Just admit to killing them. It'll be easier for you. Think about their families and friends. About what you're putting them through. This is such an obvious case. A strong case." He waited, pleading for Shaw to confess. "No? Okay. Document ninety-eight is said image of male number four. It's a still of Tony Shaw from a video captured during his first interview with me and DS Wood. Can you confirm this is a still of you, Tony?" George leaned back, a triumphant smile on his face.

Tony swallowed, closed his eyes and shook his head erratically.

"For the DIR, Tony Shaw is unresponsive and has refused to confirm that the image is of him," Wood said. She was smiling now.

"Tony Shaw, the threshold test has been passed; therefore, it is my lawful right to charge you for the murders of Rita Lawrence, Sarah Lawson and Alina Hall. Is that understood?" George asked.

"No! No!" Shaw screamed, banging the table with his hand.

"I'm being fucking framed!"

"Interview terminated," George said. They left the room. Two uniformed officers entered, handcuffs out, waiting. Shaw would spend his time in Armley Nick before his trial.

Chapter Seventeen

George smiled at his team as he walked into the squad room after announcing to the press they had charged Tony Shaw. A burst of rowdy applause erupted from the back of the room. By the look of it, Terry had set it off. Soon, they were all squished into the incident room for the last update.

"Speech!" yelled Terry, grinning at him. "Speech!" There was a euphoric atmosphere and a sense of accomplishment that seemed to go above and beyond solving a usual case. But then again, he'd caught another serial killer.

His head hurt from the interview room, and there were large sweat patches under his arms. But otherwise, he was as delighted as his team.

"This isn't just about me," he said as he gazed at the crowd of detectives, officers, and support staff. "This is about you guys, too. Without you, we wouldn't have solved this case." Yolanda whooped at him, beaming from ear to ear. Elaine was smiling at him, clapping, as were others who'd worked hard on the case.

He scanned the room for Wood's brunette curls but found nothing. It was surprising. She had been an integral part of the team. Without her, he'd have held back from the escort agency. According to the CPS, that had been the ultimate piece of the puzzle. It was the piece that had meant that Tony Shaw would finally pay for his crimes. All they needed to do now was wait for the DNA sample to come back, which was strangely taking an age compared to everything else.

"I'd like to give a toast to DS Wood," he said, his cheeks aching from smiling and laughing. "A great deputy, without whom we wouldn't have solved this case so quickly!"

They fell silent as Detective Superintendent Smith emerged with DS Wood from his office. George gave her a smile, which she didn't return.

"I think a thank you is in order for our two new detectives, DCI Peterson and DC Hambleton," George said.

A roar of cheering erupted as the DCI appeared next to George. "Thank you, DI Beaumont. I've some exciting news to share with you all. Because of the recent success with charging Tony Shaw, I've been promoted to Detective Superintendent immediately and will be leaving to meet the current Detective Superintendent at Bradford HQ."

The sound of cheering increased, mixed with hoots and laughter. He guessed the promotion was why Alex put so much pressure on him to charge Shaw.

There was more clapping as the DCI clapped George on the shoulder and whispered, "Take care, mate. See you around."

The two detectives shook hands, and as the newly promoted Detective Superintendent Alex Peterson left the squad room, George wondered whether he would see the Geordie man ever again.

As soon as there was a lull, George said, "Thank you all. Despite the lack of paid overtime, I appreciate how much you have put into this. I know you've done it for me, so I can go on paternity leave when Mia goes into labour. I've heard some of you around the office talking about it. So, thank you. Thank you so much."

He saw a lot of smiles and a few nods. He wasn't lying or exaggerating. They had worked harder, longer, and without pay for him.

"As such, the butties are on me. Tashan, go around and take orders for the truck, please."

Since about September, a mobile food truck had been parking in the ice rink car park across the road. The food was decent, better than anybody expected from a food truck, and George was rather partial to their sausage and bacon butty slathered with brown sauce.

Whenever cases were solved, especially high-profile cases such as this one, the Super would join the SIO at the front. Yet he didn't move from his position with Wood outside his office. Had something happened?

There was an inaudible murmur across the squad room as Tashan glided around and took orders on a post-it, and for a fleeting moment, George was too afraid to move. He was paranoid that something had happened.

After George had taken the orders, he and Tashan went to the food truck.

"Thank you, sir. I appreciate you putting me in with Yolanda for this case. I've learnt a lot, and I think I want to be a CCTV specialist."

George nodded. That was great news. "Ah good for you, kid. Well done."

Tashan continued, "I mean it, sir. It's thanks to you. I never knew the work that they did. She told me about the Miss Murderer and how CCTV was invaluable during that case."

George swayed for a moment, his vision blurring. He felt sick.

Tashan glanced at George. "Sir. Are you okay?"

George nodded guiltily. Something was wrong with him, something he had told nobody. "Fine, kid. I'm fine. Low blood sugar, that's all. It's been a busy day, and I haven't had a chance to eat." It was a lie, of course. He'd eaten earlier at Morrisons with Wood. But he couldn't tell Tashan how he was feeling.

After about twenty minutes, the pair returned to the station with bags filled with foiled buttys, the grease just about contained.

Soon, the squad room carried the fragrance of bacon, egg and sausage mixed with tomato and brown sauce, and all went silent as everyone tucked in.

George left his on Wood's empty desk and made his way to Smith's office.

"Everything okay, sir? I got you a butty," he said. George hadn't realised. Wood was still there. "Wood? I got you one, too."

"Sit down, Beaumont," the Super said.

He did as he was told.

"I know this was a tough case for you, George, and despite you being off fieldwork for over six months, you did a sterling job."

George gritted his teeth. "Forced off fieldwork, sir. But, with respect, I've always been ready. I hope I've proven to you how valuable I am."

"I know you have, George. And believe me, we know how valuable you are. I understand you've got a few things to sort out before you go on paternity leave, so I won't keep you long, but there are a few things we need to discuss. So first, I wanted to congratulate you and DS Wood on a job well done. The Chief Super sends his congratulations." He held out his hand.

George shook it. "Thank you, sir."

Smith lowered his voice. "Now, there are two other things we need to discuss. DS Wood, if you wouldn't mind giving us a moment?"

"Yes, sir," she said, getting up and leaving. She smelt like coffee and vanilla, a welcome from the eggy smell that had permeated the squad room.

"First, I've had a complaint."

"A complaint, sir? About what?"

"Apparently, you've been turning up to work smelling of alcohol. Is there anything in that, George? I have to know."

George instantly felt deflated. Alex Peterson had apologised for his mistake, so why had he mentioned it to Smith? "It was mouthwash, sir like I told Alex Peterson." He hated lying, but what other choice did he have? Come clean and have to speak to Professional Standards again? "I would never drink on the job, sir. I'm a professional, and I would never put my position in jeopardy."

"Well, that's the problem, George. There's been a second complaint. You've been accused of abuse of position for a sexual purpose."

"What the hell? Are you kidding me? Abuse of who?"

Chapter Eighteen

"Detective Sergeant Isabella Wood," Jim Smith said. "I've already had her side of the story, and now I want to hear yours, George."

George looked stunned and made sure Smith was well aware. "Who on earth has been spreading lies like that?" Then, when Smith said nothing, George added, "Well, what did she say?"

"You know fully that this isn't how it works, George. But unfortunately, I can't divulge the whistle-blower's identity. So, tell me your side of the story. Are you in a relationship with DS Wood, and did you use your senior position to force her into it?"

Had this come from Isabella? No. She said she wouldn't say anything, and he trusted her. He'd never used his senior position on her for anything. She barely called him sir. As far as he was concerned, they were equal. Partners. She had passed the Inspectors' Exam before he'd even met her. So no, this had come from somebody else. But who?

Whatever George said now could signal the end of his career. He was stuck. If Wood had told Smith about their relationship, it would be best for George to confirm it. But, on the other hand, if she had lied for him, and he told the truth, that would be just as bad. He knew she'd never accuse him of abusing his position with her.

"This is nonsense, sir."

"Look, George. I'm doing you a favour. I could send you to Professional Standards, and they could interrogate you. You've been there before. It's not nice. I respect you, Inspector, but I have issues if you are in a romantic relationship with a subordinate directly under your command. It's a conflict of interest. I'll be honest and tell you we don't have a policy that restricts 'fraternisation' between officers and anyone up their direct chain of command. I wish we did, George because I have seen a lot of shit. There were a ton of sexual harassment suits back in the nineties and noughties."

A conflict of interest. Jesus Christ.

"Sir, if you let me explain, I can."

"Oh, you will be explaining. But first, I need to lecture you. There are many reasons why I'm so against romantic relationships in the office, George. I've seen them first-hand. One example is an officer's partner being promoted over the better-qualified officer. I've also seen unsatisfactory performance appraisals being changed to positive ones, and let me tell you, George, the person was shit at their job."

"Sir, I must—"

"George, let me finish. I don't think you're like this for one minute, and DS Wood has amazing potential and is brilliant at her job. You know, she's next in line for DI, just as you are next for DCI. But George, I've seen more qualified people quit rather than work for the unqualified person promoted over them because they were shagging their boss. Seriously."

"Sir, I—"

"Stop interrupting me, Beaumont. One of the worst situations I've ever seen is a subordinate who had no business knowing about a performance issue with another employee coming to work and bragging about how they knew and how much trouble the other person was going to be in. But the worst thing I have seen in the workplace, and I mean absolute worse, is that once my office, Beaumont, became toxic because the relationship between a high-ranking detective and their subordinate ended. It's not worth it. Believe me. So, George, tell me the truth."

The Super made an interesting argument, yet George had no reason to tell the truth. His career was on the line, so he simply said, "The truth? We have an amazing relationship I do not want to jeopardise, sir."

Smith frowned. "And?"

"And nothing, sir. I don't know who your whistleblower is, sir, but whoever it is, has seen the incredible chemistry between DS Wood and me. Is it jealousy? Probably. I'm disappointed because it's probably come from somebody on my team. You know, they see how closely we work. How well we work. We're inseparable when we're on a case, such as the Miss Murderer or the recent Tony Shaw case. It's part of the job, but I'm sorry that it's come to this, sir. I am."

"Fine, Beaumont. You've made your point. However, I still think it's best if we separate you for now. That way, it will appease the whistleblower whilst I speak with Detective Chief Superintendent Sadiq." George shook his head, a frown on his face. "I'll assign DS Fry as your deputy on the Shaw case. He's competent, and you two seem to get on well."

"So the same as DS Wood, then? What's it going to change? It'll affect the case, swapping out my deputy now."

"Don't get smart with me, Beaumont. You're lucky this hasn't been sent to Professional Standards. Are you happy with DS Fry being your deputy?"

"If that's what you want, sir?"

* * *

That night, as George tried to fall asleep, the pictures of Sarah Lawson on her parents' mantel flashed vividly in his mind. He began to shake and felt sick. Whenever he closed his eyes, there she was. Sarah Lawson. Alive. Then dead. Then sawed into pieces. They still had found no other body parts, including any heads. Shaw denied everything. Was this guilt? Or was it something else?

A sense of overwhelming dread?

George got up and got a glass of water from the kitchen. The blood pounded in his ears, and his heart hammered in his chest. He tried to slow down his breathing and sat down on the kitchen tiles, a pain in his chest. His throat constricted. Near hyperventilating, he gripped his forehead with his free hand and drew deep breaths. Yet it became harder and harder to breathe. His heart hammered faster and faster. Finally, his hands shook, and the glass of water slipped from his grasp, shattering on the hard tiled floor, the cold water dampening his heels, soles, and toes.

His feet tingled. As he tried to stand back up, his vision blurred and swayed as if he were drunk. George needed something, anything, to get away from the nightmare he was living in. A shaky hand reached for the cupboard; a freshly bought bottle of whisky was sitting there looking at him and tempting him. His stomach churned, and he turned and threw up in the sink.

George sank back down on the hard, cold tiles, desperately

wanting to get away from the flat, desperate to return to the warmth of his home. Yet he couldn't. He'd given Mia the keys. She'd needed it for their child. He was stranded. Alone.

The fear continued to seep in.

When he attempted to fall asleep again, Sarah Lawson's head was replaced by Adam Harris'.

Thud, crash. Thud, crash. Thud, crash.

Chapter Nineteen

As DS Wood arrived, a small fire engine was pulling out of the entrance to Springhead Park. The look on the driver's face told her everything they needed to know. It was serious. A police officer was allowing traffic in and out of the car park. Wood held up her warrant card and was waved through.

She drove in and parked in the first bay she could find. Wood could already see the crime-scene perimeter in the corner and down the hill. Half a dozen vehicles, mostly marked cars and an ambulance, were parked in a cluster, people coming and going. It was a busy scene, and she noticed a CSI police van indicating Stuart Kent was probably already there.

Over the phone, control had provided all the details that morning on her way from her home in Wakefield. She was SIO, and DS Elaine Brewer was her deputy.

The fire had been called in early that morning, by which time there wasn't much that could be done. The car had still been smouldering when the dog-walker had phoned it in earlier that morning. From the recording, he'd seemed relatively unconcerned, and Isabella figured this wasn't the first time a car had been left in flames. It wasn't until the firefighters had finished dousing the burnt-out shell of the Fiat Punto and the man saw the remains of a body in the driver's seat that he panicked.

She got out, not bothering to wait for Elaine. She thought about George and how this should have been his case to manage. Detective Superintendent Smith had told her he'd given her a chance because of George's impending paternity leave, yet from the nuances in his voice, she knew they were trying to separate the two. 'A conflict of interest' is what he'd called their alleged relationship. She'd lied through her teeth to the Super, of course. For George's sake. And hers, she supposed. Isabella loved working with George, and their relationship didn't hamper that. Whoever had found out was the one putting pressure on it. She thought they were strong, but George had taken none of her calls last night. It worried her.

Wood had found herself at the blue and white police tape when she'd stopped thinking about George. Her first impressions were that the extensive park was good dog-walking territory. The car park was considerable, and the Fiat had been parked at the back, close to a grove of tall, mature oaks that would have disguised the flames and hidden the rising smoke. It was also far from the road but close enough to the park to escape. It was the perfect spot.

Wood knew the park well. She'd spent much time in Middleton with her grandparents when she was young, so she'd often been on the bus to Rothwell's Springhead Park.

"Morning, ma'am," the uniformed officer on the cordon said as he took a note of her credentials. He signed her in and offered her a white protective coverall and shoe covers.

"How are you doing?" she asked, giving him a coffee from the cardboard cup tray holders. She'd stopped by The Rhubarb

CHAPTER NINETEEN

Triangle Farm Shop for eight coffees before cutting through Carlton and then Rothwell to the park. The team of SOCOs had been here for two or three hours already. It was New Year's Eve. They deserved something.

"Thanks, ma'am," he said with a smile. "Been on nights. This was supposed to be my last shift as I was planning on getting pissed as a skunk tonight. I was supposed to be home by now. And now look what I've gotta do!"

"Yeah," Wood said, handing him the drinks and putting on her protective gear. Four SOCOs in white overalls moved around the red vehicle, carefully taking samples, only talking to document each sample as they worked. Stuart had a great team. She wondered where he was. "I reckon you'll be allowed home soon. Chin up, yeah? Midnight's not for hours yet. She winked and took the two cardboard trays from him."

"Thanks again, ma'am," he said, pulling up the tape for her.

"First thoughts?" she asked, turning back.

"A known sex worker's car."

She nodded. He told her what he knew. The car had been identified first. It was registered to Danielle Ferguson. The corpse in the driver's seat had been identified not long after from her purse. Her driving licence had survived. If she was a known sex worker, she doubted anybody would be making much of a fuss. She'd get a small team, and it wouldn't be for long.

She called DS Joshua Fry at the station and asked him to check Red Light Green Light to see if they had Danielle Ferguson working there. Tony Shaw had been sent to Armley Nick awaiting his trial, but that didn't mean they had to discount it. George had already made his feelings clear that their evidence on Shaw had come too quickly. Too readily. It all fit perfectly, like a jigsaw puzzle. He wasn't complaining, but it made him wary. "Tell George for me too, yeah? Thanks, Josh."

Wood surveyed the crime scene. The cordon wasn't massive, just one section of ground that had been taped off, large enough for a good sweep of the immediate area, but nothing more. So Kent, or whoever was in charge, must have assumed the culprit had left via their vehicle. She could see the yellow crime scene markers at the side of several rectangular patches. They had white edges, suggesting SOCOs had taken casts of car tracks. So yeah, it looked as if Kent was right. Two vehicles came in, but only one came out. Wood immediately swept the area for any signs of CCTV. She'd ask the Super for DS Yolanda William's help. The problem was that the nearest camera would probably have been out on the main road. There was certainly none in the car park, by the look of things.

It was the perfect spot.

"Hello, DS Wood," said a short, mid-to-late thirties balding man. The Crime Scene Co-ordinator, Stuart Kent, wearing his usual attire of white coverall and matching shoe covers, walked across to meet her.

"Nice to see you as always, Stuart."

He nodded at her, but he didn't look well. "You too. Inspector Beaumont not with you?"

She managed the slightest of smiles. "I'm in charge today. George is finalising everything for the Shaw case."

He failed to conceal a momentary flush of embarrassment. "Ah, good. Good. I always thought you'd make a fine SIO. Has George spoken to anybody about what we discussed? I assume he told you?"

She smiled and shrugged, not wanting to get into it. "Any

witnesses?" she asked, glancing over at the car.

"No," he said. He looked disappointed. Angry. A mix between the two. Kent had been so passionate about his theory that Shaw had been set up. Maybe there was something in it. "Her name's Danielle Ferguson. Known local sex worker, apparently," he said, his face still red. "Probably means we'll be short of resources."

She nodded. "You okay if I go in and take a look?"

"Yeah, no problem, but put some of this on your top lip." He handed her a small jar of Vicks VapoRub. He must have seen her raise her brow as he added, "Trust me, DS Wood. The smell of menthol and camphor is much better than what's about to greet you."

She already knew and smiled knowingly. But, inside, her stomach was already churning. Whenever she smelt burnt flesh, it made her feel sick and brought back memories, memories that she wished would leave her entirely.

"Thanks, Stuart. There's coffee over there in those trays if you want any. Offer it out to your guys and girls, too." She noticed Hayden Wyatt was hovering around. DS Wood opened the driver's side door, and immediately, the image of the burned and broken body that sat there brought back similar images from the past. She gagged, stepped back, and shut the door. She promised they wouldn't affect her any more and desperately attempted to push those images back into the dark recess of her brain where they belonged.

She took a deep breath of fresh air and focused. *Come on, Wood. You've got this! Don't let the past dictate your future!*

Wood opened the door and analysed the level of destruction somebody had inflicted on Danielle's body. Her bloated, shiny face was a deep purple, and congealed blood had poured out of her eyes, nostrils, ears and mouth. The deceased woman was naked, and no hair remained on her head. Danielle's expression, an expression twisted with agony. Somebody had made her suffer. But who? Who would do something so sinister? So violent?

She could only think of two people, and both were currently locked up behind bars.

"Nasty, isn't it?" Hayden Wyatt said over her shoulder.

She nodded and circled the Fiat. The ground to the front had been churned into a muddy pulp because of the work of the firefighters, and Wood was careful to move on the stepping tiles Kent had placed. The only sound was dripping water falling from the car's chassis. At least the red paintwork was still visible outside, but the fire had destroyed everything inside. The fabric seats had no chance and had burnt down to the springs. The plastic dashboard had bubbled like chocolate that had been left out in the sun.

"Morning, Wood," came a voice from behind her. "I was going to make a joke. You know, about a man and his morning wood! No? Sorry, boss."

DC Jason Scott stood there grinning at Hayden Wyatt, who had a transparent evidence bag in each hand.

"Morning, Jay," DS Wood said, looking at Hayden Wyatt and his transparent bags. "You want a coffee?"

"I'm good. Sorry, I'm late; I didn't get the call until half an hour ago. But, don't get me wrong; I'm buzzing to be working as your deputy."

She smiled and looked at Hayden Wyatt. "What are those?"

"Underwear. It looks as if they were cut off and thrown into the nearby bushes."

"Okay. Guessing you've taken DNA swabs to match them to

the deceased?" He nodded. "How'd the fire start? Any idea?" She looked at the two CSIs and her deputy.

"Petrol. Whoever did this doused the interior of the car and then left a plastic fuel container on the back seat? Well, the remains of. The burn was fairly consistent throughout," Wyatt explained.

"Someone did a good job, then?"

"Yeah, very thorough," Kent said, cutting in.

"This bag has her driving licence in it," Hayden said. She knew about that from the officer at the cordon.

"And what's in those?" Wood asked, gesturing to the other bags in the collection box.

"Remains of her clutch and purse."

Wood nodded. "Anything else?"

"Yeah," Jay said. "Hayden here found some bags under the seat. He thinks it's cannabis, right?"

Hayden shrugged. "Hard to say with the heat and everything."

Stuart cut in once again. "Once I get the toxicology report, I'll email it to you."

That's what she liked, thoroughness. Kent was good at his job, so George was conflicted about the Shaw case. Maybe it was a good idea for them to review the evidence again.

"So much for respecting the dead," Jay said, snapping him from his thoughts. The young blond SOCO moved away as a young female photographer leaned into the open door and started snapping away.

The pair of detectives moved out of the way to let her get on with it. What if Kent was right? Wood asked herself. What if Shaw was being framed so the killer could get away with his crimes? Or what if it meant he could continue killing? Maybe his MO was killing sex workers, like the Yorkshire Ripper, and not dismembering his victims à la Anthony Hardy.

Two people had mentioned Danielle was a local, but Wood needed Josh to get back to her asap.

"Anything you want me to get in particular, ma'am?" the photographer asked.

Wood looked around, still thinking about Kent and Shaw.

"Did you do the usual?" She nodded. "Inside the car?" She nodded again. "Did you take plenty of wide shots of the car park and deposition site?"

"Yep."

"From all corners of the car park? Even from exits via foot?"

"Yes, ma'am."

"Okay, thanks." Wood turned on her heels, finding the white cast marks and yellow markers. Those tracks could have just been a coincidence. If cameras were on the road, it made sense to leave by foot. Wear dark clothing. Which way would they have gone? "So, take images, 360s, as if looking out from the car? I think the culprit left on foot, and I want to try to see the quickest way out."

"Okay, ma'am, I will do it."

"What do you think, Jay?" she asked. She knew talking to another detective about your thoughts was always a good idea.

"I saw CCTV cameras on the road on the way in. So it makes sense for the culprit to leave on foot. But who knows? Maybe Danielle met her client, our culprit, in the car park. Two cars in, one out."

"Yeah, either would work. Go back to the main road and note all the cameras you see. Both ways. Ring the council and see if they own them. If they do, request the footage."

"Will do, Sarge," he said as she stepped away.

CHAPTER NINETEEN

DS Wood took a step back and watched the photographer work. She knew the park well. There was no quick way out. Not really. All exits on that side of the park led to the A654, and DS Brewer was currently seeking CCTV. The only other exits were on Park Lane, a busy road with many houses flanking it, or the A639. That road was even busier than the A654 and Park Lane.

There was no quick way out, she confirmed. She called Jay and asked him to get CCTV from the A639 and Park Lane. She'd ask the Super to ensure she had Yolanda and Tashan on her team as George didn't need them any more. And if it were connected, the Super would hopefully allow George to work with her.

***

Meanwhile, George was sitting at his desk, finalising all the evidence they had on Tony Shaw. His phone rang, and he reached for it, nearly knocking over his coffee mug.

"Hi, Dr Ross. How are you?"

"I'm good, son," Dr Ross said, his tone as warm as ever. "I've just finished the autopsy on your IC1 Jane Doe, Sarah Lawson, and I thought you'd like me to go through it with you? Well done on charging Tony Shaw, by the way. Very well done indeed."

"Thanks, Dr Ross. Going through it would be great. Hopefully, your findings will tie Shaw to Lawson. I'm ready when you are."

"Okay, son, I know you're busy, so I'll get straight to the point. Sarah Lawson died on boxing day, as per the forensic entomologist. First, I've checked for body temperature with the Glaister Equation. Then, I have cross-referenced that data with the decomposition of her internal organs to give you a more accurate time of death."

"Go on."

"Sarah Lawson died between 12 noon and 3 pm, George."

Chapter Twenty

In a large town like Leeds, finding excellent cuisine was relatively easy. Yet, despite the crowds, it was difficult to be anonymous, and George needed to be anonymous because he'd invited DS Wood out on a date.

Lorenzo's in York, on the corner opposite Fossgate and Franklins Yard, was one of the best places he had ever eaten, and he had lived in one of the biggest cities in the UK.

Isabella Wood had agreed to meet him at the small bar in the restaurant around eight, but he had gotten there early, something he was always conscious of doing. The ambience was a perfect mix of light chatter and soft music. She had beaten him there, however. He was impressed, and it gave him a flutter in his stomach. The same flutters she gave him when he first fell for her.

Deep inside, he felt like he was fortunate. Isabella was a beautiful woman with a lovely personality. She was intelligent, kind, and thoughtful. And looking at her now, he thought she was even more beautiful than he had ever thought possible. Her brunette hair was curled, with one side running down her back and the other side running down the front of a black V-neck scallop-edge dress. Her pale, toned legs were showing, and she was wearing black, open-toed heels. She looked stunning. His eyes were transfixed on the pearl chain choker she wore just above her plunging neckline.

Her dark eyes were bewitching, and he got lost in them for a moment. Then, finally, she widened them, and a broad smile crossed her face. It was effortless. And he smiled right back.

Already, he knew they were going to have a good time.

George was dressed in a royal blue shirt and black trousers with black pointy end shoes. He looked smart, but she outshone him in every way.

The maître d' showed them to their table, and people stopped eating and watched them the entire way. George had never had it happen to him before. He liked the feeling. But George was also slightly jealous that other people were looking at Isabella, taking an interest. So he shut the negative thoughts down immediately.

They were seated next to the kitchen, where they could watch Lorenzo cook their meals. The sound of knives chopping and fires burning mixed with the aroma of garlic and pine nuts had a hypnotic affect.

And having Isabella in front of him made everything just perfect.

"I've never been here before," Isabella said, looking around the restaurant. They were sitting on hickory-coloured chairs, and between them was a square table with a white tablecloth. A single red rose was seated in a vase. The side they were sitting at had the brick walls exposed, whilst the other was painted white. There were a few pictures on the walls, but the décor was subtle. It was perfect. "It's perfect. I love the décor. The music is pleasant but not too loud and being able to see and hear the chef in the kitchen is amazing!"

George smiled. It was going well.

CHAPTER TWENTY

"So, how was your day?" George asked after they had finished ordering.

"Stressful," she said and shrugged. "You've been on my mind all day, George."

George smiled, grabbed her hand, and kissed it delicately. "I'm sorry I didn't answer the phone last night. I was so mad. Not at you. Why would anybody want to ruin our relationship?"

"Maybe they see our relationship as a threat," she said to him. "Don't get me wrong, though, I enjoyed being SIO today, but—"

"But you missed me?" He grinned.

"Not a truer word was spoken. We're a good team." She shrugged. "Do we have to talk about work?"

"No. But, we haven't talked about work, that's all. Both of us denied our relationship to Smith, so the only thing Smith can do now is make us work on different cases. But, anyway, it'll make me miss you more than I already do," he said with a wink. "I love your dress, by the way. And that necklace is so unique. Just beautiful."

"Oh, I see. You were looking at the necklace, were you?" She grinned again. His eyes dropped below the necklace to the swell of her cleavage, which teased a shy grin from her. George felt giddy inside. "Well, I'm glad the dress and necklace are beautiful."

"You make them more than beautiful," he said and smiled shyly. He was sure the hot coffee was turning him rosy. He felt like a teenager again, especially when they were together.

He stared deep into those dazzling eyes, losing himself again. Isabella looked happy, which was good as he was happy too. "What did the doctor say earlier?" Wood asked.

"She told me I have PTSD from what happened with Adam

Harris and gave me some pills. I feel better already."

Isabella's drink of choice was rosé wine, so she picked out a nice bottle of Ricasoli Albia Rosé. It was citrusy and floral, and George thought he could taste red berries. It went perfectly with their shared bruschetta appetisers, an excellent start to dinner at Lorenzo's. "Should you be drinking on those new pills, George?" she asked.

He held up his hands and smiled. Isabella had been his rock, especially since the events with Adam Harris. Wood hadn't approved of his drinking and had often intervened when she could. She was great like that, and George appreciated her. "I can have a glass or two. Did I mention Alex told Smith he could smell alcohol on my breath?"

She nodded as a waitress came by, handing out their mains. George had lasagne, and Isabella had a steak. She cut a thin strip from her steak and said, "You need to stop. I know you're trying hard, and I'm proud that you're not taking the painkillers as much, but if this continues—"

"If this continues, then what?" His tone had hardened.

Wood raised her brow. "Do you want me to finish that sentence, Beaumont?" She shook her head and shrugged. "I care about you, and the drinking needs to stop."

"You're right; I'm sorry. I'm just so stuck. I want to feel better, but I find it difficult. The pills should help me with my drinking."

She nodded, a beautiful smile on her face. "Good, George. I'm glad. Smith will come around. We work well together; once they find nothing, they have no reason to separate us. Right?"

"Right."

They'd booked a hotel in York, came in separate cars and

CHAPTER TWENTY

brought separate suitcases. It was New Year's Eve, and George had got them tickets for the New Year's Eve party at Lorenzo's. It was some kind of disco with unlimited drinks. Luckily, they both had New Year's Day off. George kept his phone on loud in case Mia needed him.

"Are we okay, Isabella?" George asked.

"Why wouldn't we be?" she said.

"You've been... off." He shrugged.

"You're right, George," she said, taking a long drink. "I'm worried once the baby arrives, you'll not be interested in me, that's all. I hate feeling this way. But, of course, you've done nothing to make me feel this way, either, so I don't know why I do. But I do, okay?"

"Okay. I get it. But I don't think there's much you could do to make me disinterested in you. Mia and I are done. We have been for a long time. I don't want her, or anybody else, but you." He gripped her hand and squeezed. The elephant in the room was no more, so the two of them never stopped talking during the time they ate. Not even for a second. They hadn't had a moment together like this for a while. George wondered whether Isabella would say the words back if he said them first?

Dessert came out, and they ate that whilst talking about Isabella's childhood. She knew about his past, but hers was somewhat of a mystery.

She was telling him a story, and he couldn't keep his eyes away from her neck. It was pulsing. Bulging. The necklace was slowly moving up and down, up and down, matching her heart rate.

It was hypnotising.

"I'm sorry. What did you say?" His daydream was broken.

He had to shake his head.

"I said I didn't always look like this, you know. I used to wear braces."

"Yeah, I can tell. Beautiful smile." He smiled at her. His teeth weren't perfect, but not bad enough that his mum or dentist decided he needed a brace.

"I'm sorry I don't tell you much about my past," she said as she reached across the table and held George's hand.

"I'm sorry that you don't have great memories of your past." He squeezed back.

"You don't need to be sorry. The worst part is that I have to deal with my past while working on a case. Sometimes, places remind me of things. It pisses me right off."

"Well, I'm more than happy for you to share these memories with me. Maybe we can deal with them together?"

She laughed and nodded her head, a blazing smile on her face. George loved to hear her laugh. He loved just about every little thing about her. Was it time to tell her yet?

New Year's Eve turned into New Year's Day with the usual bangs, whooshes, crackles, fizzes, swirls, whistles, flashes, bursts, sputters, hisses, and whizzes.

"Don't read too much into this," she said as they stumbled out of Lorenzo's door, holding hands and turning right to their hotel, "but I think I love you, George Beaumont."

He couldn't stop the smile from spreading across his face. "That's good because I love you too, Isabella Wood."

Chapter Twenty-one

It was freezing outside. The weather forced Ryan Jarman to enter a café just behind City Square. It was a tiny and narrow place, one of those places where you had to part with nearly a tenner for a coffee, a place with only half a dozen tables. He wondered how people afforded it; then remembered where he was. It was a nice place, though, with shiny marble floors and ambient lighting. The heater was blowing, warming up his hands. The uniforms of the three waiting staff all looked pristine.

'Coldest January in a decade,' read the newspaper headline in the Metro. It was only the first day of January, yet he suspected the headline was correct. He'd picked up a discarded copy on the bus on his way into Leeds. Reading the paper was one of his daily rituals; knowing what was happening in the world was essential.

A woman around a similar age to him walked by, a cloud of what Ryan knew was Symphony by Louis Vuitton wafting behind her. He had bought a bottle for his mum who was back at home. The woman's clothes and shoes were all designer brands. If not for the immaculate makeup, red lipstick and expensive clothes, Ryan thought she looked similar to his mum. Both were tall and had brown, curly hair and sharp noses. Even their eyes were the same shade of brown, though hers were sharp and his mum's were dull. He had blond hair and brown eyes; clearly, his blond locks must have come from his absent dad. She turned and smiled at Ryan, slinging her Gucci bag over her shoulder, her Tiffany earrings glittering in the light.

Ryan didn't smile back.

From looking around, Ryan understood most of their trade came from those working around the area, like the businesswoman. The people working in the finance sector could obviously afford to spend that much on coffee, and whilst he could have walked across the Square to find somewhere else to drink, the place had caught his eye as he spied the nude nymphs and the Black Prince. Ryan deserved a treat after all the shit he'd suffered recently. Plus, it wasn't his money he was spending, *so fuck it,* he thought.

Ryan waited patiently for his coffee and chocolate orange muffin that had caught his eye. He was starving.

The occupants of the café were staring at him. He just knew it. They were looking down at him; the men dressed in their formal suits and ties and the women in their pantsuits and collared dresses. *How dare they!* He was a paying customer, too.

His phone rang, the Spice Girls ringtone slicing through the low hum of business conversation. They all stared at him once again. Ryan hated being at the centre of attention.

"Hi, Mum," he said in a whisper.

"Where are you?"

"I'm in Leeds," he explained. "What's wrong?"

"You shouldn't have said that to Andrés."

To Ryan's mind, he knew that protesting was a silly idea,

but Ryan hadn't set a foot wrong. Andrés had cheated on him, so he protested anyway. "I didn't do anything wrong, Mum." His voice took on an emotional edge as he spoke. "It's not my fault he cheated on me. He wants a divorce. I told him fine, but I want half."

"I get it, love; I can't really blame you," his mum continued. "I guess I would have reacted the same way myself. But you shouldn't have said—"

"I'm glad it's over, Mum—"

"Here we are, a coconut latte and a chocolate orange muffin. Can I get you anything else?"

Ryan shook his head. "Look, Mum; I've got to go. Ciao." He looked up at the handsome young man who was still standing there.

The male waiter frowned as if knowing Ryan was checking him out. "Are you sure we can't tempt you to a bacon sandwich? A croissant?"

It's not food you can tempt me with, love, he thought. "I'm a vegetarian. You got any sugar?" Ryan asked, taking a bite out of his muffin. A bacon sandwich sounded good, but if a coffee cost ten quid, then how much would a butty laced with brown sauce cost?

"I'll get you some," he said and walked away. He kept his eyes on his firm behind, wondering what he did to get such a perky ass. He'd let himself go recently, cancelling his membership to the gym and overeating. It was his prick of a soon-to-be ex-husband that had been the issue. He was an accountant, too. In fact, he probably worked with the pompous pricks who were staring at him like he didn't belong.

The place was packed with people waiting outside in the freezing rain to get in. From the looks of the waiting staff, he was obviously taking up a table in a place he didn't fit in. *Fuck 'em. Fuck 'em all.* He hoped the credit card Andrés gave him still worked. He had no means to pay for his food and drink otherwise.

Sitting back in his chair, Ryan relaxed and took a sip of his coconut coffee. A large party spanning two tables had left, and those waiting outside in the freezing rain had been allowed in, so the brief rush of trade around him had died down. There wasn't much noise other than the low hum of chatter. The young, blond waiter was busying himself, restocking the sweet counter. Once more, Ryan found his interest piqued. He can't have been much younger than him, twenty-four or twenty-five at least. Their eyes met, and Ryan winked. The young man quickly turned away, forcing Ryan to exhale deeply. He picked up his coffee once more. *He'd never be interested in a man like me.*

Who would?

It was the sexy voice of Andrés.

Who would want you now?

He stared into his cup as if seeking something at the bottom. Slowly he breathed, but his mentality had changed.

The man had been a bully. A cheating bully who had gaslighted him during the entire three years they had been married. He'd been twenty-four when they'd met. Andrés had proposed after three months, and they got married exactly a year from the day they'd first got together.

Andrés had been everything he'd ever wanted during that first year, but as soon as they were married, everything changed. Ryan chugged the remains of his coffee, delicately nibbled the last chunk of his muffin, and pulled on his ancient jacket, a jacket that really wasn't warm enough for this weather.

He tapped the credit card on the machine, not leaving a tip, and as if by miracle, it accepted his payment. With a smile, he headed towards the ornate door to leave the pompous place when a man wearing a helmet bundled into him, knocking him to the floor. Two other men on mopeds screeched to a halt outside the door. Ryan watched, bewildered, as the man who knocked him over rushed past towards the till and smacked the young, handsome waiter on the back of the head with a metal rod. The other two men, who were still wearing their helmets, entered the café, also carrying metal rods in their hands.

As Ryan lay there on the floor whimpering, the sounds of men shouting, breaking glass and screams erupted from all around him.

A fourth moped arrived at the scene, another helmeted man in tow, another metal rod in his hand.

"Get the fuck over there, you little bitch!" he said to Ryan, grabbing him by the wrist and throwing him further inside the café. He slid on the marble flooring, his knees hurting from the fall. He shut the ornate door with a slam and stood guard.

Ryan sat frozen on the spot.

Ring the police! With a shaking hand, he pulled out his phone from his jacket pocket.

"I don't think so, you little bitch!" yelled the man standing guard. His accent sounded different from the others he'd heard. Welsh, maybe?

"Please, stop! Just let me go!"

He shook his head, grabbed his phone and pulled him towards the tills. The young waiter was on the floor, shaking, his head now a crimson mess. "Stay there, you little bitch!"

He tossed Ryan's phone behind the counter, out of reach.

"Please. Let me call an ambulance or something," the young, stylish brunette said.

"Now, aren't you a pretty, young thing?" one of the helmeted men said. He took a step closer to her. "Gucci bag? Give it here."

Ryan didn't know what to do, so he drew his knees up to his chin and tried to make himself invisible. A waitress whimpered beside him while a lanky, skinny man with a beard—who he initially assumed was the owner—cowered in the corner behind the security gate. "We have little cash on the premises," the bearded man said. "It's all paid for by card. Please, take what you want and leave. The police are already on their way."

A woman's voice from inside the kitchen in the back yelled. "Police? Yes, a robbery!" Ryan heard her tell the operator the address. All he needed to do now was become invisible and stay safe until the coppers arrived.

But every instinct in his body told him to move, to run, but the fourth man, the one who'd just arrived, was watching him. He kept his guard at the door. From where he sat, Ryan could see that outside, a crowd had gathered.

Sirens. Ryan heard sirens in the distance. The four men spoke in a language he couldn't place. One man grabbed him, pulled him into the kitchen at the back, and removed his helmet. The man—no, the boy, must have been eighteen or nineteen at most. "Stay here, you little bitch." He put the helmet on Ryan's head and pulled on his balaclava. "Stay here, and I won't cut you!" He removed a long, thin knife. Ryan nodded.

A police officer suddenly ran into the kitchen, her baton drawn. The man in the balaclava stabbed her in the gut,

CHAPTER TWENTY-ONE

dropped the knife, and exited out back.

Ryan shouted for help as he crawled towards the hurt officer who had toppled to the floor. He pressed his hands against the officer's wound.

"Are you okay?" he shouted at the police officer, not removing the helmet the thug had put on him.

She ignored Ryan; her face contorted in agony. Ryan pressed harder and heard a thug yell, "We got the cash. Let's go!"

Ryan continued to put pressure on the policewoman's wound and soon found himself surrounded by armed police, all of them pointing rifles at him.

The police shouted for him to get down on the ground. He froze, and time seemed to slow down. Why were they shouting at him? Then Ryan realised. There was an officer down, a bloody knife on the floor, and he had the same helmet on as the other thugs.

"I didn't do anything," Ryan said as a firm hand shoved him down onto the kitchen tiles and pulled his bloodied hands behind his back. Before he could say anything else, he was in handcuffs.

"Please, stop. You're making a mistake," he tried to tell them. But in the chaos, nobody heard him.

Tears fell from his eyes as one of the armed officers removed the thug's helmet. "I didn't do anything," he said once again. But he knew how it looked. His hands were covered in blood, and he was wearing a helmet.

A tall, muscled Asian male officer bundled him into a waiting police car. Two coppers were sitting in the front seats wearing vests. The car smelled like a chip shop. Ryan sat there and sulked as the radio crackled to life. The policewoman he had tried to save had been pronounced dead.

Chapter Twenty-two

"How many times do I have to tell you, people? I had nothing to do with the stabbing of that policewoman, nor was I part of the gang who robbed the place."

Ryan had been put in a holding cell. He fought back the tears and pulled the cover over his head. *Why won't they believe me? I'm innocent. They must know this by now.*

But waiting wasn't the most challenging part; it was the fact that he had no idea what was going on that was upsetting him the most.

He'd been interviewed by a police detective already, a fat man with a bristling beard, who'd wanted him to answer every question he asked, yet gave no response to his own questions.

"I don't know any of those men."

"I was phoning the police when he grabbed my phone."

"I'm wearing the helmet because he forced it on me."

"He stabbed her, not me."

"He was young, about eighteen or nineteen. Blonde hair, blue eyes."

"My hands were covered in blood because I tried to help her."

"Honestly, I had nothing to do with it."

CHAPTER TWENTY-TWO

"I was a paying customer who was just trying to leave!"

After over an hour of questioning, he could finally have a wash and change into the custody clothing they'd provided. His clothes, which were covered in the deceased policewoman's blood, had been taken away and sealed in a plastic bag. It was something to do with forensics, but he wasn't listening fully to what the custody sergeant had said. He had been too upset. He just hoped he'd get them back.

Ryan had to see a nurse, who inspected his knees. They were hurting him after crashing down on the ornate floor and the kitchen tiles. They'd taken a DNA swab by rubbing a cotton bud on the inside of his mouth before putting that in a plastic tube. That was for forensics, too. Next, they took his fingerprints. He wasn't wearing gloves, though, and so he knew they would use them to eliminate him from touching the knife. Or so he hoped.

"Can I go home now?" he'd asked.

"No. An officer is dead, and you still have some explaining to do."

A sharp pain in his stomach told him something wasn't right. They believed him, right?

"Why aren't you releasing me? I didn't do anything," he said. The officer shut the metal peephole. A small lump formed in his throat as he glanced around the small room. This was a place for criminals.

Ryan drew his knees up to his chin and tried to make himself invisible again. Not that it worked last time. He wrapped the blanket around himself. He wanted to go home. This wasn't the right place for him. He wasn't a criminal.

The custody sergeant told him they had bagged up his mobile for evidence, and he had refused Ryan's requests to phone his mum.

A few hours passed, and Ryan did not know what time it was. He had to get home. His mother would panic.

He banged on the door.

The peephole slid back. "Is there a problem?"

"Yes, there bloody well is!" he shouted. "I'm innocent. You haven't given me my phone call. Why the hell am I still here? You told me I had the right to let somebody know where I was! Where's my mum?"

"You're being held in custody overnight until your DNA is back. We can't seem to get in touch with your mum, either."

* * *

Stuart Kent was standing in the squad room with his laptop tucked under his arm, waiting patiently, his nerves jingling as if he were a patient in a doctor's waiting room.

Detective Inspector Beaumont, tired despite his day off for New Year's Day, entered the squad room with a large coffee from the McDonald's around the corner. As he dumped his coat and laptop bag into his office, he saw Stuart smiling at him from the corner of his eye.

"You haven't seen DS Wood, have you?" Kent asked.

"No, not since... Monday?" he lied. "Everything okay, Stuart?"

"No, not really; I'm glad I caught you... Can we?" Stuart asked, pointing to George's office. "I think DS Wood should be involved, too."

"I think she's on leave, Stuart. As DI, run whatever it is by me, and I'll pass it on to her, yeah?"

"Okay," he said as they entered George's office. Stuart

CHAPTER TWENTY-TWO

placed his laptop on George's desk and opened it before closing the door behind him.

On the screen were images of a burnt-out red car.

A burnt-out red Fiat Punto. What does Wood have to do with this? George thought.

"What's with the car?" George asked.

"A murder inquiry DS Wood is working on. It's why I want to speak to you. To you both, actually."

"Why?"

"I need you to be honest with me, Inspector. Did you speak to Detective Superintendent Smith about my concerns?"

"No, but I spoke with Alex Peterson. We had a discussion, and ultimately, we both decided it wasn't too much of a stretch to argue the bin bags, newspaper, and receipt were stored elsewhere."

"Elsewhere?" Kent asked, a frown on his face.

"Yeah. The murder site. Did DCI Peterson not tell you about this? He said he was going to speak with you."

"I've heard nothing from anybody," Kent said with a shrug. "His promotion means he isn't in the building as much, right?"

"Right. He's in today, though, right?" Kent shrugged. "He wanted to speak to you about the fibres found. You know, the ones from the unknown place?" Kent nodded but allowed George to continue. "The three women weren't killed at Shaw's flat. You cleared both his vehicles from being involved. That means there has to be a place where he'd killed and dismembered them before trying to dispose of them."

Kent nodded. "Yes, of course. And do you know of such a place?"

"Shaw was paying a monthly direct debit for a storage company on Gelderd Road. I had one of my team, DS Joshua Fry, get a warrant from the Super to search the container. He should have gone yesterday, but as I wasn't in, and as you collared me as soon as I entered the door, I haven't had a chance to check whether they found anything yet."

"On New Year's Day?"

"They're quite flexible with opening up for customers. As soon as we produced the warrant, they were just as flexible for us. But as I say, I haven't fired up HOLMES yet. Let me ring Josh."

Kent nodded, and George pulled out his phone. Josh answered after a few rings. "Hi, Josh, it's George. I'm putting you on speaker. I have Stuart Kent here with me."

"Morning, sir. Morning Mr Kent," Josh said. "What can I help you with?"

"Did you go down to the storage place yesterday?"

"Yeah, we did, sir. Found absolutely nothing. Shaw's story checks out. It looks like he pays for the storage but doesn't actually use it."

"That doesn't explain the CCTV footage we received, though, does it? I used that as evidence when I called the CPS. Who did you speak to? Jason Perkins?"

"No, sir," Josh replied, a tone of doubt in his voice. "He was called Nick and came in, especially with it being New Year's Day."

"Jason Perkins made a positive ID for Tony Shaw. He said he saw him on Christmas Eve. He was the one who provided the CCTV footage you gave me. Why didn't you ask for him to show you to the storage container?"

"I—I didn't think, sir. I was just happy they allowed us in with it being a bank holiday."

"Did this Nick say anything?"

"No. But I didn't really ask. I thought—I thought you wanted a search of the place. Mr Kent, some of your SOCOs were there."

"Do you know which ones?" Kent asked.

"Wyatt, Billy and Idina. And, err, a black woman with blonde hair?"

Hayden Wyatt's name keeps coming up, George thought.

"Harmony?"

"Harmony, that's the one."

"What was the floor like in the storage container? Carpet, stone, wood or laminate?"

"Laminate, Mr Kent. There was a carpet rolled up in the corner, though. When we rolled it out, there wasn't anything interesting about it."

"What colour was the carpet?"

"Red. Like a scarlet, or something dark red like that."

"And my team took samples?"

"I assume so. They said they'd send all the results to you and DI Beaumont."

Kent nodded, smiling. "Thanks, Josh," George said as he hung up.

"Right, well, that was good timing. The reason I wanted to talk to you was that I needed to discuss fibres. Specifically, protective coverall fibres and carpet fibres."

"Okay?"

"On Tuesday, DS Wood was appointed SIO of a murder inquiry. The deceased was found in a burnt-out red Fiat Punto by a local dog walker in Springhead Park, Rothwell." George didn't speak but raised his brows, indicating for Kent to continue. "Her bra and knickers had been cut off and were thrown into the nearby bushes. We tested them for DNA, of course, and it matches the deceased. We also found fibres on the underwear."

"Fibres?"

Kent nodded. "Fibres. They match the fibres found on the newspaper, bin bags and receipt from Shaw's flat. The ones I said I thought were planted there."

"Okay. And the coverall fibres?"

"Protective coverall suits, like the ones you and I wear when inspecting a scene, are specifically designed not to shed fibres."

The information dawned on George, and Kent must have seen the sheer look of panic on his face as he said, "I'm worried too, DI Beaumont. When we compared the white fibres from the victim's underwear with the reference database, it was a match to the polythene of coveralls worn by investigators at crime scenes."

"So that means it's a CSI or a detective?"

Kent nodded his head and grimaced. "That's not all, Inspector. Wood's murder victim was a well-known sex worker, one that worked for Red Light Green Light. One that was reported missing this morning just as the DNA profile hit the database. We found her driving licence in the burnt-out vehicle but needed DNA to confirm it was her. But that's not all we found—" Kent said and paused for effect. "I found another of those blond hairs, George, its follicle intact."

"Shit." He thought once more of Hayden Wyatt. The hairs, the knowledge, the coverall. It was probably time to bring him in for questioning.

"Shit indeed, Inspector. It looks like your killer is free and is changing his MO to keep you off his scent."

* * *

CHAPTER TWENTY-TWO

George needed to speak to the Super and fast. What Kent said really disturbed him. If what Kent was saying was true, and George had no reason to believe otherwise, then they needed to do two things. One, release Shaw, and two, find out where those stray coverall fibres and crimson carpet fibres came from.

After looking around the squad room and knocking on all the office doors, he couldn't find them anywhere, so George opened the door to the stairwell.

As he started to walk down the steps, the stairwell echoed with the sounds of voices. Male voices. Voices he was sure he recognised. The echo didn't help.

"Is everything okay?" a man with a Geordie accent asked. George recognised the voice; he was sure but wasn't sure where from. Again, the echo didn't help.

"No, it's not. That's what I want to talk to you about."

"Right. I see." There was a nervousness in the voice. "Are you sure we can't talk about this over a cup of tea or coffee?"

"No. I have little time, so I'm just going to ask you, and I want an honest answer. What the hell is going on?"

"What's going on? I—I don't know what you mean."

The second voice took on a tone, one of authority, one that showed he was angry. "You are a Crime Scene Co-ordinator. You might be the forensics expert and have an area of expertise I don't, but essentially I'm your boss, and you answer to me. Are we clear?"

"Crystal," the nervous man replied.

"If so, why are you questioning my assessment of the forensics? We have him. Yet, for some reason, you're preventing justice. Why?"

"Look, I get it. You're upset. I understand why. But if the

suspect is innocent, then that is justice—"

"The suspect isn't innocent," the aggressive man cut in.

"That's not what the evidence suggests. You're clearly being emotional. I know how important this is to you, especially with you going up for—"

"Don't make out as if you know me or what's important to me. I'm being emotional because you're saying I'm wrong. Yet, instead of coming to me, you went behind my back. What the fuck?"

A long, suffocating pause drew out for what was probably ten or twenty seconds but felt like hours before the aggressive man spoke once more. "See. You can't even fucking tell me the truth, can you? I thought we had mutual respect?"

"Clearly not if this is the way you speak to me. You know, the whole 'I'm your boss, and you answer to me' bullshit. I had no choice but to speak to Detective—"

"Bullshit. You're the one who's full of shit. You had every choice and every chance to talk to me first. I know what this is. A witch hunt."

"Nonsense. I tried to speak to you."

"Don't give me that bullshit. You made a perfunctory effort to email me about a few slight irregularities in the evidence *you* and *your* team recovered."

"They were hardly slight. That evidence is being used to put an innocent victim away! And yes, we recovered the evidence. So what?"

"Well, your young American friend comes across as rather dodgy, to be honest. He was the one who bagged up the evidence. Maybe your American is trying to frame him? It makes sense to me."

"You said... I thought you said—"

CHAPTER TWENTY-TWO

"You're the one who said he was being framed, not me. I'm just trying to come up with an explanation," the aggressive man shouted. "And anyway, why are you calling him an 'innocent victim'? He's not a victim, and he's certainly not innocent. He's the perpetrator! This has been a complex case which has created a mountain of evidence. It was my job to interpret the evidence and consider whether the case went to the CPS. You forget, the investigating officer agreed with me; he recognised the truth."

"That's bullshit, and you know it!" the nervous man said. His voice was getting quieter as if he were heading down the stairwell. George didn't move, not wanting to risk alerting them. "The evidence is the truth! It's not for you to interpret. Facts are facts, and it's a fact that no traces were found to link your suspect to the evidence. And now it seems the evidence is linked to a different—"

"If you force this, and our culprit goes free, you will come to regret it. You hear me?" The aggressive man's voice was louder now, more commanding.

"I hear you," the nervous man said, his voice trembling. "But there's the possibility of another suspect. And for some reason, you seem to be blind to it!"

"Another suspect? What other suspect? There is no other suspect, you blathering idiot!"

"You're wrong. The blond hairs. Calder Park is building a DNA profile as we speak, if they haven't emailed me the results already."

"Blond hairs? What blond hairs?"

There was another suffocating silence.

"What fucking blond hairs?"

A hollow laugh. It was hard to tell which male it came from, but George had the impression the tables had turned. The nervous man was now the one commanding the conversation. "We found a blond hair on the manuscript at Shaw's flat. We also found one in the boot of the red Fiat Punto, which had been burnt out. Explain that to me?"

"Your American friend is blond. Could they be his? Have you got a match on the DNA database? What about the Contamination Elimination Database?" The nervous man must have shaken his head because the aggressive man continued. "Then they could be different people. Many people have blond hair, and even if they don't, they dye it. If it is the same person, maybe it's a victim; the hair could have been a female—"

"It's male. Calder Park already checked; I'm just waiting for email confirmation of the DNA profile."

"You think you've got this all figured out, huh? Well, you're wrong. Tony Shaw is the killer, and those items of evidence were kept separate from his flat. As for the hairs, they've got to be Wyatt's. Same for the coverall fibres. Yes, I've read HOLMES today. It's the transference of fibres, that's all. Do you know your problem, Kent? It's that you take a narrow view of your own field. I don't. I'm the boss. Only the DCS is higher than me, and so it's my job to evaluate and interpret."

"No! No! No! No!" Kent shouted in between deep breaths. An audible, raging scream erupted from deep down the stairwell that got louder as time went on. Kent must have walked back up the stairs towards the aggressive stranger.

"You're angry. Of course, you are. Truth hurts, huh?"

"Just who the fuck do you think you are?" Kent asked. There was a sound barely audible to George, a sound of metal pinging.

"Did you just push me? Are you fucking kidding me right now?" There was a laugh, a laugh that got louder the longer it

CHAPTER TWENTY-TWO

went on.

"You need to see that I'm right. Tony Shaw's innocent. You know it. Why won't you admit it?"

"No. I'm not wrong. All I see is a narrow-minded Crime Scene Co-ordinator who can't admit that he's the one that's wrong. It's rather that, or you're protecting Hayden Wyatt. This is my career, remember? I will not have a narrow-minded wanker mess that up!"

"Oh, so I'm suddenly a 'narrow-minded wanker', am I? Why don't you frame me so you can lock me up?"

"Oh fuck off, not this again. I did not frame Shaw."

"That's not what he said. And anyway, you did everything in your power to make sure an innocent man was charged!"

"He's not innocent, Stuart. He's guilty. Hayden Wyatt is probably working with him. I always had the inkling there was another person involved. I want him brought in for questioning."

"No! No! No! No!" Kent shouted again, gasping for air. "Hayden wouldn't do something like this." There was a louder metallic sound and a sharp cry of pain. "Get the fuck out of my face!"

"Oh, now you've gone and fucking done it, Stuart Cunt!" the stranger uttered, the sound of his voice low and mournful. "You stupid bastard, you've just assaulted a police officer!"

George didn't know quite what to do and considered slamming the door and walking down the stairwell nonchalantly. Unfortunately, the choice was taken away from him.

The door behind George slammed into him, pushing him into the metal railing. It was DS Fry. "Ah, DI Beaumont, finally! Have you seen the Chief or the Super anywhere, sir?"

George shook his head as the sound of a door slamming shut

carried up the stairwell.

Chapter Twenty-three

Ryan slept badly, not really knowing how many hours he'd managed. He banged on the door but got no reply.

When are they going to let me go?

After what felt like an age but was only about an hour or two, an officer poked his head around the door. "Are you okay, Ryan?"

He nodded.

"The SIO is back and wants to have a word with you."

Ryan didn't move.

"Come on."

Draped in his blanket, Ryan got off the bench and crept towards the door. "What's an SIO, and what do they want with me?" he asked.

"You'll find out soon enough."

He followed the man down a long corridor and into a smouldering interrogation room.

"Take a seat, Ryan. The SIO will be here shortly."

Ryan nodded but stayed standing. He removed his blanket and looked around. The two chairs on his side of the table, including the table itself, were bolted to the floor. In the corner was a stack of three chairs. Up in the corner, a camera was angled down at the table. Was someone watching him?

Suddenly, he felt terrified. His mouth went dry, and his heart pounded.

A few moments later, the door opened, and a tall blond man stepped in. He wasn't what he had been expecting. In Ryan's eyes, detectives were fat and ugly. Not this man. He was tall, but not too tall. His hair was messy but was obviously styled that way, tousled at the top and undercut at the sides. He removed his stone-coloured trench coat, grinning as he did so, before pulling a chair from the stack and leaving his coat on top of the others. It matched the colour of his trousers. *Was this trendy guy really a detective?* He was well-muscled, too. Not a bodybuilder, but obviously somebody who looked after himself.

"You're the SIO?" Ryan asked, taking in his green-coloured eyes. He was absolutely gorgeous.

"Yeah. Detective Inspector George Beaumont." He sat down, his legs stretching under the table. The inspector held out his hand, an offer for him to take a seat.

He obliged and said, "You don't look like a detective."

He grinned. "Oh, really? What do I look like? And how is a detective supposed to look?"

Shit! Ryan knew he couldn't say the detective was too handsome to be a detective, and instead said, "I don't know. You're only the second detective I've ever met."

He chuckled and shrugged. "I believe you refused a lawyer. Why?"

Ryan studied him warily. "I'm not a criminal. Only criminals need lawyers."

He glanced down at a document in a folder he'd brought in with him. "Fair enough. I'm going to record this conversation." He nodded as the detective placed a disc in the machine and clicked the button. He pressed another button. "Okay, you're now being filmed on that camera, too. Ryan Jarman, twenty-eight?" He nodded again. "You're not known to us, nor any other police force. That's good. Tell me, what was your role in the café robbery?"

"I had no role."

"I know, but I needed you to confirm it for me." He closed the file. "CCTV in the café confirmed your story. As of now, you're no longer under arrest for the murder of a police officer."

Ryan frowned. "Then why am I here, detective?"

"We had to wait for your DNA results to come back. You could have been here longer, but my boss expedited the results."

Ryan remembered the swab. "Why did you take it?"

"It's procedure. And to be honest, it's a good job we did."

He blinked, holding back tears as he said, "What does that even mean? Stop being so cryptic!"

"I'm not being cryptic. I'm doing my job. Tell me your name."

"Ryan."

He sighed. "Look, Ryan. I've got as long as this takes. Ryan, what?"

Ryan shrugged. "You have the document in that file. You already know my name and age."

"I want you to confirm it for me. I've told you my name."

"You haven't told me your age, relationship status or your sexual orientation, though." He was so happy he'd pawned the ring Andrés had given him. Ryan mustered up his most sexy grin.

Ryan was met with silence. The detective inspector sat there, saying nothing. He could feel the heat crawling up his neck and settling on his face. Had he just made a dick of himself?

"Jarman. Ryan Jarman."

"How old are you, Ryan Jarman?"

"Twenty-eight."

"Where do you live?"

"In Holbeck."

He read out an address, and Ryan nodded. "With your mum?"

"For now. I recently got out of a long-term relationship. I'm single, and you?"

He ignored the question. "Is it just your mum, or do you live with your dad, too?"

"Dad? No."

He glanced at the table. He'd never had a dad. His mum had been his only parent.

The detective opened his folder again, took out a photograph, and slid it across the table to him. "Have you ever seen this man before?"

He stared at the picture. "Nope."

"Look again."

The man was a complete stranger, but he picked up the photo. Looking back at him was an enormous man in his late fifties or early sixties with a bald head and greasy beard.

"I don't know. Who is he?"

The detective nodded his head and smiled at Ryan. "Tony Shaw. Anthony Shields. He goes by either name. Do you recognise him now?"

He shook his head. "Nope. Was he one of the guys under the moped helmets? The one I saw was very young, though."

He mirrored Ryan and shook his head. "This man has nothing to do with the café robbery."

CHAPTER TWENTY-THREE

Ryan didn't exactly consider himself clever, but he wasn't dumb, and the gorgeous detective wasn't making any sense at all. "I'm baffled, Detective." He glanced at the camera above and shook his head, his palms up and out. "I really don't understand what's going on."

"This man, Tony Shaw, is currently in custody for the murders of three women."

Ryan raised an eyebrow and shrugged. "Right, and what's that got to do with me?"

"Thirty years ago, Tony Shaw was involved in a very similar set of murders but was released due to lack of evidence. We found some DNA inside one of those victims, and it's been stored on our database since 1995."

Ryan raised his other brow and shrugged. "Right. I wasn't even born then. What's this got to do with me?"

He smiled that gorgeous grin of his leant on the table. He was close, too close. Ryan could smell his aftershave. "This has everything to do with you, Ryan. During a recent murder investigation, we found blond hairs at different crime scenes. Those blond hairs were sent to the lab, and forensic scientists were able to obtain a DNA profile."

"You think I had something to do with your recent murder investigation? Not me."

"You're right. But Ryan, whoever killed those women thirty years ago, left that DNA. And whoever left those blond hairs behind recently killed and dismembered three women."

"And?"

"And, Ryan, you're a familial match."

Ryan glanced at him. "Right. A familial match? What does that even mean?"

The detective leaned even closer, his eyes sparkling. "Well, it means two things, Ryan. One, your grandad, dad, or brother killed four innocent women thirty years ago. And two, your grandad, dad, or brother recently killed and dismembered three innocent women."

* * *

George studied the man sitting in front of him. He had a pale complexion and was tall and slender. His hair was an ash blond, a nest that would probably have been styled into a quiff or a pompadour. He stared back at George with dark eyes inside dark shadows. Ryan reminded him of somebody he knew. He just couldn't place it.

After the robbery in the city centre, the police rounded up everyone involved and brought them to Elland Road Station for processing. They'd been lucky. The DSU had allowed their DNA to be sent along with more DNA from the Shaw case. As soon as his DNA had flagged an alert on the system, he'd received a call.

"I don't have any brothers. Nor do I know my dad," Ryan said and nodded to the photograph of Shaw. "Unless you're saying this guy's my dad?"

George narrowed his eyes. The swab they'd taken from Shaw had been compromised, and so they had needed to take another one. That one, according to Alex Peterson, had also been compromised. So, they'd had to take another one. They couldn't be sure of anything, so George changed tact.

"That's not something I can confirm or deny," George said.

Ryan folded his arms across his chest. "Well, what has this got to do with me, then?"

"Both DNA profiles are a familial match to both you and

CHAPTER TWENTY-THREE

themselves. They could be your brothers or your dad and brother. We need to find out who the DNA belonged to and what it was doing there," George explained.

Ryan's eyes burnt holes into the table. "Then you'll have to ask my mum. I've got no idea who my dad is."

"Where is she? You provided us with her contact number, yet we've been unable to contact her."

"I don't know," Ryan said with a shrug.

"As I pulled your file, I sent an officer to check your home in Holbeck. She isn't there. Is there somewhere else she could be?"

"Yeah, she could have stayed with that dick, Andy. That's her dickhead boyfriend. Since I moved back in, she's stayed at his place a lot."

Dick. Dickhead. He clearly wasn't a fan of his mum's boyfriend, then.

"Does this dickhead boyfriend have a surname?"

"Gillespie."

George glanced at Ryan. "Do you know Andy Gillespie's address?" He was expecting another shrug.

To his surprise, Ryan said, "I don't know the address. But I know he lives on the Ingrams, opposite the car dealer. It's number thirty-five, I think."

"Thank you, Ryan," George said, firing off a text to DS Brewer. "That's very helpful."

"Can I leave now? You said I'm not under arrest, right?"

"Right, but I can't let you leave just yet. Have you had breakfast?" He knew they'd kept him in overnight, but he'd been called into the station early. It was only eight.

He nodded and fired off a text to DC Blackburn, who he knew was in, asking him to speak to the custody sergeant to get Ryan

Jarman some breakfast.

"Whilst we wait for your breakfast, Ryan, I'd like to ask you some questions."

Ryan laughed. "Go on."

"I don't know what happened between your mum and dad and why he didn't stick around, but this investigation might uncover some truths you don't like." Ryan nodded sullenly. He understood, at least. That was good. "We may find your dad. We can keep your name out of it, of course. Keep you away from him. But if this goes to court, then—"

"I'd like to know who he is. But then, if he's a killer, maybe not."

"I'll be honest with you, Ryan. We're not sure if he's the killer or whether he was just a customer of the victims."

"A customer. You mean?"

Shit! George knew he had said too much. But then, it was only a matter of time before the press found out they had another Yorkshire Ripper on their hands.

"Yeah." There was no point in lying to the guy. "We found semen in the mouth of one of our culprit's victims."

Ryan narrowed his eyes. "Sounds gross. So what, it matches a family member of mine?"

"Yeah. We can only get the Y chromosome DNA from a male. Yours matches the sample we have on the database. It isn't you, as you weren't born, and the full profile doesn't match. It means it could be a brother of yours, but most likely, it means it's your dad's."

Ryan sniffed and cleared his throat. "I'm sorry, but I can't help you with that."

George shot him a pointed look. "Are you sure? What's your mum's name?"

CHAPTER TWENTY-THREE

"Kelly Jarman. I'm sure. I have no siblings and no dad. Well, I do, obviously. My mum isn't the Virgin Mary. But he's never been around, and when I've asked, my mum shut me down. She said it could be anyone."

George nodded and made a note. Then he looked up at Ryan and frowned. "What do you mean?"

"My mum. Before she had me, she used to be a sex worker, too."

Chapter Twenty-four

George called DS Josh Fry and asked him to get Kelly Jarman's file printed and put on his desk. Meanwhile, Josh had given George the contact number of Kelly's old social worker.

He dialled, and after a few rings, a female voice said, "Hello, Kimmy Dixon speaking."

"Hi, Kimmy, my name is George Beaumont. I'm a Detective Inspector down at Elland Road Station. I wonder whether you could answer some questions about Ryan and Kelly Jarman."

"Wow, okay. I haven't heard those names in a while. Sure, go ahead."

"Are you okay if I record the call for my notes later?"

"Yeah, go for it."

"Is it true Kelly was once a sex worker?" George asked the social worker.

"Sadly, yes. Kelly Jarman was a sex worker for probably a decade before she had Ryan. She was also a chronic drug user and alcohol drinker. That's why I got involved. At one point, when Ryan wasn't even a year old, we nearly took him away and put him in foster care. Then suddenly, Kelly cleaned up her act. She stopped the alcohol and the drugs and stopped prostitution. Kelly proved she could pay the rent and the bills, so we left Ryan where he was. She bought the place from the council, eventually."

George knew they tried to keep the family unit together if possible. "Do you know who Ryan's dad is? Does he have any siblings?"

"No to both questions, I'm afraid. He isn't on Ryan's birth certificate, and Kelly never gave us that information. Ryan was an only child as far as I was aware, too."

"I'm guessing you checked on them?"

"Of course we did. At first, we conducted monthly checks, and everything seemed to be okay. She got a cleaning job that paid well. All were legitimate from what we saw."

"Thanks. And after those monthly checks stopped?" He couldn't explain it, but there was something about Ryan that he recognised. Did he know his dad?

"Other cases took priority, especially once we knew Kelly was stable. We rarely followed up as often. When we visited, and they were surprise visits, everything was normal. We were aware Kelly still liked a drink or two in the evenings and had replaced her drug use by smoking cigarettes. But she wasn't soliciting on the street any more, and the drug tests showed us she was clean. Kelly was also doing a great job of looking after her child."

"Thanks for answering my questions, Kimmy."

"Of course. My pleasure. Oh, and a great job with capturing the Miss Murderer, by the way."

* * *

Kelly Jarman was almost as thin as her son, but whilst he was pale and fair, Kelly was tanned and had dark features. Whilst she may have once been beautiful enough to sell her body, the alcohol, drugs, and cigarettes had taken their toll, meaning she now looked haggard.

Her guarded eyes stared back at George. "Look, officer. I ain't done anything wrong."

"Detective," George said and took a seat. He told her he was recording her and placed a disc inside the machine. Tashan sat beside him, taking notes. She'd waived her right to a solicitor, which would make this easier. She would talk to him without a solicitor getting in the way.

"You're not under arrest. That's not why you're here, Mrs Jarman." He attempted a smile he thought would put her at ease.

She scowled. "It's Miss, actually. If I've done nothing wrong, then why the hell am I here?"

Ryan looked nothing like her. He must look more like his dad. And if that was the case, George was sure he'd seen Ryan's dad before; he just didn't know where.

"I want to ask you some questions about someone you may have known thirty years ago."

"Jesus. Thirty years ago? Who?" Her eyes narrowed. From the file he'd just read, George, suspected she'd known a few dodgy characters in her life. She'd been arrested for soliciting, but as Kimmy Dixon had said, that had been nearly thirty years ago. She had received a caution for using cocaine, but other than that, her record was cleaner than he'd expected.

According to the records from HMRC, Kelly got a job and began paying taxes in early two thousand. Kimmy Dixon was obviously correct when she said Kelly had cleaned up her act when Ryan was younger. But what had she been doing before her job? From the file, Ryan would have just turned six then.

CHAPTER TWENTY-FOUR

What had she done for six years, lived on benefits? He was still waiting on more information from the data clerk.

"I want to know, Kelly, whether you knew any men named Anthony Shields or Tony Shaw?"

She frowned and shook her head. "Nope. Sorry, love. Those names don't ring any bells. Should they?"

"Never had any clients go by that name?"

She snorted. "I mean, it's been a while since I had those kinds of clients, love. And let's be frank, they never used their real names, anyway. You got a picture of this guy?"

"This was taken recently, Miss Jarman, so he'll be older," George said, handing her the photo of Shaw. He wanted to save a younger picture of Shaw for later.

She stared at the picture. "Nope."

Like mother, like son. "Look again."

"Seriously. Never seen this guy in my life. Is that all?"

"No. Miss Jarman, would you mind giving us a DNA sample?"

"Why?" she said, instantly going on the defensive.

"Because I'm looking into the murders of four women that happened thirty years ago. We found DNA, and there's a chance it might be yours as it's a familial match to your son's," he said. It was a lie, of course. A small lie to open up questions about Ryan's dad.

She frowned. "Right. And if the DNA matches mine. What does that mean?"

"Then we know you had ties to the women." He forced a smile. It was a thin, phoney smile. He grimaced immediately, knowing she would know. "To use your word, Miss Jarman, I'll be frank with you. Three of the four women dismembered back in 1994 were sex workers. Maybe you knew them, but maybe you didn't. I've checked the case files, and you were never brought in for questioning. That strikes me as odd."

Her frown turned to a scowl. "Odd? Why? Probably because I had nothing to do with any murder. After all this time—you're trying to pin the murders on me, aren't you?"

"Definitely not, Miss Jarman. To repeat, we found DNA that is a familial match to your son, Ryan. That means it must have come from any siblings or parents. We simply want to rule you out of the investigation."

She thought for a moment and smiled. "Okay. If it'll rule me out, then fine."

George gave a smile and a nod. "Amazing. Thank you for your cooperation."

"As I said, if it rules me out, then fine. You wanna do it now?"

"Yes, but I'll get a forensic officer up from the lab to come and do it in a moment. There are a few things I'd like to ask you."

She sighed. "Like what?"

"Tell me about Ryan's dad."

"I knew this was coming, and I'll be frank with you, Detective. I fucked a lot of men back in the day. To be honest, I was rather pissed or stoned, or worse. Some of those dickheads would say they were using protection when they weren't. Do you get where I'm going with this? I have no idea who Ryan's dad is."

George feared this was coming. "Does Ryan have any siblings? If this happened to you a lot, did you give birth and, say, give up a child for adoption?"

There was a slight hesitation, but she said, "No."

He paused. The room was silent.

"Look, I had a few abortions, okay?"

CHAPTER TWENTY-FOUR

"What was different about Ryan?"

"Honestly?"

He paused once again, inviting her to talk.

"I wanted out. Back in the nineties, I could get a better house and decent benefits by having a child. It happened at a time when I was at my lowest, and to tell you the truth, Ryan saved me. Alright? There. That blond bastard saved my life, and I fucking love him. I don't know who his dad is. Honestly, detective."

George studied her. Whilst he had asked the questions, there was no tightening of her lips, no dilation of her pupils, no tension in her body language. Yes, she had hesitated, but the word abortion rarely encouraged a positive discussion. Kelly Jarman was clearly embarrassed by her past, an embarrassment George thought was unnecessary. They all had pasts, and he wasn't really the person to judge. So, from all of that, George didn't think she was lying, but of course, she could have been. He just hoped she was telling the truth.

"Okay, Miss Jarman. Thanks so much. We'll leave it there for now. I need you to wait in here whilst I get the forensic officer up to take the DNA swab."

Kelly grunted a reply.

He gathered up the folder and, before leaving, handed her his card. "Call me. In case you remember anything about Ryan's dad."

He made his way back upstairs to the squad room to speak to DC Jason Scott, who had been watching the interviews from a live video link. "What do you think, Jay?"

"I think she was lying, sir."

"Lying about what? The dad or the abortions?"

"Both," DC Scott said. "It was the hesitation. The look in

her eyes."

"She didn't seem to know Shaw, though."

"Yeah, people change in thirty years," he said.

"Right, okay. I'll get the DNA Sent to the Calder lab, and then we can go from there. Did we get Shaw's new sample back yet? I can't believe the first one was messed up. Also, do we know who took the sample yet?"

"No. I heard Peter Alexander apparently had a bit of a slagging match with one of the forensic officers downstairs. They're each blaming the other. Pretty funny, especially as the newly promoted Super doesn't seem the type to like to fail," Jay said.

George frowned. "Well, whoever messed it up has caused more work for us. I charged Shaw under pressure from him to close the case. All we can do now is wait for both sets of results to come back; then, we'll know for sure if it was him and whether he's Ryan's dad. In the meantime, I want you and DC Blackburn to look into Kelly's background and see if we can find a link between her and the other victims. A group of prostitutes in Holbeck in the nineties must have been a close-knit group, right?"

"So, you still think she's involved in some way?" DC Scott asked.

George grinned at him. "It's odd she wasn't questioned when so many other sex workers were. That's fishy to me, Jay. We're only just seeing the tip of the iceberg. I just know it."

Chapter Twenty-five

"Got some news for you, boss," DS Joshua Fry said that Friday morning. He clicked his mouse to show George. "As expected, Kelly is a partial match to Ryan. We got Shaw's back." Josh paused for a moment, reading. "It's not him, sir. His DNA isn't the DNA they found thirty years ago."

"Bollocks," George said. "We're going to have to let him go. The CPS didn't think the fibres from the burnt-out Fiat Punto were enough to release him, but if we're connecting the two cases, then they'll have to."

"There's more, sir." Josh scrutinised the on-screen report. He'd gone quiet.

George frowned. "What is it?"

"Well, it's good news, I suppose. The blond hairs Kent found in the Punto match the one found on Shaw's manuscript."

"We thought that, anyway. Still no match on the database?"

"No, sir. They don't match any from the Contamination Elimination Database, either. At least it's not a police officer. That's good, right, sir?"

George shrugged. "It's not mandatory, Josh. Quite a lot of officers aren't on the CED." Kent had told him Alex Peterson wasn't on there, which he still found strange. He was blond, too, and had a Geordie accent. Was there something in that? Especially after the argument, he'd heard in the stairwell yesterday.

"Are you okay, sir?"

"Yeah, fine. Just thinking we're now back at square one. Four bodies and not a single suspect. Fucking hell! Ring DS Wood for me, will you? Tell her we need all the information about Danielle Ferguson transferring to us. I'll speak to the Super, let him know what's going on."

"Will do, sir."

George went to inform Detective Superintendent Smith.

"What is it, George?" He looked up from his laptop.

"DNA from DS Wood's case has come back, sir. The blond hairs found in the burnt-out Punto match the one on Shaw's manuscript. It proves the murder of Danielle Ferguson is connected to my case. I've asked Josh to get the details from DS Wood. I'll need all the information transferred over. Is that okay?"

"Yes, I'll email her confirming. What about Shaw's DNA? The new swabs were sent in with that batch, right?" Smith said, wincing as he picked up his coffee mug.

"Are you okay, sir?" George asked, noticing the brace on his wrist.

"Am I okay?" Smith looked confused and shook his head before realising. "Oh, this?" Smith placed the mug down and shrugged. "I was walking down the stairwell, getting in my steps as usual, and somebody must have spilt something because I suddenly went careering into the metal barrier. Hurt my wrist."

"Right, well, I'm glad you're okay." Was it Smith he'd heard speaking to Stuart Kent in the stairwell? He still wasn't sure.

Smith was a Geordie, though. "As for Shaw's DNA, I hate to tell you this, but it wasn't him, sir. The DNA doesn't match the profile we got from the semen. I'm sorry, I really am. I thought we had him."

Jim Smith looked down and worn out. Unsolved cases were the bane of a detective's life. They affected you more than you ever let on. They'd given Smith hope it was Shaw, only to have to pull that hope away. "Look, sir. We still have Ryan and Kelly Jarman. Your case and mine are still connected. Ryan's brother or dad is still our prime suspect. And one of those is yours, too. We just need to find out who they are."

"Excellent news, George. I take it you'll be bringing Kelly Jarman in for questioning again?"

"Correct, sir," he said. "She must know who Ryan's dad was. That, or she might remember who her clients were. Josh and I are going to put a ton of pressure on her. She'll crack."

There was a brief pause. Smith's eyes narrowed. "Don't put too much pressure on her, George. The last thing we need is our case thrown out because you intimidated a witness. Shaw's solicitor nearly had us with that."

"I understand, sir. Look, I know you've been separating the pair of us because of the whistleblowing, but I want her back on my team. She's an incredible detective, and to be frank, I need all the help I can get. I have no concrete suspects, and she's my best interviewer. Is that okay?"

"Fine. But if you're the one who is interviewing, DS Wood has to watch from a live video link. Is that everything, for now, George?"

Beaumont nodded, but Smith's eyes were already back on his screen.

* * *

"I'm not liking the fact you keep dragging me down here in a marked car, Inspector Beaumont," Kelly Jarman said. "Why am I here now?"

DS Josh Fry sat beside him, taking notes. Like yesterday, Kelly had surrendered her right to a solicitor, which would again make this easier. George wondered how long she'd talk to him without a solicitor getting in the way.

"Respectfully, I think you were dishonest in your interview yesterday, Miss Jarman."

"Dishonest. How so?"

"To reiterate something I mentioned yesterday, I checked the case files, and you were never brought in for questioning. That still strikes me as odd. In fact, I lost sleep over it. So here," George said, handing over six photographs. The photographs were of six women, four of Jack the Butcher's victims and two dummies. "Take a long look. Do you recognise these women?"

Kelly stared long and hard at the photographs, picking each one up in turn and making three piles. "Okay. I don't know these two," she said, accurately identifying the fakes. "These three," she said and pointed at the middle pile, "were women who I worked with regularly. We solicited the streets together. Nicole Green, Joanne Cox and Stacey Lumb. Right?"

"Right? What do you know about this woman?" George asked, pointing to the image of the fourth victim, Anna Hill.

"I recognise her. She was also a prostitute: a new one, a little green around the ears. Word around was her husband pimped her out. Used to drop her off and pick her up. I don't know her name, though."

"Anna Hill. Our intelligence suggests she wasn't a sex

CHAPTER TWENTY-FIVE

worker. You're sure it's her, you remember?"

"Definitely."

"Yet you don't remember your clients? Josh?"

Josh checked his notes. "Yesterday, Miss Jarman, you said, and I quote, 'I'll be frank with you, Detective. I fucked a lot of men back in the day. To be honest, I was rather pissed or stoned, or worse.'"

"How are we supposed to believe you when you've told us something like this already, Miss Jarman?" George asked.

"Look. I've been doing a lot of thinking since I saw you yesterday. If you'd asked me yesterday, I wouldn't have remembered. But today, I do."

"Okay, brilliant," George said, a fake smile plastered on his face. "So tell me, who is Ryan's dad?"

"I don't know."

"Stop with the bullshit!"

"Keep going, Detective Inspector Beaumont, and I will withdraw my cooperation."

George smiled, his teeth and fists clenched. He had worked on his anger after the Miss Murderer case, but Kelly Jarman knew something, yet she wasn't being honest with them.

"Ryan obviously has a dad, unless you're telling me Ryan was conceived immaculately?"

"Don't be stupid. I already told you I was so fucked up; my clients took advantage of me. I had many abortions."

"I'm this close to asking for a solicitor, Inspector Beaumont," she said, pinching her thumb and index finger together. "You've asked me this question already."

George feared this was coming. "Just tell us the truth, Kelly. Does Ryan have any siblings? Did you say give up a child for adoption? Please, Kelly!"

"No. I didn't."

Defeated, George tried his next line of questioning. "So tell me what you remember about your male clients? One of them was obviously Ryan's dad."

She shrugged. "I don't know. They were men who paid me for a quick fuck. A blow job here, a hand job there. I was young. Hot. Dependent on drugs and alcohol. You're lucky I remembered Nicole, Joanne, and Stacey."

He took a six-pack of photographs from his folder. A six-pack was a set of six photos with five fillers and a suspect. They contained images of detectives and officers who worked on the case thirty years ago who had a similar look to the young Tony Shaw, along with a picture of a young Tony Shaw. "Here, have a look at these images. It might help."

She stared long and hard at the photographs. "You might be onto something here. Yeah. I knew this guy," she said. "He was one of my regulars. Why?"

George's pulse rocketed. Was she about to bring Shaw back into the equation? She pointed at an image he hadn't been expecting her to. "This guy?" He picked up the image and passed it to her.

"Yes, love. This guy."

"Are you sure?"

She smiled and looked a decade younger. "Certain."

* * *

"Tell me his name," George asked, the shock in his voice unmistakable.

"Oh love, after everything I told you already. I don't know his first name. And to be frank, even if I remembered, which

I don't, it'll have been fake, anyway." She nodded at the photograph. "I remember this guy simply because he was special. We had a great time together."

"How often did you see him?"

"Erm, every couple of weeks, usually mid-week. As I said, we had a great time together."

"A great time in what way?"

"He didn't hire me just for sex. His home life was tough, and his job was stressful, not that he shared with me what job he had. His wife hadn't touched him since becoming pregnant. He found that hard. She didn't want to go anywhere or do anything with him. So, we used to go to Newcastle and Liverpool and Manchester," she said with a smile. "We'd go out as if we were a couple. There was never a set day, but we'd stay over or go back to mine. Sometimes he'd go home. Now that I remember those days, it hurts me that he just disappeared. I guess once his kid had been born, that was it." She wiped a tear from a watery eye just below a perfectly plucked eyebrow.

George nodded, not speaking. This was more than she'd given him before, and he didn't want to jeopardise it.

"And you stopped seeing him because his baby was born?"

She shrugged. "It was just a guess. I don't know, to be honest. But all good things come to an end, don't they? Especially relationships. One day, he just stopped showing up. I figured his wife had found out, or he'd moved away, or something. But back then, there was always another client, always."

"When did you last see him?"

She looked down and scratched her forehead with a manicured nail. She shrugged. "I dunno. It was years ago. Decades, even."

"Thirty years ago," George clarified.

"If you say so." She threw up her arms, a frown on her face.

"This is important," George said. "Try to think," he urged. "Could this guy be Ryan's dad?"

Josh glanced at him. It obviously hadn't occurred to him that the guy in the photo could be Ryan Jarman's dad.

Kelly rubbed her chin. "Could be. But so could a hundred other guys. Do I really need to keep going over and over?"

"We've got time. Think about it."

She dropped her head into her hands, and George waited. Was she really trying to recall, or was she desperately trying to come up with an excuse?

Kelly lifted her head up, nodded, and smiled.

Both George and Josh stared at her. "Do you remember?" prompted George.

"Sorry. No dice. Ryan's dad could have been anybody. I'm trying to think whether or not it was him," she said, pointing to the blond man in the picture George was still holding. "I want to say the last time I saw him was on a weeknight. He took me down to London." She smiled. "His little girl had just been born, and so his wife stayed home, and I went to London with him instead," she said and rolled her eyes.

Nothing she was saying made any sense.

"He can't have been the dad, then." She gave a sad smile. "It's a shame, you know. I'd have liked to have asked why he left us. You know?"

"Us?" DS Fry asked.

"Yeah. Sorry, it's the way I speak. I use us for me. He let me down when he left me. I should have known he was leaving me. We stayed over in London and had breakfast together. He dropped me off back home in Holbeck, and then he left. Never saw him again." She paused. "Shit, it's crazy how easy you remember things at times, even if they were impossible before. But as for anything else, I'm sorry. I got nothing."

"It's a lot of detail for somebody who was at the time, 'pissed or stoned or worse'," George said.

She shrugged, and George nodded to Josh, who arranged the rest of the six-pack out on the table in front of her. "Were they 'clients' of yours too?" asked Josh.

She frowned and leaned closer to study their faces. "No. I don't think so. Nope, I don't recognise any of them." She shrugged. "I was pissed or stoned or worse, remember? But they could have been, I guess. I don't remember every cock, you know."

Chapter Twenty-six

"How did you get on with the searches on Kelly Jarman, Josh?" George asked Josh late that Friday afternoon. After allowing Kelly home, he'd ordered Josh to contact the Adoptions Section in Southport to look into any adoptions in Leeds, where the birth mother was named Kelly Jarman. Kelly's medical history made for interesting reading. They found out Kelly had given birth to another child before she'd given birth to Ryan.

"Still waiting, sir. They've sent two through already, but they were no good. It isn't a common name, so I'm hoping I get good news soon."

"What about the forensics on the Jarman's accounts?"

"They hadn't come back when I checked ten minutes ago. Let me look again." Josh clacked away on his keyboard. "Nope, still nothing. Sorry, sir."

"Okay. Keep me informed, Josh, yeah?" George asked, walking towards his office.

* * *

There was a loud knock on George's open office door, and he looked up to find DS Joshua Fry.

CHAPTER TWENTY-SIX

"What did you find?" George asked, scratching his chin.

"Ryan's account is meagre. He didn't work but received some kind of allowance. But other than that, there were zero miscellaneous payments. Overall, nothing dodgy. A couple of cash withdrawals, but that's normal. I checked into the allowance. He was married to a guy called Andrés. Ryan is now living with Kelly because of the divorce filed by Andrés. I spoke with the café Ryan was on the day he was arrested, and he paid by credit card. I checked that, and it's one that belongs to Andrés García. Ryan is clean."

George raised an eyebrow and asked, "What about Kelly's?"

"I'll start with her recent statements," Josh said, his eyes glittering. George got the feeling he had something worth sharing but was holding it back. He wanted Josh to get straight to the juicy morsels but allowed the sergeant to continue it his way. "Compared with Ryan, Kelly is a big spender. She doesn't have any vices, and by that, I mean no sports gambling, no online bingo, that kind of thing. She gets a regular wage which she spends on clothes and hair, and makeup. There are no suspicious payments going into the account, and she has no rent because her mortgage was paid off years ago."

"So nothing dodgy?" sighed George.

"Not in the last ten years, no," clarified Josh. "Now, here's where it gets interesting."

"Come on," George said, urging his sergeant to continue.

"For five years, Kelly was being sent monthly maintenance payments," Josh said with a flourish.

George stared at her. "Maintenance payments? Are you sure?"

"Yep. The maintenance payments were being paid into a separate account."

George whistled under his breath. "Nice work, Josh." He clapped Josh on the shoulder. "Tell me you checked the account number of the sender."

"That I did, sir. It matches the name you told me it would. Shall I get Uniform to bring her in?"

Josh's screen pinged, and an email popped up on his screen. Josh clicked, opening the email for George to see. It was from the Adoptions Section. There was also an unopened email from Calder Park, too, with the report on the extra DNA analysis they'd asked for.

"Absolutely, Josh," George replied. "Miss Jarman has some explaining to do."

* * *

Kelly Jarman looked up as George and Josh marched in. She brightened up the dull interrogation room with an oversized green tracksuit and platinum hair. A sweet, spicy aroma drifted around the room, a pleasant alternative to BO and sick. He'd only seen Kelly Jarman four hours ago, and yet she'd dyed her hair and had an entirely new wardrobe.

"This is the second time today you've had me hauled in here in a marked police vehicle like some common criminal," she complained as George took a seat. "Not to mention, it's the third time in two days. People are already talking about it!"

"Hello, Kelly," George said cordially. "You remember Detective Sergeant Fry? You're under caution, but you've decided not to have a solicitor present. This conversation will be both audio and video recorded. Okay?"

"What for? I ain't done anything."

"Are you sure you don't want a solicitor?" George asked.

CHAPTER TWENTY-SIX

She shook her head and then shrugged. "Do I need a solicitor?"

"I can't make that decision for you, Kelly." He shrugged. "Anyway, we need to ask you a few more questions." George would not argue. It wasn't for him to tell her she should have a solicitor present. They'd only ask her to say, 'no comment'. He opened the folder on the desk. "I can't believe I'm going to say this, but you lied to me, Kelly." He fixed his eyes on her, giving her nowhere else to look. "I thought we had a mutual understanding? I trusted you."

Kelly began a sucking motion, pursing her lips.

"You knew this guy's name, didn't you?" George said, passing over the photo of the blond man from his folder.

Unresponsive, she stared at him.

"Fine, don't answer. See document ten," George said, sliding over a folder for Kelly to look through. "Document ten shows evidence that this man," George said, pointing at the photo, "was sending you five-hundred quid a month." He leaned forward, inhaling the sweet and spicy scent. "Why?"

She held out a hand, palm up. "You know what I did for a living. Use your bloody imagination!" she snapped.

"Come off it. That would have been in cash, not by BACS. Don't lie to me. What was the money for?"

"No comment."

George smiled whilst he studied her. Her shoulders were tense, her eyes watery. It was the face of a rattled woman who stared back. Detective Superintendent Smith had told him not to intimidate her. But in that moment, as she pouted petulantly, he knew he couldn't keep his promise to Smith. "Come off it, Kelly. It doesn't take a detective to work out that he began paying you maintenance for Ryan, does it?" They'd cross-checked Ryan's birth certificate with the dates on the bank statements. They matched perfectly. "Ryan is his son, isn't he?" He pointed at the photo once more.

She coughed and tried to speak. She stopped and coughed again. A dry throat. A sign of a liar. "Don't be daft. I told you that man disappeared on me."

"What's the point of lying to me? It's there in black and white. He was sending you money for over five years. If it wasn't maintenance for Ryan, then what was it?"

Kelly said nothing. "Tell me. Otherwise, I will arrest you for obstructing a murder investigation."

"Why? I'm not obstructing your murder investigation."

George thought it was time to disclose the nature of the DNA they'd found to Kelly.

"Look, Kelly. Have a look at documents twelve and thirteen in your folder. Those documents contain information about two cases. A cold case from thirty years ago and a current case I'm working on."

"The Bone Saw Ripper?" George nodded. "I have nothing to do with it. Honestly," she said.

"We don't think you do, Kelly. Take a look at documents fourteen and fifteen. Document fourteen is a report from the pathologist during the Jack the Butcher case. You know about it?" She nodded. "Now, DNA was found in the mouth and stomach of one of the victims. Stacey Lumb." Kelly nodded again. "It was semen, and the labs extracted a DNA profile from it. In 1995, when the DNA database was created, it was added to the database, and it's checked every week against all the profiles on there. We received a familial match on Thursday morning."

"A match to Ryan?"

CHAPTER TWENTY-SIX

"Correct. It's a match to Ryan's Y chromosome. It means the semen came from his dad or his brother."

"Okay, I follow you."

"So if this guy is Ryan's dad," George said, pointing to the blond man in the photo, "then there's a chance he could have been the killer."

"No. Not him. He wouldn't—"

"We're not accusing him," DS Fry interrupted. "We just need you to confirm it's him so we can A, find him and request a DNA swab, and B, question him about it. It's important," Josh said.

"It is important," George agreed. "Very important. It's important because of several reasons. You said you'd heard about the Bone Saw Ripper. That's the case I'm in charge of. We found DNA that is a familial match to Ryan's dad. So we need to speak to him about two cases. Who is he? Tell us?"

"No. I know how you guys operate," she said.

George smiled and shook his head. "You've no idea, Kelly. Who is Ryan's dad? Tell us. Now!" He ground his teeth.

She avoided his gaze. The room was silent.

Kelly eventually mumbled a name.

"I didn't catch that," George advised.

"Look, I don't want to get in trouble for lying before. Can you promise me that?"

"Absolutely. Tell me the truth. Now!"

"Okay, Detective. Okay. Yes, he's Ryan's dad. I did some research last night and found out he died, which was obviously why the payments stopped." She stopped and thought for a moment about how to proceed. "I thought his wife had found out, or something like I said before. I was worried about telling you earlier today because they still haven't found the killer, and I didn't want you to think I did it. You know, I didn't want you to accuse me of being a crazy escort woman. Or something like that."

He exhaled. "Why didn't you tell us earlier? I assumed you had something to hide. And anyway, why would you have a motive for his murder? He was paying you maintenance. Why would you want to kill him and stop that?"

"Fair enough. Look, I panicked, okay? You obviously know who Ryan's dad is already, as you haven't asked me for his name."

George said nothing but continued to glare at her.

"Oh, come on. Let's quit the charade. You didn't tell me you needed to speak to him about a murder investigation, did you? And it's shit because now you can't, as he's dead. I tried to call him, you know, but he didn't pick up. He had a mobile number he called my house phone on, but when I called him after he stopped coming, it kept going to voicemail. I guessed it was a burner phone and eventually gave up. I only had a name, really, so even thinking about going to the courts for CSA wasn't feasible. And anyway, with the money stopping, I couldn't afford to hire anyone to look into it. Solicitors cost a fortune."

George nodded. He'd already discussed maintenance with Mia, and they'd agreed he'd continue to pay the mortgage and let them live there rent-free.

"Okay, so to confirm. He was paying money for Ryan?" As George said it, he pointed at the image of the blond man.

She sighed. "Yes. When I got pregnant, he talked to me about leaving his wife and coming to live with us. But he couldn't do it. His daughter was going to be two, and well, he became distant. Until he left," she said as a tear dropped from her eye, "he continued to spend as much time with us as possible, staying over and taking us away. He loved being a dad to Ryan. But something happened. I'm not sure what it was, but he only stayed in Ryan's life for a year, eighteen months. Ryan doesn't even remember him. He continued to pay but ignored any attempt at contact."

"How did you cope when the money stopped?" said George.

"Not very good. It was a shit time." She started to chew her manicured fingernails. "We relied on the money. I had no home address for him; no work address either. All I had was a phone number that went to voicemail. So I did what any mother would do for their son. I got a job. I couldn't carry on being a prostitute with a kid at home, so I got work and got off the drugs."

George nodded. It's precisely what the social worker had said.

"So this guy?" he said and pointed to the photo. "He's Ryan's dad?"

"Correct."

"Okay, so going back to the Bone Saw Ripper. Well, the DNA found at a crime scene also belongs to your son."

"No. Ryan wouldn't. He's a good boy; he wouldn't kill anybody."

George shook his head and exhaled. "No, not Ryan. Thomas."

The colour drained from her face. "Thomas?" she asked, the name slow off her tongue. She looked around the room in a dazed manner. "How did you—"

"See document twenty. It's the adoption certificate. DS Fry checked up on your medical history, and we found that you lied about both having an abortion and giving birth to Ryan's sibling… Why?"

"Their dad… He didn't want me to be involved. Said it was to protect me. I didn't want a kid, but I couldn't—I couldn't abort him."

"This piece of evidence suggests you knew their dad much longer than you've admitted to us. Why didn't you tell the truth?" George asked.

"I remember little from that period… I was fully fucked up. You might not believe me, but I sobered up a lot."

"So, the adoption was your choice?"

"Yes," she said, curling up into a ball in her chair, tears dripping down her cheeks. She was chewing her lower lip, otherwise unmoving. "That's how you know his name already? He—he wanted to be on the certificate too so the child could contact him when he turned eighteen. At the time—at the time, I didn't—"

"Do you know what happened to Thomas?"

She took a deep breath and began to shake. Eventually, she said, "He went with a nice family to live in South Shields. That's all I know." More tears fell down her face, smudging her makeup.

George wasn't sure how much more information he could get out of her, so he changed tack.

"Ryan doesn't know who his dad is, does he?"

Kelly shook her head, unable to speak. It was obvious to George she was tired, both physically and mentally. Tears were now freely flowing down her face.

"It's probably time you told him," George suggested. It was none of his business, but as a soon-to-be dad, he thought it was only right a son deserves to know their father. "I think Ryan has a right to know who his dad was."

"He's dead. What does it matter?"

"A child has the right to know who their parents are, Kelly. As you know, Ryan has a half-sister." She nodded. "To be able to confirm Ryan is Peter's son, I'm going to have to speak to his daughter and ask her for a voluntary DNA sample. We can compare them, despite being half-siblings."

"And you know Peter's daughter?" she asked.

"Yeah," he said, biting his lip. "She's my ex-fiancée and soon-to-be mother of my child."

Chapter Twenty-seven

DI Beaumont and DS Fry pulled their jackets around them as they left the Honda and made their way up the path towards the front door. It had been recently painted a glossy crimson colour, and George wondered who had painted it and why Mia hadn't called him for permission. A new video doorbell greeted them, daring them to press the button.

Instead, George thumped on the door and stood back, nearly knocking into the forensics officer who had followed them from Elland Road HQ.

It took a while, but a woman with an oval face and blonde curls opened the door. She frowned and shook her head. "George," she said. The blonde woman looked at the lanky unshaven, Ray-Ban-wearing detective who had accompanied her ex-fiancé. "No DS Wood?" she questioned, looking at Josh Fry, inspecting the bird's nest atop his head.

"No." A hesitant smile. "No DS Wood today, Mia," George said. He thought she looked ready to burst, wearing leggings and an oversized, knitted jumper that, despite the pregnant belly, reached her knees. George could feel intense heat coming at him from the doorway and said, "Can we come in please, Mia?"

CHAPTER TWENTY-SEVEN

Her face wrinkled with concern. "Sure. Is everything alright, George?"

"Yeah, fine. I'll make the introductions once we're inside. It's freezing out here."

"Oh, okay then. Come in, come in."

The heavily pregnant Mia showed them into the living room. It was stylishly decorated, and a gigantic vase of lilies stood on a low coffee table. "This is a nice house, sir," DS Fry said.

"Thanks, Josh." George sat opposite Mia but couldn't see her through the flowers, so he asked her if he could move them. Mia watched him without comment until he sat down again.

"You know, George, I haven't seen you in a week. What's this all about?" she asked. She didn't offer them tea or coffee, but that was Mia's way.

"Mia, this is DS Josh Fry. He's my deputy on a triple murder case. It's why I've been so busy. You know I love coming to see you. You look ready to burst," he said with a smile.

She frowned, then rolled her eyes. "Hello, Josh. And her?"

"This is Anabel Spencer, a forensics officer from Elland Road."

She raised a perfectly plucked eyebrow. "Right, and?"

"And I need to speak to you about something… sensitive."

"Sensitive?" She raised a brow and scrunched up her face.

She looked cute. It was the same face she used to make when she was confused. It distracted him.

"It—It involves your dad, Peter." He watched her for a reaction, but her cornflower blue eyes barely wavered.

"My dad?"

"Yeah. Have you ever heard the name, Kelly Jarman? Ryan Jarman?"

"Other than the famous Ryan Jarman? The one from The

Cribs?"

He was such an idiot. The name had sounded very familiar, yet he hadn't known why. That was why. Mia's favourite band. "Not Jarman from The Cribs. Ryan Jarman from Holbeck?" She shook her head. Again, her blue eyes barely wavered. "What about Thomas Tweedy?"

"What about it?"

"Do you recognise the name?" asked George, his tone showing impatience.

"No, George, and I'm very good with names. Comes with being a teacher."

George nodded his head. He didn't want to disclose the information that her dad may have been a serial killer, but they needed her to give them a DNA swab they could use in court.

He hesitated. "We have reason to believe that your dad, Peter Alexander, had two children with a woman named Kelly Jarman. Ryan Jarman and Thomas Tweedy. The reason Anabel is here is that we would like you to provide a voluntary DNA sample so we can prove that you're related. We believe Ryan and Thomas are your half-brothers."

"You believe?" she said and stood up, her face turning beetroot. "So you don't actually know? You know what, George, I thought you'd changed. You come here with your half-truths, trying to piss me off!"

George stood up and smiled, holding up his hands. "That's not what I'm trying to do, Mia."

She sighed and sank back onto the sofa. "What makes you think my father slept with this woman, this Kelly Jarman, anyway?"

He nodded his understanding at her question, and Josh attempted a smile. "Because she told us," said George. "There's other evidence, too. The name Peter Alexander appears on Thomas' birth certificate, for example."

"And your evidence for Ryan?"

He looked at Josh Fry, who shrugged. "You're the boss."

"Your father was paying child maintenance for him. Monthly. It was like clockwork until he died."

"Until he was murdered," Mia remarked.

He nodded. "Murdered. Yes. Kelly told us everything. If she's lying, your DNA swab will prove this, and we can move on. Please, Mia."

"All this time, I thought I was alone. If they are my brothers, am I allowed to see them?" she asked.

"I don't see why not. Are you happy for Anabel to take the swabs now?"

She nodded, and Anabel said, "Any allergies to latex?" Mia shook her head, and Anabel put on a pair of blue latex gloves.

After Anabel had taken a DNA swab by rubbing a cotton bud on the inside of Mia's mouth, she put it in a plastic tube and asked if she could drop the sample off at Calder Park. DS Fry saw her out, giving George some privacy with Mia.

"How are you coping?" he asked.

She sighed, then glanced at the clock on the wall. "About as well as expected. I'm fat, I can't see my toes, and I'm alone." She smiled sweetly. "I miss you." He knew she missed him. It was all she spoke about when they were together. Mia wanted the three of them to live in the East Ardsley house together as a family.

"Please, Mia. Don't. Don't make it harder than it has to be. For either of us."

"Suit yourself, Beaumont. If there isn't anything else, then

I think you should leave. I imagine you're busy?"

George nodded. Fair enough. "Have you spoken with any doctors? You're past your due date, right?"

"Yes," she said. "To both questions. They allow you to go a week or two over. Well, no longer than forty-two weeks."

George frowned. "I've got my phone on loud constantly, and I never let it go below fifty per cent charge. You call me when you need me, yeah?"

"Yeah." She looked sad. "I'm sorry for what I—" She took a steadying breath. "Why can't we do this together?"

"We are doing this together. Just separately. It's the best way."

"The best way for who? This isn't what I want."

There was a brief pause as George collected his thoughts. He knew he couldn't tell her this was all her fault, that it was Adam Harris who was stopping them from getting back together. She should never have cheated on him, but George had Isabella Wood now, not that he could share that with Mia. And even if he felt safe sharing it with her, he wouldn't. There was no point in rubbing salt in the wound.

Her mobile phone rang, and after looking down at the caller ID, she got up to answer it. "I need to take this. I'll be right back."

He nodded and took the time to think about whether to broach the subject of the Jack the Butcher murders with her. By the time she got back, he'd decided against it.

"That was the midwife." He nodded. "She was just checking in to see how I feel. I told her I was fine."

George swallowed. "Are you? Fine?"

She nodded. "I am."

"Good. Well, okay. I'd better be off. You ring me when you

CHAPTER TWENTY-SEVEN

need me, yeah? I'll call you every night. I promise."

She nodded and rolled her eyes. "You know me, George. I plan everything. I don't need you to check in with me every night."

George studied her, and Mia watched him studying her. "I know you don't need me to, but I want to. Okay?"

She scowled but raised her brow to show she was joking. "Whatever you say, Detective Inspector."

"Good." He smiled.

George inhaled. "Look, before I go, Mia. I really hope you don't mind me asking this, but did you ever suspect your dad of being unfaithful?"

"You what?" Her eyes blazed. "No, why would I? What a stupid question. Why on earth would you ask me that?"

He hesitated. "I just wanted to know whether you thought he had any other kids he'd —"

"Abandoned?" Mia's eyes widened. "Is that what you were going to say, abandoned?"

He shook his head, watching her reaction. She had every right to be mad, yet it was sincere anger. She knew nothing. "I'm sorry, Mia. That was a terrible mistake I made." He held up his hands. "Abandoned wasn't the word I was going to use. I just need to speak to as many men as I can who would have your dad's DNA. Did he have any brothers or uncles? Is his father still alive?"

She clutched her phone in her lap, and George saw her typing. "My grandpa is still alive. Peter Alexander. Confusing, I know."

"Would you ask him if I could take a DNA sample from him, too? Please, Mia? It's important."

"My grandparents told me they always wanted more grandchildren," she whispered. "My aunt can't have kids, and so

I'm their only grandchild. They'll probably have some of my dad's old stuff you could use to try and get DNA from. I'll call him and ask. I'll ask about a DNA swab, too. Okay?"

George nodded. "That's great," he said. "Thank you, Mia. I really appreciate it."

She walked with George to the door in a trance.

"Thank you, Mia," George said. "You're sure you're okay?"

"Yeah, I'm fine," she croaked, clutching the door handle. "Can you speak with Ryan and Thomas for me, see if they're willing to meet me? I think—I think Nana and Grandpa would like to meet them, too. Oh, and my aunt."

"Okay, if you're sure that's what you want."

She nodded and closed the door. He desperately wanted to go back inside, to see her and comfort her, but he knew it wasn't the right time.

Chapter Twenty-eight

One of the hardest parts of being a detective was admitting you were wrong all along. It was even more challenging when your chief suspect had been framed. George Beaumont had done his job expertly. His attention to detail had been spot on. The interviews had gone smoothly. All the evidence was there. It was plentiful. George used it. He had his man. The CPS told him he had a watertight case. Yet, it was all worthless.

Tony Shaw was innocent. He hadn't killed Rita Lawrence, Alina Hall, Roxy and Sarah Lawson. Nor had he killed Danielle Ferguson. Yet despite knowing that, there was something bugging George, something that made little sense.

He'd gone through the evidence. Twice. Three times. Something that Shaw said. It had been niggling at him. What was it? The librarian? No, it was something else, something he had misinterpreted, something he hadn't worked out. He knew it was there, though, waiting for him, staring at him in the face.

Then he realised it suddenly. Like the sun rising, the light piercing through the darkness. Why on earth was Shaw so adamant it was detectives Smith and Alexander who had framed him? What was their motive? Was it because Alexander had murdered the women thirty years ago?

Maybe. He called DS Fry and ordered him to get Tony Shaw into an interview room at Armley Nick immediately.

* * *

Tony Shaw sat dishevelled and defeated with his pixie solicitor sitting next to him. Even she looked knackered. They informed him he was still under caution. DS Wood was watching from a live video link from a room upstairs in prison.

"I'm being framed," Tony said in a whisper. "Please. Let me go. I'm innocent."

"Explain?" George asked. Despite his friendly tone, Tony Shaw jumped at George's voice and fixed him with a watery look. The man was crying again.

"I was framed thirty years ago, and I'm being framed now," Shaw said.

"Go on, Shaw. Tell me everything."

There was a look of surprise on his worn face. "DI Alexander. And to an extent, DS Smith. Those two bastards were after me thirty years ago. And you're no different, DI Beaumont."

"You're wrong, Shaw," George advised. "As a detective, I have no bias. If I didn't have the evidence to charge you, then I'd have moved on. I don't care about gender, race or creed. Women were killed, and the evidence led back to you. Stop taking this so personal, Shaw."

"How can I not take it personally?" Shaw asked and furiously rubbed his nose. "It was personal thirty years ago, and so it must be now. You detectives don't change!"

"Explain, Shaw. Give me everything. Better you're in here with me than out there?"

CHAPTER TWENTY-EIGHT

Shaw nodded, a look of fear on his face. "DI Alexander framed me for the murders because he didn't like what I was doing."

George frowned. "What were you doing?"

"I was frequenting a prostitute. One DI Alexander thought he had some kind of ownership over." Shaw must have seen the look on George's face as he clarified. "Yes, detective, the DI was a customer, too."

"And you mentioned it at the time?"

"Of course, but everything was recorded differently back then. He used to interview me alone. And when he didn't, it was always DS Smith."

"So you're telling me the reason you were targeted thirty years ago was that DI Peter Alexander wanted you to stop frequenting a certain prostitute?"

"Correct, DI Beaumont."

"Who is she?"

"You expect me to remember some whore's name from thirty years ago? You must be joking. I'm sure you've seen my record, DI Beaumont. I've been done time and time again paying for prostitutes. It doesn't embarrass me. But that one, she was something else. Your DI must have noticed that, too."

George knew who he was talking about. He took out his phone and found the image of Kelly Jarman. "Look familiar?"

Shaw held the mobile phone close to his face. "Yeah, it could be. Is this what all of this is still about? Alexander was a DI thirty years ago. What's he now, a Chief Superintendent? Higher?" George frowned. Clearly, the man knew nothing about Alexander's death. "What?" What's that face for?"

George ignored him for a moment. "This is Kelly Jarman."

"Kelly. Yes. That's her. I—I frequented her regularly.

DI Alexander didn't like it. I wouldn't stop seeing her. He threatened me. Repeatedly. But I never gave up. I wasn't easily intimidated back then, and so I guess when the murders happened, he tried to frame me for them. You still haven't told me why the look on your face changed." He looked at his solicitor, who shrugged.

"What are you not telling us, DI Beaumont?" she asked.

"Peter Alexander was killed in the line of duty over twenty years ago. He's not here pulling the strings trying to frame you, Shaw. But somebody is. Who that somebody is, we're yet to find out, but we're close. Very close."

A look of relief spread across Shaw's face.

"Don't, Shaw. We have a lot of evidence that ties you to the crimes. For all we know, you're involved. You're to remain in remand until further evidence is found that proves otherwise. You understand?"

"Let me make a second bail application," Shaw said. He must have seen the look of hesitation on George's face as he added, "Please, DI Beaumont. I can't be locked up here any more."

"My client has proved valuable to your inquiries. He's been fully cooperative and has helped with further investigation into the murders of three women. He's told you the truth, Inspector, even when you doubted him. If you no longer oppose it, Tony Shaw will willingly surrender his passport and reside at his home address." Shaw nodded. "He will also accept being monitored by an electronic tag."

Shaw nodded again. "Please, DI Beaumont. Don't oppose it. I need to be let out of this terrible fucking place. Please?"

George nodded and stood up. "Thanks, Tony."

He called DS Fry on his way out of Armley Nick. "Josh, send

a marked car to Kelly Shaw's place. Drag her back down to the station, pronto!"

* * *

Mia Alexander had come through for him. Her grandpa had offered a voluntary DNA swab and had given the forensic officer a box of old notebooks and diaries his son, Peter Alexander, had stored at their house in the nineties.

By the time George got them later on that night, they'd already been swabbed and checked for both prints and DNA. Calder Park would get back to him within forty-eight hours with their results, but at least he had the diaries to read through. George hoped they would offer something. Answers as to why he gave up a son, maybe? A reason why his DNA would have been found.

Halfway through, George found something. He wasn't disappointed.

* * *

If looks could kill, then George would be dead four times over. Kelly Jarman didn't speak. She didn't need to. George grinned and took his seat. DS Wood took her rightful place next to him.

"You're under caution, but you have again refused to have a solicitor present. This conversation will be both audio and video recorded. Okay?"

She ignored him.

"Kelly, do you understand what DI Beaumont has just told you?" DS Wood asked.

"Yes. I understand I've refused a solicitor. What I don't

understand is why I've been dragged down here for the fourth time!"

"Something has come up from one of our earlier interviews," DS Wood said. "We need some clarification." She handed Kelly a document.

"That's the initial transcript, and so you can refer to that when necessary," George explained. "Kelly, do you know, or have you ever known, a man called Anthony Shields or Tony Shaw?"

She frowned and shook her head. "Nope." Kelly looked down at her sheet and read it back to George, word for word. "Sorry, love. Those names don't ring any bells. Should they?"

Two can play that game, he thought. "Never had any clients go by that name?"

She grinned and snorted. "I mean, it's been a while since I had those kinds of clients, love. And let's be frank, they never used their real names, anyway. You got a picture of this guy?" Kelly was clearly up for playing games.

So was George. "This was taken recently, Miss Jarman, so he'll be older," George said, handing her the photo of Shaw. He wanted to play the same game with Kelly and so saved the younger picture of Shaw for later.

She didn't even stare at the picture. "Nope."

"Look again."

"Seriously," she said and shook her head. "I'm sick of games, detective. I've never seen this guy in my life. Is that all?" She got up to leave.

"Sit down. You're under caution. One more move, and I'll arrest you," George said.

"On what charge?" She bared her teeth at him.

"Perverting the course of justice," DS Wood said. "Sit down.

CHAPTER TWENTY-EIGHT

Now!"

"I think I might need a solicitor after all."

"Maybe. We can pause this interview at any minute. You just let us know. But all we want to know is whether you recognise this man. Okay?" Wood said and slid the younger image of Shaw across to her.

"Why do you want to know?" Kelly asked.

"Because he's the guy we recently charged for triple murder. He's also the guy who says he's being framed. We believe him. We want to know who is framing him. And you can help. Do you know this man, Kelly?" DS Wood asked.

She held up her hands and looked down at the table. "Fine. Yes. He was an old customer of mine, a greasy bastard who paid well. Anthony Shields. It was regular as clockwork. You see when you're down and out like I was, and you need cash, guys like that are useful. They might be greasy and smelly, but they're reliable."

"If you knew him, why did you lie before? By lying to us, you're impeding our investigation. You are literally—"

"Perverting the course of justice," DS Wood interrupted. "And I will arrest you if you lie to us one more time!"

"I like this woman, Beaumont," Kelly said with a grin. "Where's she been all this time?"

George laughed. "Yeah, she's great. Answer the question."

Kelly held up her hands as if surrendering. "I'm sorry, alright? I've been hiding everything. It was Peter. Okay? He was jealous and possessive and tried to intimidate Shields. Or Shaw. Whatever his name is now. I lied because I didn't want to be involved. That's the truth. Peter intimidated Shaw. Threatened him. But it wasn't just him, though. It was every repeat customer of mine. At first, I didn't know about it. I lost a lot of money, and a few of the punters went elsewhere. I was furious with him."

"Shaw believes Peter tried to frame him for the murders of Hill, Green, Cox and Lumb. Your colleagues," George said. "What do you know about that?"

"I know Peter struggled with the case. They couldn't find the guy. His behaviour became erratic. It wouldn't surprise me if he framed Shaw just to get the case closed. He was under so much pressure. And with his daughter being a few months old, it broke the man down."

DS Wood moved on quickly. "Were you aware of Peter Alexander paying any other prostitutes for sex? Other than yourself, is what I mean. Specifically Hill, Green, Cox or Lumb?"

A dark look stretched across her face. "Once. We had a fight. He took it out on me and got back at me by paying Stacey Lumb for a blowjob."

"Do you remember when this was?" DS Wood asked.

She snorted and shook her head. "Are you kidding me? That entire time period merges into one. It was during the murder cases, though. Jack the Butcher. I know because we'd been fighting about me being out on the streets. He wanted me home and safe, not out working. Endearing, yes. Financially sound, no. I needed the money. He told me he'd give me money. But he couldn't give me enough. I was very dependent on drugs and alcohol, you see? It wasn't enough. I was fucked."

"Okay, thanks, Kelly," George said. Maybe Peter Alexander was innocent after all? What Kelly had just told them explained why his DNA if it was his DNA, was in Stacey Lumb's mouth and stomach. "I have one more question for you. And we won't hesitate to arrest you if we even think that you're thinking

CHAPTER TWENTY-EIGHT

about lying. Okay?"

"Okay."

George thought about the diaries and the entry he'd read just before coming into the interview room. "Did Pete ever mention anything to you about wanting to see Thomas?"

She didn't even think about it. "Once or twice. He felt guilty."

"Did he ever succeed?"

"I've no idea." She looked at both detectives with pleading eyes.

DS Wood slid another piece of paper across the table. There was an image of a page from a diary, its entry transcribed below. Kelly read it and said, "Holy shit."

Chapter Twenty-nine

Saturday morning was icy, dark, and damp when George awoke early and looked out the window of his dingy flat. It had been over a week now since the initial torso and body parts had been found in the bins behind the takeaways in Middleton, yet he didn't feel as if they were any closer to catching the killer. He'd requested a meeting with DSU Smith. Smith didn't work weekends but would come in early on a Saturday if necessary.

It was necessary; he'd told the Super. But only necessary for an hour or two. Smith had promised his wife a day out. He worried the DSU would not like what he had to share.

George needed coffee and so drove to the McDonald's opposite the stadium. After ordering a McMuffin with extra sausage and a large toffee latte, he doubled his order as an afterthought, a bribe for Smith. George appreciated his boss giving him the SIO position after his failings with Adam Harris, and the gift of a McMuffin wouldn't harm his future.

The pills were helping George, too, but the nightmares weren't going away. Last night, he dreamt about Mia and Adam in the woods again and woke up screaming. The face of the murderer he had killed was engrained in his mind. George had to kill Adam before he killed him or Mia. He'd used a rock to beat his brains out before he could do anything to harm either of them. With his mind's eye, he could see Adam's face disintegrating beneath the blows and feel Adam's blood speckling his skin.

They called his memories and nightmares PTSD. A psychiatric disorder that can affect people who have experienced or witnessed a traumatic event. It was a disorder of the brain, the magnificent, complex organ that was compensating for the horror it had encountered. Mia struggled. The last time they spoke on the phone, she admitted she still struggled.

He was a fighter, a warrior. George knew he would recover from the PTSD eventually, but it was not knowing how long it would take to recover that made George even more anxious. The therapist who had cleared him to be back at work six months ago didn't know half of what was going on inside his head, the turmoil indescribable. Killing another human with a rock in his hands had, quite rightly, fucked him up. The only way he could deal with that was by drinking alcohol, but Isabella and his doctor had soon become aware the alcohol made him detached and desensitised to the people he loved and his surroundings. He thought the alcohol was helping him to survive and adapt, yet all it was doing was dulling his brain, making his symptoms worse rather than better. It's why he felt the way he did at the Lawson house.

"Thanks for putting me as SIO on the triple murder case, sir," George said, offering the goods from McDonald's.

Smith laughed and raised a brow. "I'm getting a bit of déjà vu. Are you bribing me, Beaumont?"

George placed the items on Smith's desk and was nodded to a chair to sit down. "No, sir. Just showing my appreciation. Thanks again. Do you want me to come back, or can we start the briefing now?"

"We can do it now, Beaumont, as long as you're happy to talk whilst I eat?"

"That's fine with me, sir," George said with a laugh. "I haven't updated HOLMES yet because I wanted to tell you in person."

Smith looked up from unwrapping his McMuffin and nodded before frowning. "Tell me what in person?"

George hesitated, and Smith raised a questioning brow. "Jack the Butcher?" Smith nodded. "We have firm evidence that points to Peter Alexander as being the killer."

"You what, Beaumont? Peter Alexander was SIO on the case! What're you trying to pull?" He took a bite out of the muffin, the grease from the sausage dripping onto the table.

George shook his head with a smile. "Nothing, sir. I'm sorry to tell you, but it looks as if it was him."

His boss' gaze dropped to the coffee cup George had placed on his desk. When he eventually looked back up, there was no smile there. "Tell me everything."

George did, explaining the DNA profile they'd extracted from the semen found thirty years ago was a familial match to a man named Ryan Jarman, who was wrongly arrested in the city centre for burgling a café and stabbing a police officer. The DNA from the Y chromosome matched, meaning Ryan's grandad, dad, or brother, was the one who most likely murdered the four women thirty years ago.

Smith nodded his understanding. "I always wondered how long it would take before we got a match on the system. I expected a while, but not thirty years. So from what you're saying, Peter was Ryan's dad?"

"Correct, sir. We pulled in Kelly Jarman, Ryan's mum, as

you know."

"Aye, I remember you telling me. I didn't realise it was connected."

"Well, sir, she confirmed Peter was a regular customer of hers. She told us eventually that he was Ryan's dad. Mia's half-brother. It turns out he was paying Kelly maintenance for Ryan until he died."

"Murdered, Beaumont. He was murdered. We still haven't found the bastard who did it."

George nodded. "At first, she wouldn't tell us who Ryan's dad was; her story was that she got knocked up a lot as she was a sex worker and men used to refuse to wear condoms. She told us she had quite a few abortions."

"And you checked her medical records?"

"Correct, sir. Well, Josh Fry did. It turns out she'd given birth to a child but gave said child up for adoption. Josh spoke with the Adoptions Section in Southport, and they provided the adoption certificate. She had a child they'd named Thomas, who was adopted by a family in South Shields with the surname Tweedy. I've got Josh on it as we speak."

"On what, Beaumont?"

"Well, as you already know, sir. During the search of Tony Shaw's flat, Stuart Kent found a blond hair, its follicle intact. Calder Park extracted a DNA profile from it, but it didn't match any of the profiles on the databases. Now," he said with a grin, "it *was* a familial match to Ryan Jarman's DNA profile, and the DNA profile we suspect is Peter Alexander's from thirty years ago."

"Right. A match to both Ryan and Peter?"

George nodded. "A familial match. It means it wasn't them, but our culprit, Jack the Butcher, is related to them."

"And?"

"And, sir, Stuart Kent found a blond hair in the burnt-out Fiat Punto. DS Wood's case."

Smith frowned once more. "Yeah, he did. And it matched the one from Shaw's flat, right?" George nodded. "So you believe the female body found in Springhead Park is related to the triple murder case you're working on?"

George nodded. "The Bone Saw Ripper case."

"Fucking press and their stupid names... I don't see it, George," Smith said. "Are we sure it isn't contamination of the scene? DCI Peterson was wary of Hayden Wyatt, the American SOCO. Apparently, he wasn't the most skilled at leaving no traces behind."

"I didn't see it at first either, sir. I also had my doubts about Wyatt. But look at it this way. The killer must have known we charged Shaw. To keep killing, they have to change the way they kill or risk Shaw being released. But they don't have to change why. I don't think the MO is dismembering any more. I think it's killing sex workers and escorts. Danielle Ferguson, according to DS Wood's reports on HOLMES, was well known for being a sex worker and an escort. The fact that we have two blond hairs that are A, from the same person, and B were found during two separate murder investigations means to me they're related."

Smith thought for a quick moment, and George could see the cogs turning. "So you're saying Peter and Kelly's child, Thomas, is the Bone Saw Ripper?"

George tried to hide his smile. "Yes. Actually. That's exactly what I'm saying, sir. As I said, Josh has asked the Royal Courts of Justice for any information regarding a name change for Thomas Tweedy. We have his date of birth from Kelly's medical records and the date of adoption and full name from the adoption certificate. We find Thomas, or whatever he's called now, and we find the killer. As soon as that information comes back, I want a warrant so that I can arrest him."

The Super was nodding. "What do we do about Peter Alexander, sir?" George asked. "I went down to Mia Alexander's house with a forensic officer. She gave a voluntary DNA swab so we can confirm that Ryan and Thomas are related to Mia. Same for her grandad, Peter Alexander Sr., as he's apparently the only male still alive."

"Fine, Beaumont. Good work."

George could see Smith looked hurt. There was a change in his body language, a darkening of his expression. "Does his DNA being in the mouth of a victim mean he was the killer, sir?" George asked, referring to Peter Alexander being Jack the Butcher.

"I don't know." Jim Smith looked defeated. "Have you shared this with anybody else, George?"

"No, sir," he said, shaking his head. "Other than Josh, anyway. He was in the interview room with me. The forensic scientist who matched the profiles also knows. I haven't updated HOLMES yet."

"Okay, leave it with me. I'm not convinced Peter was Jack the Butcher. He was very passionate during the case. And he loved his wife, Mia's mother. I remember him being so excited about her being pregnant. But that semen had to get into the victim's mouth somehow. Whether that was Peter himself or whether he was framed, I don't know. Neither makes any sense." The Super said nothing for a minute, or two and George sat patiently. "Leave it with me, George. Please?"

"Okay, sir. Let me know when you want me to include his

name on HOLMES, okay?"

The Super nodded. "Is there anything else?" George shook his head, not wanting to discuss what he'd heard in the stairwell. There were three Geordies involved with the triple murder, and Jim Smith was one of them. The Super got up and opened his office door. "I'll let you get back to whatever it was you were doing, George."

A clear dismissal. George got up, thanked his boss and headed towards his own office.

* * *

A couple of hours later, and after finally updating HOLMES with information regarding Ryan and Kelly Jarman, George thought it was time to go home. It had been a busy day, and as it was the weekend, it may be Monday now until he had all the information he needed to seek the killer. He'd done exactly as DSU Smith had requested and left Alex Peterson's name out of the reports, knowing he could update them on Monday once Smith gave him the go-ahead.

He stood up, and his phone rang.

"Sir, it's Josh. I've just got the info you wanted back from the Royal Courts of Justice, and I've emailed it to you. You're not going to believe who it is."

George clacked away at his keyboard and opened up the email. A smile spread across his face. They'd found the fucker.

"I knew it was him, Josh. Holy shit!"

Chapter Thirty

"I want a tail on DSU Peterson twenty-four seven, sir," George bellowed down the phone.

"The Detective Chief Superintendent won't allow it," came DSU Smith's calm response. "I'm sorry, George, he's put his foot down. He's the same rank as me now, and so I need authorisation. You have no direct evidence implicating DSU Peterson in the murders, and we're over budget already. I have to tell you, he's thinking about pulling the plug."

"No, sir! You can't let that happen. We have plenty of evidence. Information received from the Royal Courts of Justice strongly suggests DSU Peterson is Thomas Tweedy, the son of Peter Alexander and Kelly Jarman, who was adopted by the Tweedy family up in South Shields. We have familial DNA, which proves Ryan Jarman's sibling murdered and dismembered four women. I'm waiting for Mia's DNA results, but I don't need to. I'm confident it's him. If you can't authorise a tail, can you at least authorise the collection of a DNA sample?" George held his breath, and when the DSU didn't reply, he added, "DCS Sadiq is letting his loyalty impede justice. We're so close, sir. He did it. I know he did."

"Your gut feeling isn't enough, Beaumont," Smith said. "Peterson is a high-ranking officer of the law. You need more."

"For fuck's sake!" George slammed his hand on his desk. "Sorry, sir. Somebody is blocking the investigation. I know it! Even his disclosure checks back from when he entered the force show he used to be Thomas Tweedy. Please, sir, for me. Call the Chief Super. Tell him about the name and the adoption certificate. Explain Peterson's not on the CED, and we need a DNA sample to eliminate Peterson from our inquiry."

"Fine, Beaumont. But it's late—"

"It's only half five, sir."

"He never answers his phone when he's not at the station, and I know for a fact he went home. Once I speak with the Chief Super, I'll let you know what he says. Don't be doing anything stupid in the meantime."

DSU Jim Smith ended the call, and George immediately called DS Wood. He filled her in on what the Super advised him.

"I'll have to tail him, then. Peterson knows we're onto him, and I think he's going to run."

"You can't tail him by yourself. Don't be an idiot, George."

"Why not? Nobody else is going to do it. It's him; I know it is." He scratched his beard. George could feel the stress elevating his blood pressure.

"Okay, George, but promise me you'll be careful," Wood said. "If he is the Bone Saw Ripper, then he's dangerous and unpredictable. The man's meticulous and highly trained. He's a big fucker, too. If you put him in a tight spot, you don't know how he'll react."

"He might go to the gym a lot, but he's a desk jockey, Wood. I think he'll do a runner."

"Fine, keep me informed. If he does a runner, let me know, and I'll send uniform over."

"Thanks, Gorgeous."

CHAPTER THIRTY

George hung up, then tried Stuart Kent, wanting to know if they'd found anything else in the burnt-out Punto. It went straight to voicemail.

Next, he called DS Josh Fry. "I need you back at the station."

"Okay, sir. On my way. Is everything okay?"

"Yeah. The—the Super has authorised a tail on Alex Peterson," he lied. "Me. I want you here to run ops. Okay?"

"Sir."

* * *

Josh texted him Peterson's registration number as he made the journey to Bradford. After finding the underground police car park, it took him ten or fifteen minutes to find the Toyota Corolla navy blue hatchback. Then he parked up on a side street where he could monitor the exit.

An hour later, Alex's Toyota exited the car park, and George slunk down in the Honda's seat as Alex drove by. He counted to twenty and then pulled out and followed, keeping a safe distance away. Josh had already sent another text with Alex Peterson's home address, and from the route, he was taking, that was where he was headed. Hopefully, the Chief Super hadn't made him aware of their knowledge, but it was just his luck. Sadiq had let the cat out of the bag. He hoped it was the other way around, that he'd give George a warrant. Would there be a warning issued out of loyalty? One that left little time for him to get out of the city?

George hoped not.

George took the familiar roads back from Bradford to Churwell, where Alex lived. Alex reversed into his drive, and George pulled in behind a white Ford van and switched off the engine.

From his vantage, he saw Alex climb out of the car. Alex walked to the end of his drive and stood still for a moment, glancing up and down the street. Had the DCS warned him? Were they in it together?

After a minute of watching, obviously satisfied, DSU Peterson went into his house.

George knew he could be there all night, so he settled down to wait. The best time to leave would be during the early hours, under cover of darkness.

Kent's phone was still going straight to voicemail. Was it the guy's day off? Even if it were, a man like Stuart Kent wouldn't be the type of guy to turn it off. Something deep within his chest told him he should worry.

His phone rang, interrupting his thoughts, and instead of allowing it to go to the speaker system in the Honda, he answered his mobile.

"How's the tail going, sir?" It was Josh.

"It's fine. I'm outside his house. If he leaves, I'll let you know."

"DS Wood is here with me. She took down Mia's sample to Calder Park personally. Pulled a few strings," he said. "It's a match for both samples."

He'd thought they would, but it was nice to be confirmed. All they needed now was another profile to cross-reference, and bingo! "Good. All we need now is Alex Peterson's DNA to match."

"Do you think a court will be convinced it's DSU Peterson?" Josh asked. "All we have is the blond hairs." He heard the concern in Josh's voice. They still had no heads. Alina's torso was still missing, as were limbs from Sarah Lawson and Rita Lawrence. He felt for their friends and families, especially as they couldn't bury or cremate their loved ones until the investigation was over. If they found those body parts, then they may find other pieces of evidence to tie the DSU to the crimes. "It worries me because we might only get him for Danielle Ferguson's murder because the other three had a different MO, and his hair could be explained as being transferred from his DC during the search. Do you think Holly was involved?"

George thought for a moment before speaking. "Nah, a man like that does all the dirty himself. Holly is a great DC. I don't think she's involved at all. Too risky. He's probably working alone." George hadn't told Josh about his concerns about the DCS. He was also a Geordie, and he still wasn't sure it was Alex who Stuart was arguing with in the stairwell. "As for a court, it depends whether he confesses. All we can do is provide what we have and hope for the best. What we won't do is stop. The Super refused warrants to check Alex's call and text history and to impound his phone for location data purposes."

"Okay, sir. Keep in touch with us, yeah?"

Why was the Super obstructing the investigation? It made no sense. George thought back to the argument in the stairwell. A Geordie. Stuart's boss. It wasn't DSU Smith, was it? Was he leading them in the wrong direction? No. He trusted the man. Smith had done nothing that George doubted.

George tried Kent again, wanting to know if they'd found anything else in the burnt-out Punto. It went straight to voicemail.

***

It was half-past one in the morning when the door opened,

and Alex Peterson came out. The house was in darkness. He wondered whether Alex had a family. A wife and kids, like his dad, had when he'd murdered those four innocent women thirty years ago.

George followed Alex with his eyes, noticing he was carrying a large sports bag, which he tossed into the back seat of the Toyota. After another satisfying look around, he climbed in behind the wheel and switched on the engine.

All he'd taken was one large sports bag. This guy wasn't running. No. But he was going somewhere, and George needed to know where.

Peterson headed north on the A6110, eventually turning right onto Gelderd Road. He wasn't fleeing the country going that way, and George smiled. It worried him at first, as continuing down the A6110 would take him to Leeds and Bradford Airport. Alex probably had no clue he was being followed; he probably did not know he was even a suspect. Good.

George followed him, keeping out of sight, which was difficult because of the hour. There were barely any cars on the road, but more than George had expected. That was also good.

Peterson continued down Gelderd Road and took the third exit on the roundabout onto Domestic Road. George followed, passing the storage company. Had DSU Alex Peterson dressed up as Tony Shaw to plant evidence? As far as George could tell, Shaw and Peterson didn't know each other from Adam, their only link being Alex's biological father.

George called Josh, who told him DS Wood, DC Tashan Blackburn, and DC Terry Morton had met him at the station. George gave them an update on where he was. The connection

CHAPTER THIRTY

was awful, and he knew by the echo Josh had put him on speakerphone.

"I'm going to get in my car and follow you," DS Wood said tersely. "Something has me worried, George. I think you'll need backup."

"I'm coming too. We're leaving in separate cars now," Tashan added.

"I'm staying here, sir," Josh said. "I'll keep running ops. You need me, you call. Yeah?"

"Yeah, cheers, Josh."

Peterson made a loop around the city of Leeds, first heading past the escort agency down Water Lane, turning right at The Dalek building, the affectionate nickname of Bridgewater Place, before looping back up Great Wilson Street onto Crown Point Road and over the River Aire. Both Wood and Tashan checked in with him every five minutes, taking it in turns. George could hear them talking between themselves, clearly having brought radios from the station.

"We're about ten minutes behind you, sir," Tashan said as George reached the roundabout where the former Leeds police HQ, Millgarth police station, had been demolished and replaced by a shopping centre. He was surprised Tashan and Wood hadn't made up any of the distance.

Despite that, it felt good knowing he wasn't alone and that they were coming. Especially DS Wood. The lights of the city flickered in the darkness. It had started raining, and the darkness above continued to swallow up the moon. Now and then, George saw it darting behind low-lying clouds as if it was anxious about what was about to happen.

George hadn't thought about what he was going to do when Alex eventually stopped. There was a reason he'd put on his soft vest and duty belt, though. These days, he made sure they were always in his car or on his person.

Peterson indicated left but raced around the roundabout, heading back down the A61 down Duke Street. George saw the Toyota as it sped through a red light down the A61 towards the Richmond Hill area of the city. From there, he could just about get anywhere. It was a stupid place to lose him. *Fucking hell!* George raced through the red light himself and hurriedly dialled DS Wood's number. "I think I might have lost him, Wood," he yelled.

"Shit! Do you need me to put out an APB?" Wood asked.

George felt stupid. The Honda had followed Alex for miles. It was obvious he knew. *Fucking hell!* "Hold off for now. I'm going to keep looking around. Wait, I think I see him." On the other side of the barrier, George saw Alex's navy Corolla blasting down the A61 north. "I've found him, Wood. He's heading back into the city centre."

With the traffic light on the roads, George risked a right, taking him on the opposite side of the road on Cross Green Lane, praying he wouldn't meet any vehicles coming the other way. He didn't. George's tyres screeched again as he took another sharp right, back onto the A61 north. As he did so, he saw the navy Corolla head left down a slip road before turning left again down by the River Aire.

George followed slowly, turning off his lights and coasting down the hill. At the bottom was a housing complex that went by the name Secret Garden. *What was Alex doing here?*

Whatever it was, neither Wood nor Tashan wouldn't make it in time. If Peterson were waiting for him, he'd have no choice but to take him down alone. Surely Alex had already realised it was the same set of headlights that had followed him all the way from home. Hopefully not, but as they'd left the city centre, the lack of traffic meant it was possible. He hoped the presence of delivery vans, lorries, and shift workers going about their business would have helped him blend in and stay unnoticed.

He opened his window and smelled the water from the river. It was stagnant. He heard the sound of a car door being slammed as his tyres crunched on the gravel track. Was Alex waiting for him around the corner? Probably. He pulled over and switched off the engine. After sending a quick text to Wood with the words, 'Secret Garden,' he retrieved his vest and belt from the backseat and got out of the car quietly. He crept down the gravel track and around the corner, following the indents Peterson's car had made.

He rounded a bend and saw Alex unlocking the door to one of the houses, his sports bag in one hand.

Oh, shit. Now what?

There could be anybody in that house. At least out here, he had the advantage. He called Wood and placed the phone in his pocket.

"DSU Peterson, stop what you're doing now!" he shouted, shattering the stillness of the silence.

He spun around and looked at George. "Beaumont? George, is that you? Jesus, what's wrong with you?"

"Nothing, sir. I'm arresting you on suspicion of the murders of Danielle Ferguson, Rita Lawrence, Alina Hall, and Sarah Lawson—"

"I'm innocent, you prick," Alex Peterson said, walking towards George, dropping his bag and placing his hands up in the air. "Trust me; I'm not your guy. I'm here, following a lead. Call DCS Sadiq." He placed a hand inside his pocket and said, "Here, use my phone."

"Hands where I can see them, Peterson." Alex placed both hands up in the air. "You do not have to say anything. But, it may harm your defence if you do not mention when questioned, something which you later rely on in court. Anything you do say may be given in evidence."

George took a step closer, reaching for the cuffs on his duty belt, momentarily distracted.

It was enough. Alex Peterson noticed the distraction and relaxed his body. He placed his left leg forward and his right leg back, clenching his fist. George wasn't looking up; he was looking down, wondering why the cuffs wouldn't come free.

Then Alex stepped into the punch, twisting his hips to generate maximum force. At the exact moment Alex stepped in, George felt a chill at the base of his neck. He didn't know what it was, but the signal was too late, as Alex's fist crashed into his head directly between the hairline and the eyebrows, his knuckles following through. George's head snapped to the side, the force of the blow causing George's brain to swing violently against the skull lining.

Like a marionette with its strings cut, George plunged to the ground.

All went black.

Chapter Thirty-one

As Alex Peterson dragged DI Beaumont down the cellar steps, he whistled a silly tune. George was still unconscious, and there was blood dripping from his mouth. Alex sat him on the floor and used cable ties to fasten George's hands to a lally column.

Kelly Jarman opened her eyes, groggy from the drugs, and screamed when she saw George. It was a distressed scream. She had been hysterical all day, and it pissed Alex off. He had to threaten to saw off a limb to shut her up.

Crime Scene Co-ordinator Stuart Kent was still unconscious, and Ryan Jarman had been quiet, considering his precious mum was also tied up and injured in a cellar. The four of them were each sitting on the floor, their hands tied to a separate lally column arranged into a square. The only light in the cellar came from a single low-wattage bulb that swung on its wire above, making it impossible to see into the corners of the dingy room.

The arrival of George hadn't changed the dynamic of the room. Despite knowing he was terrified, Ryan's calm demeanour had surprised Alex, but his mum's hadn't. The slut. The abandoner. Filthy whore! She continued to wail, begging for mercy, pleading for forgiveness. The dirty bitch! Before the night was up, she'd pay most of all. Alex smiled at her, and her distress became uncontrollable again.

He switched on the spotlight.

"Stop crying, Kelly or I'll saw Ryan to bits right in front of you," Alex said, matter of fact. He looked at her and grinned. "Or should I call you Mam?" Kelly groaned. "Oh, don't groan at me like that. You're mi mum. You gave birth to me, after all." He shrugged. "What makes him so much more special than me?" he asked, waving his surgical bone saw at Ryan. She said nothing. "Mam? Huh? No? Answer me!" Kelly Jarman closed her eyes as he waved about the surgical saw and tried to pretend she was somewhere else. She stopped crying to protect her child. "Ah, silence. That's better."

Stuart Kent's head snapped around the room, blinking against the glare, the room coming into focus.

"Ah, Kent the cunt. Did you know Kelly was mi birth mam?" Alex asked, smiling. Kent had seen Kelly Jarman in images on HOLMES 2, yet he barely recognised the older lady that looked back at him. She had been crying; her eyes were red and swollen. "Say hello to Stuart Kent, the cunt, Mam," Alex said. Kelly blinked at Alex and then scowled at him. Then she focused her eyes on the floor. "Don't be rude, Mam. When I ask you to do something, you fucking do it. Say hello!"

"I'm not your fucking mum!" she snapped. "I knew you were evil from the moment I first held you. If this is about getting back at me, then fine, but let the others go. Especially Ryan. He's innocent, Alex. He knew nothing about you until you kidnapped him. Let everybody else go. Please."

"Are you going to say hello to the idiot Crime Scene Co-ordinator?"

"No! Let them all go, Alex. Please. They're innocent."

CHAPTER THIRTY-ONE

"Even my own flesh and blood won't greet you, Stuart Cunt. I apologise for her rudeness," Alex said.

George awoke and groaned as his eyes focused. There was a metallic taste in his mouth. He looked around and examined the situation. It wasn't looking good. Alex Peterson, dressed in a white protective coverall with his hood up, blue shoe covers and blue disposable gloves, looked as if he had finally lost his mind. There was an air of menace that surrounded him, an aura of evil. George twisted his wrists slightly to test his bonds. They were secure. George's heart thrummed as a man across the room, also tied to a lally column, caught his eye. It was Stuart Kent, battered and bruised. To his right were the Jarmans, Kelly and Ryan.

"Look who's finally awake," Peterson said as he kicked George in the ribs. "I'm glad you're finally with us, Detective." He followed his gaze to the Jarmans. "You've noticed my other guests? Are you impressed?"

"What... What's going on, Alex?" George asked, in pain. His words sounded funny. His jaw hurt. "Why are we all here?"

"For my hobby, George."

"Hobby?"

"To be butchered, of course. I'm the Bone Saw Ripper! My father, Jack the Butcher, managed four bodies. I've already managed four of my own. You four are next. I'll be fucking famous!"

"So you were the Ripper, after all. I was right?" George said. He noticed the bone saw in Alex's hand. If he could get it, they could tie that weapon to the victims.

"You've known it was me for a while, Detective."

"No. I didn't. Not fully." George looked around the room. They were all sitting on a scarlet-coloured carpet. "Not until now, anyway. The carpet and the saw are dead giveaways."

He nodded. "Soaks up bloodstains. You don't seem surprised to see me, though, Detective Beaumont."

"I'm not. It was you in the stairwell with Stuart?"

Peterson frowned but nodded in answer. "You'll notice your phone is missing. Do you think I'm stupid, Beaumont? Did you think I wouldn't notice you had DS Wood on the line? You're the idiot, Beaumont. I led you here. To your death. You should have done as you were told and kept Shaw in remand." George shook his head and grimaced. He vaguely remembered being hit. "Then again, that's your biggest problem. Despite having a clear suspect, you kept looking elsewhere. I guess that's why you and my sister broke up; why you've been shagging your DS?"

"You're the biggest problem, Alex," Kelly said, interrupting him. "From the day you were born, you were a problem. I think back and always wonder why your dad never stuck around. It was you! He sorted out the adoption because he couldn't stand you," she shouted and shook her head.

"Do kindly shut up, Mam," Alex said. "My adopted mum always said, 'If you can't say anything nice, say nothing at all.' She was a pleasant woman. Not at all a bitch or a slut like you!"

"Pleasant? I hope so. She clearly didn't do a good job raising you, though, if this is how you turned out!" she screamed. "Fucking psychopath!"

"Shut up, Mam." The Geordie in his voice became more pronounced the angrier he got. He flushed red. "You're doing my fucking head in!"

"Your head is already fucking done in!" Kelly said. "What the hell do you think you're doing? Ryan is your family, Alex, and so am I. Let us go. Turn yourself in. Please."

CHAPTER THIRTY-ONE

"I don't fucking think so. Once I'm done with you, Mam, I'm going to teach both Beaumont and Stuart Cunt a lesson," Alex said. The atmosphere was tense, and Alex looked utterly unpredictable. Stuart Kent looked up and listened; George watched in silence. George could sense Alex was on edge. "That stupid cunt couldn't let it go." He turned and faced Kent. "You went behind my back. I bet you two had a right laugh talking about me, didn't you? Stuart?" Stuart shook his head. "I'll lose everything if I let you go. So you all need to know it's not happening."

"They're innocent people, Alex. Let them go. Please?" his mum asked.

"No. They let an innocent man free, and they must take his place."

"Shaw is innocent," Kent piped up.

"Shaw isn't an innocent man!" Peterson said, his tone childlike. "No, he's far from innocent. I'll give him a year or two and kill him myself. If I kill him now, everything will be connected. I won't let that happen again."

"There's only one person in this room who deserves to die!" she shouted. "Let the others go!"

"Be quiet, Mam, or I'll saw out your voice box and hand it to you whilst it's still warm!" Alex looked at her, and she glared back. He wasn't sure where this bravado had come from, especially as all she had done earlier was cry, cry, and cry again.

George sent a warning glare her way. He didn't think Alex was bluffing. George could see it in Alex's eyes. There was nothing there, just eyes completely void of emotion. The woman opposite George may have been Alex's blood mother, but it meant absolutely nothing to him. George could see that. He wondered whether she was the reason he had initially targeted sex workers. The look in Alex's eyes told him he was right. To Alex, she was a slut, a dirty bitch; he didn't care she had given birth to him.

"You don't frighten me, Peter," she said. "I always thought there would be a day you'd turn up. I'll be honest and say I wasn't expecting it like this, but I never once thought you'd greet me with open arms. This is my fault. I'll take responsibility because your piece of shit father can't. He forced me to give you up, you know—"

"I won't tell you again, Mam. Shut the fuck up!" There was a menace in his voice, a menace that scared George. He glared at Kelly again, trying to let her know she was pushing her luck. He continued to try to slip out of the cable ties.

She shook her head. "It's me you want. The slut. The whore bitch. I abandoned you. Let Ryan go. He's an innocent boy."

Alex walked over and stood next to Kelly. She looked up at him with fierce eyes. He grasped her brown curls with his left hand, tilted her head back, and drew the surgical saw across her throat.

Chapter Thirty-two

Kelly Jarman struggled violently against her ties as Alex continued to saw backwards and forwards. Ryan screamed, the sound of metal ripping through flesh and bone distressing to hear.

Crimson gushed from the wound, and Peterson held her chocolate curls in his hand. Soon her head was severed from her neck, and the light had left her eyes. Kelly Jarman's body fell to the carpet and twitched. Soon, the smell of Kelly's blood that was dripping on the carpet filled the air. Alex brought the severed head to his eye level and looked her dead in the eye.

For the first time, George thought Alex looked disturbed. A single tear fell from his left eye. The bone saw, bloodied by his mum's blood, clattered to the floor. George knew this might be his only moment to break free, so he shuffled up against the column and turned his wrists, so they faced inwards. He tried to get his thumb out first, but they had been tied securely. George continued to try to slip his hands out of the ties.

George stopped when Alex Peterson looked his way, his body still. He didn't want to attract his attention and be next. He knew it would only take one wrong move to set Alex off.

"Ryan, I'm sorry about Mam. It was her own fault. She didn't listen," Alex said, shrugging. "I told her to shut up. You're a witness," he said as he wiped the blood from his gloved hands onto a rag tied to his coverall. "Was she always like that, Ryan?" Alex asked as he stepped closer to his brother. Ryan shook his head. "Are you sure? The stupid cow blamed me for Dad leaving. That's bullshit. I know the reason he left, and it wasn't because of me. He left because he wanted me but didn't want your whore of a mum to know! You cried all the fucking time, apparently. You were always in their bed, ruining whatever fun Dad wanted. A hooker with a baby. Dad lost interest in you both."

Ryan Jarman was trying to hold it together, but panic came in waves. He didn't want to antagonise his brother like their mum had done and was choking back sobs, his breathing short and sharp. Tears were freely flowing down his face.

"You not interested in Dad, then Ryan?"

Stuart Kent kept eye contact with him, trying to reassure him. Exactly what Kent could reassure him about was beyond George. As far as George was concerned, their position couldn't get any worse. They were trapped. Helpless. He wasn't even sure where they were.

Ryan looked at his brother and eventually shook his head.

"No? Why? Because he was a murderer, too? I have a plan, you know—a good one. I think you'll like it. The two of us could become a team. Kill George, Stuart, and then Andrés García. I know what he did to you, Ryan. After that, your fourth will be Tony Shaw. I think it's a fucking fantastic idea. Don't you?"

Peterson walked toward his brother and handed him the saw. When Ryan refused to take it, Peterson forced it into his hands.

Ryan knew then the chances of them getting out of the cellar alive were practically zero. So did Stuart; Ryan's prints were now on the murder weapon. For Ryan, his brother had moved from being a stalker and a hunter to snatching his family and the police. He'd also killed their mother. There was no way to return from this. The two men knew.

But not George. George had a plan; he just needed to keep Peterson talking. His demeanour had changed. Killing his mother had affected him. That was clear. It looked to George as if he was disintegrating from the inside out. Yet the consequences of Alex's actions were no longer of any concern to him, and that was what worried George. He'd encountered men like that before, men who no longer cared what happened to them. The endings were never good.

The last time it had happened, George had killed the man.

Thud, crash. Thud, crash. Thud, crash.

"You don't look so good, George," Peterson said. He sounded concerned. "Do you need to be sick? Is it the meds? Oh, don't look so surprised. I know all about the PTSD and the meds your doctor gave you. It gives me great pleasure, you know. You may have survived Adam Harris, but you won't survive me!"

George said nothing but met his gaze.

"Scary, scary. You know, George, you're making me edgy, and I'm not sure it's good for me or you if I'm edgy. All it takes is one little slip of the wrist, and you end up like mi Mam. Okay? You too, Ryan!" Alex said, turning and facing his brother. With his back to George, he tried to slip his thumb out of the cable tie again.

As George struggled with his bindings, Ryan Jarman shook his head, his eyes bulging. He took a few breaths to calm down.

"Good, Brother. That's better. You don't need to be afraid of me. Well, not unless you decide to turn me down. You're not going to do that, though, are you?" When his brother said or did nothing, he walked over to Stuart Kent. "Now then, Stuart. You've been quiet. Too fucking quiet! Here we are, face to face, again. The last time we spoke, you got all high and mighty. You even pushed me in the stairwell, you cunt!" he screamed in his face, spit flying in all directions.

Stuart Kent closed his eyes, unable to speak as his mouth was dry with fear. George thought that was a good thing as he watched the pair in between fighting his bonds. He'd got both thumbs free, but his fingers were swollen, and he was struggling to get them free. He didn't like what he saw, though. His grip on reality was loosening, the murdering detective slipping further and further into madness.

"This is all your fault, Stuart. I hope you know that. We had Shaw wrapped up neatly with a bow on top," Peterson said, looking at him. "I even had this idiot eating out of the palm of my hand." Peterson pointed at George. "Call yourself a detective, Beaumont? Every time I put pressure on you, you did as you were told. And when that didn't work, I went hot and cold. It was so easy to knock you down a peg and then apologise for it. You were so willing to please me, so willing to do what you were told."

"That's why you apologised, then?" George asked. Alex nodded and laughed. "Tell me about Shaw," George said. "He told me Peter Alexander tried to frame him thirty years ago because he kept paying to fuck your mum!"

The look on Peterson's face was priceless, and George continued. "Kelly agreed. She told me Peter was jealous and possessive, and after noticing Shaw frequented her, Peter tried to intimidate him; keep him away from his woman. I've read the reports on HOLMES, as I assume you have. They had plenty of eyewitness testimony that proved Shaw frequented prostitutes, especially your mum and the victims, Green, Cox and Lumb. But that was it. They found DNA, but it wasn't a match for the sample Shaw provided. Alexander and Smith couldn't make any charges stick. It sounds to me as if your dad was trying to frame Shaw. Is that why you were doing the same?"

"Something like that," Alex said.

"Tell me, Alex, it was you in the CCTV footage dumping the body parts, wasn't it?"

"Of course, it was, you idiot."

"And in Sainsbury's? You purchased the items with cash, dressing up to look like Shaw? We had you on CCTV, and the checkout girl identified Shaw."

"My disguise was perfect," Alex said with a sneer.

"It was the same for storage manager Jason Perkins, right?"

"Right. I was going to leave the heads in Shaw's storage container, but that blathering idiot wouldn't let me in without the key. Anything else?"

"The purchase from Sainsbury's tied the bin bags and newspaper to Shaw. What I can't figure out is how you got them into Shaw's flat without him noticing," George said.

"I didn't. I took them down with me when we searched the place."

"But my team was there. You didn't enter the flat. How?" Kent asked.

"As you are already aware, I'm not on the Contamination Elimination Database, so I can't enter a crime scene. The woman guarding the tape took a personal call. I told her I'd handle it, logging everybody in and out whilst she went outside. The room was empty. It was easy to put on a pair of gloves and overshoes and then place the items under the manuscript. I guess that was my downfall, my blond hair. Not that it matters, however, because DNA is useless without a profile to match it against! I don't plan on leaving any behind."

"You were the one who pointed out the bin bags to Hayden Wyatt, the American SOCO?" Kent asked.

"Bingo. I'd hoped if the charges against Shaw were quashed, that Wyatt would take the fall instead. He's a useless bastard, anyway."

"Is that why you wore the coverall when killing and dismembering your victims, Peterson?"

"What, to frame Wyatt?" George nodded. "Not initially, no. I wore the coverall to protect myself. It was a happy coincidence you found the polyethene fibres. Made Wyatt look even guiltier."

"What about the victims themselves, Alex?" George asked. "We spoke to the escort agency, and it was Shaw's mobile which made the calls for the bookings."

Alex raised his brow and laughed. "Never heard of a cloned phone, Beaumont? Fucking hell, what do they teach you these days? I even went and ordered the sluts from outside Shaw's flat to make sure the location data would fit before turning the device off."

"And the money being paid for the storage?" George asked.

"That was his own fault. His mistake. I searched his bins and found un-shredded bank statements. Fucking idiot!"

"It was all you?" Alex nodded, the grin on his face stretching wider. "Shaw was innocent then?" Stuart said.

"Shaw wasn't innocent. No, he's far from innocent. He's a sick, dirty pervert. Dad told me Shaw tried to fuck a couple of kids when he was young. Oh yeah, I never finished mi story, did I?" He turned to face his brother and chuckled. "Dad came

CHAPTER THIRTY-TWO

to see me not long before he was murdered. You know he was murdered, right?" Peterson asked.

Ryan nodded.

"He told me how it was his fault I got adopted. He was sorry. Our dad regretted ever letting me go. What a cunt. It's bullshit. All of it! It was like he needed me as some kind of sounding board. Like I was a priest, and he was at a confessional. He explained how he was involved in a murder investigation and how the press had coined the killer Jack the Butcher. Dad admitted it was him. He'd done it to frame a guy called Tony Shaw. A paedo. I tried to frame him. Initially, Dad had killed one woman. That was enough to put Shaw away. Then he thought it'd be best to kill another, make it a double murder. But that's the problem. When you start, you can't stop. Do you think I'm a sick monster? No, no, no. Peter Alexander was the monster, not me. Our Dad."

"Is that why you changed your name to Alexander Peterson? Alexander because of Pete's surname, and your surname because it means Peter's son?"

"A massive fucking hint if I do say so. And a homage. He was my muse, my inspiration. He was the reason I killed. I wanted to carry on his legacy!"

"You can't blame your dad for the deaths you caused, Alex," Kent said.

"Oh, I'm not even trying to do that, Stuart Cunt. No, no, no. Definitely not." George could see the last slither of sanity slipping away.

"Our dad, Ryan, killed a third woman because he couldn't help it. He told me a triple murder would put Shaw away for the rest of his life, but you know what?" Ryan shook his head. "Something happened to Dad. He couldn't help himself. I ended up murdering a fourth just for the hell of it. The press labelled her an innocent. Our dad convinced himself Anna Hill was innocent, too. It's why he stopped. But she wasn't innocent, no." He shook his head. "Her husband pimped her out for cash. I dropped her off and picked her up. That man let his wife be fucked for money by any Tom, Dick and Harry. She was just like our Mam." Ryan Jarman shook his head. "Yes! Just like our Mam! Eventually, I knew our dad was right. His work was just. I told him I wanted to be just like him when I was older. You know, join the police and put bad people behind bars. I wanted justice. I also wanted to cut the dirty whores to bits as he did. You know, those women who sell themselves for money, just like our Mam?"

Alex Peterson strutted back and forth across the cellar, eyeing each man as he did so. Ryan was shaking his head erratically. George knew the man was becoming agitated and could feel the mood darkening. He needed to escape and fast.

"I asked Dad how he got away with the murders, you know, because of DNA and stuff?" He pointed the finger at Kent. "You're the expert on DNA. Tell my brother what happens to semen that's ingested?" He turned to his brother. "I bet you've ingested a ton of semen, haven't you? Yeah, you gay bastard. If you weren't my brother, I'd have cut your cock and bollocks off already. Dirty bastard! But you can change. Once you get an escort sucking your cock, you'll be back for more. Trust me, I know." He turned back to Kent. "Kent. Tell my brother what happens to semen that's ingested. Now!"

"Stomach acid makes it so we can't use it for DNA purposes," Stuart Kent said.

"Yeah. And then we have to use bleach. It gets stuck in their teeth, under the tongue. It's that, or you make sure they spit it all out. But that gives a similar result. The best idea is to hide the heads. No head, no evidence."

"Where are the heads, Alex?" George asked.

"You know, DI Beaumont, I forgot for a moment that you were here. It's unlike you to be quiet. I..." He shrugged. "I may as well tell you. The heads are weighted down in a bin bag in Middleton Park pond. They're in the end next to the visitor centre where the anglers avoid. Nobody will ever know."

"That's just sick! Think of the victims' families and friends."

Peterson shrugged. "They should have thought about that before they parted their legs for money. They're the sick ones." Peterson began to shake and took a deep breath to calm himself. "And you're just as bad! What you did to our sister was sick! Knocking her up and then fucking off."

"I'm not talking to you about Mia," George said.

"You shut your mouth," Peterson snapped. "How dare you use her name? That poor woman went through her pregnancy alone whilst you were fucking your DS." He paused, waiting for George to reply. "Somebody told the Super about you and Wood. I bet you think it was me, right? Well, it wasn't. You have a rotten seed in your team, Beaumont, one that needs weeding out. Mia deserves better."

"You stay the fuck away from Mia!"

"Oh, we're getting brave, are we?" Alex stepped forward and planted a boot on George's right temple, knocking him down.

George felt sick and dizzy. He hoped he didn't have brain damage.

"So, Ryan. Back to Dad." Ryan didn't dare speak. "Dad fucked off back to his wife after he got rid of me. He did the same to you, though you got to live the life I didn't. You took that away from me, I guess. I should be angry with you, but I'm a reasonable man. You were innocent. That's why I'm giving you a chance." He sighed and shook his head before picking up the surgical saw. "But you know, finding out about how Kelly kept you and finding out that Dad allowed Kelly to keep you, it... Do you have any idea how it made me feel?" Peterson asked.

Ryan shook his head. George watched, transfixed, but continued to slip his fingers free. The look on Ryan's face was one that showed he was terrified, the fear in his eyes evident. "It... Well, it made me very, very sad. It made me feel unloved, Ryan because there was nothing I could do about it. Nothing at all. Have you ever felt unloved, Ryan?" Ryan didn't answer. "Of course, you have, though not like I did. Andrés García made you feel this way, didn't he? Oh, how I wish I could have him here in this cellar right now. The puff. The faggot. Fucking bummer! I love you, Ryan. It's why I'm giving you a chance, brother. Imagine how nice it'll feel as you draw this saw blade across his throat."

"What do I need to do?"

"Good." Alex Peterson smiled. "I'll tell you later. Stay there and shut up! It's time I dealt with Stuart Cunt!"

Alex walked over towards the short, balding figure of Stuart Kent. He was visibly shaking. "Do you feel helpless, Stuart?"

He nodded his head. Alex took a deep breath.

"I don't think I believe you. I think I need to teach you what helplessness feels like. You need to suffer. This is all happening because of you. If you hadn't gone to George behind my back, none of this would have happened. That little puppy over there was doing everything I wanted him to! You just had to fuck it up, and you made me feel helpless. Disrespected.

Angry. I'm still angry, but I'm going to show you disrespect and make you feel helpless. Okay?" Stuart shook his head. "Defiance. Good. Good!"

George strained as he pulled his fingers free. All he needed now was to wait for the right chance to strike. He was sure something depraved was about to happen, and he wanted to be ready for it.

"I really don't want to kill you, Stuart," Peterson said. He sounded calm. He looked the complete opposite. "I've only ever killed women. I don't want to kill you, Stuart," Alex said, looking at the balding man.

"Good, because I don't want to die," Stuart said. George didn't think Stuart was making the right move by trying to communicate. Alex was on edge, and it wouldn't take long for him to tip the scales. "Look, I was doing my job, Alex. I'm sorry I messed up your plan. Let us go. We won't say anything. I'll make something up and plant something to frame Shaw. He's a piece of shit, anyway!"

"No, that's not good enough. I don't believe you!" Peterson shouted. "What I want is for you to suffer. You need to suffer. Just like I had to. So don't go dying on me, yeah?"

Stuart tried to speak, but his lips were opening, and closing and no words were coming out.

"Cat got your tongue? You've no idea what sorry means, Stuart, but you will." Peterson took a deep breath and grinned. "I'm going to be fair. Kill George Beaumont, and I'll let you live longer, Stuart." Stuart looked at George as Alex Peterson walked over to the corner of the cellar where his large sports bag lay. He carried a larger surgical bone saw back and offered it to Stuart. A second weapon, murder weapon? If so, they needed that one, too.

"George was only doing his job, Alex," Stuart said, his voice shaky. He tried to smile at Alex, but it didn't work. "Let us go," he said to Peterson, who frowned back. "I won't kill George. He's done nothing wrong."

"But you're wrong, Stuart," Peterson said. "George has wronged my family. And so, he deserves to pay!"

"Please, Alex."

"Shut up, Stuart," Peterson snapped. He shook his head. He had the look of a madman. "I can't think straight when you speak to me so calmly. Why aren't you crying and begging for your life? Do you think I won't do it?" Alex sprinted over to where he had placed his mother's decapitated head and brought it back to Stuart. "Look at what I did to mi own mum! Look at what I did, you cunt. See? Now!" Stuart looked at the floor, realising he had pushed Peterson too far. "This is what I'm capable of! Don't you forget it!"

"Let us go, Alex."

Alex Peterson looked at George and walked over to him. "You're very quiet, DI Beaumont," he said. "Will you please explain to Stuart that he's annoying me?"

"I would listen to what Alex has to say if I were you, Stuart," George said calmly. He looked between Alex and Stuart, reinforcing the message by making eye contact.

Stuart nodded. "Okay, I'm listening. I'm sorry, Alex," Stuart said.

"Good. Now, what's your decision? Kill Beaumont, or suffer?"

"That's not a choice!" Stuart said, as his bottom lip quivered. George could see he was close to losing it.

"Oh fuck off, of course, it's a choice. Kill the stupid DI and live longer, or suffer," Peterson said, offering Kent the larger surgical saw. "Don't make me repeat myself."

"I don't... I don't want to kill George. Stop this, Alex, please?" As Stuart pleaded, Alex smiled.

"Okay." Peterson lowered the bone saw; Stuart moaned but choked the tears back. George watched and listened. "I'll decide for you, shall I?"

"Please, Alex. Don't do this," Stuart said, tears running down his face.

"Don't take your eyes off him, Stuart. And make sure you listen to him," George said, not wanting Peterson to pay any attention to him. All he needed was one moment to strike.

"Thank you for your wisdom, George," Peterson said with a nod. "The DI is right. But time's up." Alex Peterson crossed the room and took a handful of cable ties back to Stuart. "Want to see something fun, Bro?" he asked Ryan.

Ryan shook his head as Alex head-butted Stuart, the hard part of his forehead crunching against Stuart's nose. Crimson splattered everywhere, and Stuart fell down.

Next, Alex cut Stuart's ties with a small knife and arranged him in the centre of the four lally columns. George continued to watch, not daring to move, as Alex still had the knife in his hand.

Ryan watched with morbid curiosity as his brother tied Stuart's limbs to each column. First, Alex tied Stuart's left ankle to the same column Kelly's body was still tied to. Next, he tied Stuart's right ankle to the column he had been bound to. Then Stuart's right wrist was tied to George's column, and finally, Stuart's left wrist was tied to Ryan's column.

From above, Stuart was the Vitruvian Man, spreadeagled in the centre of the four columns. Stuart awoke a few seconds later, shaking. He looked around and soon realised he was bound. Looking down at him was his captor. "You're a sick bastard." He spat at Alex, who laughed and wiped away the bloodied spit with his gloved hand.

"Are you ready, Stuart?" He threw the knife to the ground, taking the bone saw in one hand. Alex stepped closer, choosing to saw Stuart's left leg first, his back to Beaumont.

Stuart spasmed, desperately trying to pull his limbs free from the cable ties. It was futile. A smiling Alex Peterson stamped his foot on Stuart's pelvis, above Stuart's left thigh. Kent let out a cry of both pain and fear.

George only had seconds left. He sprung from the ground, gripping the knife with one hand and steadying himself with the other. Time seemed to slow, as it had with Adam Harris. The steps George took closer towards the Bone Saw Ripper took an age to complete. As the jagged steel tore through Stuart's flesh, George gripped the knife tighter and thrust.

Chapter Thirty-three

DSU Alex Peterson heard the sirens coming; they seemed to bring him back to reality. He studied the surrounding carnage. Stuart Kent was thrashing about on the floor. Blood soaked the cellar floor and the walls. But that wasn't all. He was in excruciating pain, and his shirt was stuck to his back.

He felt the place where his back hurt the most, wincing. It was sticky. He withdrew his hand and looked at it, the crimson, sticky fluid contrasting against the blue latex. Alex turned and looked at George.

"Drop the knife, DI Beaumont. You may have gotten in a lucky shot, but I'm still in control here." Despite what he was saying, George could see Alex seemed surprised at what George had done. George watched him, his heart racing. Luckily, one of his team had traced the call, just like he knew they would.

"Give it up, Thomas!" George shouted. "Armed police will be on their way. Let me tend to Stuart." George stepped forward, but Alex jumped in the way.

He appeared bemused by the situation. He looked at George and shook his head. "Thomas? I haven't used that name for an age. Your friends sound far away. We have time to play for a little while."

"Tell me the truth, Thomas. Why did you kill those women?"

"Because they're dirt!" he spat. "Whores. Abandoners. Sluts. My slut of a mother abandoned me when I was a child. She was far too interested in getting fucked for money. I didn't want another Thomas Tweedy living in this world. Every whore has the potential to breed, to abandon. I decided to take that potential away!"

"See, I thought you had daddy issues. I figured mummy issues, too. It's why you fucked them before killing them. See, that's the problem, right? You enjoyed fucking them. Did you imagine it was Kelly as you fucked them, Thomas? Your own birth mother? Did you?"

"You keep that filthy whore's name out of your mouth. I don't want to hear it! My dad wanted me. He loved me. From an early age, he attempted to be involved in my life. I didn't tell the Tweedy family. They never knew. But until he was murdered, I saw him a lot. He loved me, George. He really loved me. He told me he was going to speak to my parents and see if they could make a deal. We were going to start a life together. Father and son."

"That's not what I meant. You're just like him—you're both women killers. Were you just imitating him?" George thought back to the diaries. There was something off with Peterson's story.

"Of course, Beaumont. He was everything to me. Jack the Butcher. What a guy. I couldn't believe it when he contacted me."

"Right."

"What do you mean by that? Have I missed something?" George didn't answer but had a smirk on his face. His smirk was hiding the fear inside. He needed help to arrive, and fast;

CHAPTER THIRTY-THREE

otherwise, Stuart wouldn't make it. "Your report on HOLMES made for interesting reading earlier, and I figured with all the familial DNA searches, it was only a matter of time before you linked both my dad and me to the crimes. What are you hiding behind that smirk, Beaumont? Tell me."

"I believe Peter Alexander was innocent. That somebody else killed those women. In fact, are you even sure it was Peter Alexander who was visiting you when you were young?"

A look of doubt spread across Peterson's face. *Good.* "I see your game. Do you think I'm fucking stupid, Beaumont? I won't fall for it. I know it was Peter who visited me."

"Where's Alina Hall's torso and the rest of the limbs? The families and friends of the victims deserve to know," George asked, changing tact. He wasn't sure it would work on Alex.

"There's no point telling you, as you won't ever leave this place," he muttered. Peterson listened to the sirens. They were louder. "They're nearly here. I guess it's time to say goodbye." He stepped closer to George, who gripped the knife. His vest and belt had been removed. He felt vulnerable.

"Humour me, dickhead," George said with the same smirk. "Give me this before you kill me. Tell me where they are. I may have failed as SIO. Again. So give me this. I deserve it."

"Fine. They're in Ardsley Reservoir. I didn't think you'd point your finger at Shaw so quickly, so I kept them as a backup. They smelled, so I moved them from here. I assume you realise this is the place I butchered them?"

George nodded. "I'm hiding a secret from you, Peterson. I've had access to Peter Alexander's personal diaries from the nineties. Did you know he wanted to be a writer once he retired?"

He saw Alex grit his teeth before shaking his head. "So what,

Beaumont? There are no fucking secrets. I've read everything on HOLMES. Are you trying to buy time? Is that it?"

George shook, wanting to keep Alex talking but struggling to stand. He'd taken an enormous blow to each temple, and his brain felt funny. His legs were wobbly. "No. Peter. He tried to find you. Just once. Every time he—" George stumbled.

"You know, Beaumont, you don't look so good. Drop the knife, and maybe I'll let you survive. I'll take Ryan with me. A hostage. Just in case. You tell them how serious I am. I killed mi mum; I won't hesitate to kill mi brother. Hey, I might even kill mi sister!"

"Don't you fucking dare talk about Mia like that." He blinked the pain away.

"I'm surprised you even care. DS Wood is delicious." He licked his lips. "I can see why you got with her. How is she in the sack? Good? No, I bet she's excellent. She must be if she's worth your career. You see, Beaumont, no woman is worth anything. They're good for a blow job or a quick fuck, but that's it. They let you down. My DC, Holly, was gagging for it. I let her have a little taste once, though I haven't recently. I respect my career too much, but she just wants me. Constantly. And it's good. It feels good. She's mine whenever I want. She doesn't fuck other guys because she knows if she does, it's over. That's loyalty. And it's rare. DS Wood has no loyalty to you. Even mi sister didn't. She fucked a serial killer behind your back. She told him all about your investigation. Mia Alexander is a whore. A two-faced rat. It's simple. And that baby, was it even yours in the first place? Did you care?"

"Stop it, Alex. Shut the fuck up."

"Or what? Are you going to cave my head in?" He looked around with a grin on his face. "Uh oh, I don't see any boulders,

Beaumont. And I'm not some fucking amateur like Harris. What are you going to do?"

"I said, shut the fuck up!"

"Brave boy. You forgot the 'sir'," Alex said as he swiftly closed the distance between the two. Alex lashed out with the bone saw, the surgical stainless steel blade glinting in the spotlight. George saw it late but stepped back, out of reach, safe. He felt the displaced air on his neck.

"Sprightly fella, aren't you?" He laughed dryly. "I'm surprised. I hit you very, very hard. You have my respect. From the sounds of the sirens, we have two minutes before I have to leave. Ask me a question. Anything. I'll answer it honestly."

"You said your dad was Jack the Butcher, and he told you that when he visited you. I told you I knew a secret. So, is what you told me really true?"

"What a question, Beaumont." He scratched his head through his blond hair. A devilish grin split his face, his teeth gleaming in the spotlight. The spots of blood on his face added to the visage, as did the white hood, luminous against the spotlight.

"Do you want to know my secret?" George asked. The sirens were even louder now. "It wasn't your dad who visited you as a child in Newcastle. It was your paedophile uncle, Boris Jarman. Kelly's brother. She'd told him all about you. He's in HMP Northumberland, ironically, for forcing underage boys to have sex with him. He's a sick, perverted man. And I'm guessing he groomed you. Bought you toys? Gave you money? Want to know who put him away?" he whispered.

Alex stood there, stunned.

"You were one of the lucky ones!" George shouted. "If not for Peter, who notified Northumbria Police, that sick, depraved predator would still be roaming the streets. He'd have fucked you like he did the other little boys!"

"No. That's not true."

"Yes, it is, Alex. You know it is. He also tried to fuck your mum. Drugged her. Had his cock inside her. If not for your DNA matching Mia's, then I'd have sworn you were his! You're both sick, depraved bastards!"

"You cunt! Don't you dare!"

"That's what Pete wrote in one of his diaries. Boris confessed everything. It's all on the system. Why didn't we make the connection? Well, who knows? I certainly didn't. I'm getting it looked into, but to hazard a guess, I think Peter made sure the connection wouldn't ever happen. But Boris liked sex workers. I suppose they were the only ones willing to have sex with him."

DSU Peterson shook his head. "Stop lying to me! It was Peter who visited me."

"No. As I said, Peter got a full confession from your uncle Boris. He actively sought you out. Boris thought you were his son. You know, after raping his prostitute sister?"

"Don't you fucking dare, Beaumont. Stop!"

"During this case. Didn't you look up Peter? Make sure he looked like the man who visited you all those years ago?" Alex looked down at his gloved hands before closing his eyes. "Of course you did. They're similar looking, yet starkly different. You were a kid. You didn't know. You were a victim, that's all. What I want to know is whether Boris admitted to being Jack the Butcher. Tell me, Alex?"

Alex tightened his grip on the saw and opened his eyes. "There's no need to answer that. It's been nice knowing you." Another grin broke out on his face. "Nah, who am I kidding?

CHAPTER THIRTY-THREE

You're a cunt, Beaumont," Peterson said. He raised the steel saw at George and sprinted towards him as the sound of the front and back doors being breached echoed down into the cellar.

"Armed police!" Alex heard. The shout made Alex hesitate, and George didn't waste his chance. He pushed the Bone Saw Ripper away and sprinted towards Stuart, pulling off his shirt and binding it around Kent's thigh to put pressure on the wound. "I've got you, Stuart. I've got you. Everything's going to be okay."

The cellar door shattered open. "The order is Fahrenheit!"

Alex stood there, still and silent. The voices in his head were fading. He felt himself sliding away into the darkness. "I forgot to answer you, didn't I? The truth? He told me he was Jack the Butcher. He told me he was Peter Alexander. But for all I know, he was fucking Peter Sutcliffe! It doesn't matter, anyway. I'll go down in fucking history, George!" Alex Peterson rushed towards him, and just as he was about to slash at George's throat, George saw blood splatter all over the walls and ceiling, felt the blood on his naked torso, and smelt the metallic tinge in the air.

As the first team of armed officers stormed down the stairs, DSU Alex Peterson's body crumpled to the carpeted floor. George craned his neck and saw an armed officer, his Heckler & Koch G36C rifle smoking. DS Wood was behind him.

Chapter Thirty-four

If an AFO, an authorised firearms officer, believes someone poses a threat to their life or to the life of others, then reasonable force may be used. The decision is theirs, and theirs alone. AFOs are legally responsible for each and every shot they decide to fire. The official policy says AFOs must 'shoot to incapacitate'. What does that even mean? Well, they're trained to target the centre of the chest to 'incapacitate' a subject, even though it is highly likely that this will kill.

That's where AFOs have to tread a fine line; as for the shots to be legal, they must prove they were acting in defence of themselves or others and that their actions were reasonable.

Danny Corbett, a Tactical and Strategic Firearms Commander, had made the decision to take the shot, the shot that had hit Alexander Peterson in the upper right part of the chest, away from the heart and any other vital organs. The bullet had passed straight through, and the DSU would recover to stand trial.

Not only had Danny Corbett incapacitated DSU Peterson safely, but he had also saved DI George Beaumont's life. A second or two later, and he'd have ended up like Kelly Jarman.

* * *

CHAPTER THIRTY-FOUR

George was moved away from the cellar, up the stairs and outside by an ambulance. On his way out, he raised a hand in thank you to Danny Corbett and received a nod back. As soon as George was out of sight, DS Wood flew into his arms.

"You stupid, stupid man!" she screamed. "You could have been killed. What were you thinking?"

"I wasn't," he said with a grin. "We got him, though. He confessed to everything. Ryan and Stuart were witnesses." George's face dropped. "Stuart!" He tried to move but fell to his knees. He'd been given a jacket but was shivering uncontrollably.

"It's okay, George," DS Wood said. "Don't try to move. You need to be checked over." She ran off and, after a minute, appeared with a blanket and draped it over the pair of them; they huddled together for warmth. "Doctor will be here soon."

George didn't know how long they stayed that way, but when his vision stabilised long enough for him to see properly, he stared at what he recognised was a team of SOCOs, led by Dr Ross, heading into the house.

Every shiver made him feel sick. "I was hit in the head. Twice. I don't feel so good."

"A doctor's on their way, George. They're making sure Stuart lives."

"Good. I'm glad. What about Peterson?" he asked.

"The bullet passed straight through. He's alive. Danny Corbett, the Tactical and Strategic Firearms Commander, hit Peterson in the upper right part of his chest, away from the heart and any other vital organs. Peterson was lucky—"

"So was I, thanks to him. And you. Thanks, Isabella; I owe you my life. You called for the firearms unit, right?"

"Right. But you owe Josh, too." She grinned. "He traced

your phone when our call ended. Without him—"

"We don't need to think about what ifs, alright?"

She nodded as a doctor appeared. "You have bruising and a couple of nasty bumps," he said. With DS Wood's help, they sat George delicately on the ledge at the back of the ambulance. "Tell me what happened."

"He hit me here," George said, pointing to his temple, "and I blacked out. He struck me hard, and it hurt. A lot. Then he hit me on the other side. Not as hard, but it still hurt."

The doctor nodded. "Nasty." He touched George's temple, and George winced. "Very nasty indeed. We need to do some scans back at the hospital, but from what you're describing, the force of the blow caused your brain to swing violently against your skull lining. That would cause a blackout." George nodded. The doctor looked at DS Wood. "Your colleagues can debrief you at the hospital. I'll get the EMTs to take you to St James'."

They had a moment together, alone. She encircled him with her arms and held him close.

"I love you, Isabella," he said.

She smiled, buried herself in his nook and whispered, "I love you more, George Beaumont."

The EMTs put him on a gurney and strapped him up tight. "Are you coming?" a tall, broad, balding black man with a London accent asked DS Wood.

She nodded and stepped up into the back of the ambulance.

Epilogue

One month later

Ryan Jarman sat in George Beaumont's Honda outside Mia Alexander's house, his heart pounding.

"You're sure about this?" George asked him.

He nodded. They had the same father, even if he might have been a serial killer. George told him they were still questioning his uncle, Boris Jarman, about the Jack the Butcher murders. Boris was being difficult.

Ever since he'd found out about his half-sibling, Mia, he'd been desperate to meet her. When George had called her and told her Ryan Jarman had asked to see her, she was so happy. Mia had never expected to have any other family than her aunt or grandparents. She thought she was alone in the world, other than baby Jack Beaumont, of course. And Mia had George, too. Though not in the way she wanted.

"Come on, then." Both men got out of George's car, but as they walked up the path, Ryan hesitated.

Before George could knock on the front door, it swung open, and a woman stood there, holding a handsome blond baby. They had matching curls and oval faces. Their chins were sharp, their noses like buttons. And he swore that when he looked deep into his boy's emerald-green eyes, the same colour as his own, it was like his boy could see within his very soul.

"Hi Ryan," she said. "Nice to meet you."

Ryan nodded and looked down at the floor.

"I'm Mia, and this is your nephew, Jack. Come on in. We've been expecting you."

Ryan glanced back at George, who nodded encouragingly, so he followed his half-sister into her house. She stood at the door to the kitchen and gestured for him to enter the living room, where Ryan came to a halt so suddenly that George bumped into him.

There were so many people! And they were all staring directly at him.

Ryan didn't know where to look and gulped, glad he'd showered and worn clean clothes.

"Let me introduce you to your family," said Mia. She was nervous too, and Ryan was relieved to hear the tremor in her voice.

Until recently, George wasn't aware that Mia had any other family. She'd never spoken to George about them before. All he knew was her mum and dad had died when she was younger, her dad when she was seven and her mum when she was sixteen.

"This is Nana and Grandpa—Emilia and Peter Alexander—our dad's parents." Her face fell as she said the word, dad. "They're your grandparents, too, Ryan."

Ryan smiled and nodded, heading towards the sofa to greet them.

"It's very nice to meet you, Ryan," Emilia said whilst beaming. Ryan liked her. His mum's parents had died years before Ryan was born, and so he'd never had grandparents. He especially liked how, despite looking old, she looked fierce and determined but still kind. Ryan wanted to ask her about her life, devour her stories, and ask her how she looked so beautiful despite the crow's feet.

His Grandpa Peter had been chiselled by time, but he saw the resemblance. Especially from the scintillating smile, he was giving him. That's what he'd look like when he got older. Ryan just knew it.

"Hello Ryan, I'm your grandpa," he said, offering rheumatic, trembling fingers to shake. Ryan squeezed them gently as a tinge of excitement ran down his spine. He wasn't expecting it, but he received a firm squeeze back. His grandpa's voice was also deeper than he'd been expecting, with an accent he didn't recognise.

"Thank you. Both of you. It's lovely to meet you all finally."

A woman entered the living room from outside, the glass door sliding open, revealing his small garden. "This is Melissa," Mia said. "She's your dad's younger sister. Our aunt."

Ryan grinned and said, "Hi." She had an hourglass figure, a pixie's nose, pencil-thin eyebrows, and a glowing complexion. She was everything he'd ever seen on the covers of fashion magazines and more, with her Gucci bag slung over her shoulder and Tiffany earrings glittering in the light. Blonde spools plunged around her smooth, oval face. Melissa was something else and somehow outshone Mia's own natural beauty. She broke into a smile, and her beguiling, pearly whites lit up the room. Ryan couldn't believe how young she looked.

"Would you like a drink?" Melissa asked.

"Tea, please."

Emilia patted the seat between her and Peter on the three-seater sofa, and so Ryan went over and sat. George remained by the door, trying his best not to take in the two blonde bombshells. It was obvious which family line Mia had got her superb looks from. She saw him looking and smiled. She nodded him over.

"Hey there, Detective," she said, his son in her arms.

"He's so beautiful. Just like you," George said, kissing them both on the cheek.

"I think he looks like you, George. He changes every day, yet he still looks just like you. I pushed him out, you know. He should bloody look like me!"

George laughed and watched as Ryan was fussed by his grandparents. "I know it's a shock, Ryan dear, especially hearing about your older brother, Thomas. We didn't know, either. Our son never told us about you two boys. We wish he had; we could have—"

"It's okay, Nana," Ryan said. "You're here now. None of this was your fault."

The public hadn't been made aware of the crimes their brother and grandson, Alex Peterson, had committed, but they soon would. Trials were terrible things, where no secrets were left unturned. They'd find out all about the confessions from Alex, about how he pretended to be Tony Shaw to lead four women to their deaths, even dressing up as him to fool a Sainsbury's checkout girl and the storage company manager. He'd even fooled George and his team. They'd never once cottoned on it was Alex, and not Shaw, on the CCTV footage.

Peterson's DNA profile matched the profile extracted from the blond hairs, and with two bone saws taken in for evidence, they'd also tied the murder weapons to the murders of all four victims. Peter's diaries proved his DNA was a match to the one on the database, but they still weren't sure he was Jack the Butcher. Peterson had told George the killer had visited him as a child, and as far as they could tell, Peter never did.

The cellar was a treasure trove for Dr Ross and Kent's SOCO team. The carpet fibre deposits found on the black bin bags matched the crimson carpet. Forensic scientists had also proved the stray fibres found in the Fiat Punto where Danielle Ferguson had been burnt alive came from the protective coverall Peterson was wearing in the cellar that day.

During searches of the house above the cellar, they found a mobile phone which had been used to call the escort agency. As Alex had said, he'd cloned Shaw's number.

The OSU, the Operational Support Unit, are officers who work across the force and have a wide range of skills. A team specialised in underwater searches dredged Ardsley Reservoir for ten hours a day for over two weeks before they found Alina Hall's torso and the rest of Sarah Lawson's and Rita Lawrence's limbs. It only took them a few days to find the heads in Middleton Park pond. Being in the water for such a time meant all traces of DNA had disappeared, but Peterson had incriminated himself by confessing where he'd disposed of them.

After finding those pieces of evidence, everything fit, and George tied everything into a neat bow. Shaw was an innocent man, as was Hayden Wyatt. George was sure the charges of five counts of murder and two counts of attempted murder would stick. Shit always stuck.

Ryan held his nana's hand, and she cried, her blood-flecked eyes trying to blink the tears away. "I meant it when I said none of this was your fault."

"We didn't know that... Well, we still don't know if he was involved with those murders thirty years ago, do we—"

"It was a shock to us all, Nana," Mia said.

"Nobody ever knew, mum," Melissa confirmed.

"Your dad was a good man. He clearly had his flaws, especially if it's true. And well, there's no excuse. But he was a good man, Ryan. He locked away a lot of dangerous criminals. It is a shame he—"

"Thanks." Ryan nodded and smiled. From what George had already told him, he already knew his dad had put many killers behind bars. If Peter did what they thought he may have done, why he did what he did was anybody's guess. He'd ask his brother, Alex or Thomas, whatever his name was, and find out why he committed the crimes he did. Maybe there would be something there. A hint? Anything. At least they'd saved Stuart Kent from him and George, too. "Tell me about Dad," he finally said. "I want to know why he was such a good man."

Emilia smiled. Ryan knew her warmth was genuine. He was worried he'd be shunned—a prostitute's son. There wasn't a hint of that coming from his new family. After his brother had killed their mum, Ryan had sat on that blood-soaked carpeted cellar floor, empty and alone. He missed her and would never replace her, but being here felt right.

"Well, it only makes sense we start at the beginning," Emilia said. "Peter was born early. He couldn't wait to get out of the womb."

George took Jack from Mia and sat with him in the chair, gazing down into those emerald eyes, and listened as Emilia told Ryan everything she knew. During the brief moments he looked up, George saw Ryan listening intently, the look on his face increasingly happy and full of amazement. The way Emilia told her story made Peter Alexander out to be bright and fun-loving, just like Ryan. It was nice to see. A boy brought up in poverty with just a single family member. Now he had six at least. George had included himself in that number; he'd be Uncle Ryan to Jack, after all.

"I'm told you wanted to be a writer. You went to University and studied writing?" Emilia said.

Ryan nodded. "That's right, Nana. Creative Writing at Leeds University."

"Your dad was going to be a writer. He said once he retired from being a detective, he was going to write crime fiction, using his experiences. I have some notebooks at home if you want to look. We took them from the house when Mia's mother died."

Ryan looked at Mia. He'd never been told that both of Mia's parents had died. She smiled back at him and nodded. "Take them," she mouthed.

They'd used the notebooks to extract a DNA profile. It had come back as a match to the profile extracted thirty years ago. DSU Smith said it didn't matter; Peter could have visited the sex worker before she was killed. George wasn't sure, but the case had been handed over.

DS Wood had also spoken to the Tweedy family, Alex's adopted parents, and informed them of what happened. Alex couldn't have murdered his biological dad because he was at a Newcastle United game that day. His adopted dad even showed recorded footage of them being shown on television. Alex had lied through his teeth, and DSU Smith had used that as his basis, moving forward in his attempts to prove his old boss, Peter Alexander, was innocent.

Ryan's grandparents continued to talk about Peter, and even Melissa supplied stories about their childhood and what kind of brother he was like. George stopped listening and focused on the mother of his child.

"How long have you been back in their lives then?" he asked Mia with a smile.

Her face darkened slightly. "After Adam, I didn't want to be alone any more. You didn't—" She breathed. "Look, I don't blame you. I needed to; I don't know, not feel alone or unsafe any more. And having family around helped. A lot."

"I'm sorry, Mia."

"You saved my life, Beaumont. Don't be sorry. You saved Jack's too. Don't you ever forget that? I won't."

His phone rang. He glanced at the number. It was work. Mia shrugged and went to get Jack when she saw him press the red button. "This is more important than work," he said.

She smiled. It was a smile he realised he had missed—one of those genuine ones, full of love and warmth. For once, George felt complete. His relationship with Isabella Wood was stronger than ever, and he had his son. George had Mia, though not in the way she wanted him. He also had Ryan, too, in a way. And Melissa, Emilia and Peter. This was the other half of the family he so desperately wanted to be involved in, his son's half. This was what he'd been missing.

A small tear fell from his eye, and he blinked it away immediately. Mia saw. She wiped it away, kissing him on the forehead. "You good?" she asked.

"Yeah, I'm good, Mia." He gripped her hand, and she smiled back. He was good.

Very good.

The nightmares had finally stopped, and he felt complete.

Afterword

Thank you, kind reader, for reading the follow-up to my debut novel. That you bought and read my book is incredible. I'm so encouraged by and very grateful for your lovely reviews. It's been a humbling experience, and I appreciate it hugely.

Like my first novel, I opted to stay close to South Leeds, based in my hometown of Middleton. I had so much fun with the geography of the diverse area, and the parade of shops and takeaways where the initial set of torsos and limbs are found are real. The cafe there is exceptionally moreish, and I've come up with some of my best ideas sitting there with a cup of tea and a sausage butty. Don't forget the HP Fruity brown sauce!

I left the burnt-out car in Springhead Park in Rothwell, having used Middleton Park in my debut. Both are lovely places to visit, and I highly recommend visiting them. I've spent a lot of time in both areas with my family.

I'm excited to take you to more amazing places in Leeds as you follow George and his team heading to Headingley and Beeston next time. I hope you enjoy the adventures.

If you enjoyed this book, I'd appreciate it if you could leave an honest review on Amazon.

George Beaumont will be back soon in The Blonde Delilah.

Thanks again and take care,

Lee

Also by Lee Brook

The Detective George Beaumont West Yorkshire Crime Thriller series in order:

The Miss Murderer

The Bone Saw Ripper

The Blonde Delilah

The Cross Flatts Snatcher

The Middleton Woods Stalker

The Naughty List

More titles coming soon.

Printed in Great Britain
by Amazon